THE INTIMIDATION GAME

C.L STEWART

Cover by Natasha Snow
www.natashasnowdesigns.com

ISBN: 978-1-9993193-6-6

In Memory of Maureen

I hope you knew how happy you made me the day we met.

PROLOGUE

I hate him. Lying in his bed I watch him with complete and utter contempt, thankful that today is the day I get the hell away from this evil controlling man. The pristine white shirt, the collar starched to within an inch of its life. The bespoke suit…God forbid he should wear anything off the peg. The multitude of hair products taking pride of place on the dresser.

As he pushes his hands through his salt and pepper strands he asks; "Nik you going to get up and make an effort today?"

Ugh I hate being called that and he knows it. My name is Nikki. His condescending tone makes me feel nauseous. I nod; I can't speak. I'm struggling to hold back my tears, but I refuse to cry in front of him again. My misery seems to feed his ego.

I roll my eyes and sigh. He shakes his head and sneers, stalking towards where I lie. I shoot across the bed as quickly as I can, but I'm not fast enough.

He grabs my jaw in one of his strong hands. His face so

close to mine, he talks quietly through gritted teeth. "Who the fuck do you think you are?"

My heart thumps so hard and fast that I think it is about to burst out from my chest. I curl myself into a ball, hoping he might relent. He doesn't though, his grip intensifies and my jaw aches. "You're a lazy little bitch. You're nothing without me. Say it. Tell me I'm right."

I look at him wide eyed. I can't believe he's going to make me do this again, but I know if I don't, he won't leave, so I give him what he wants. "I'm a lazy little bitch." I can't form the words properly since my jaw feels like it is in a vice.

"And?" He shouts this time.

"And I'm nothing without you." My voice sounds weak and pathetic.

His smile is nothing more than a nasty grin and I notice his pupils are huge. *Oh my God, he's getting off on this!*

"Fucking know your place you little idiot." He loosens his grip and pushes me back into the bed, laughing to himself as he leaves the room.

I take a shuddering breath in and listen as he goes about his morning rituals. The coffee machine whirring, the clinking of the mugs and the fridge door opening and closing. When I hear the front door opening, I know he is giving himself a final check over in the mirror; narcissistic prick.

As soon as I hear the rumble of his precious Porsche, that he spends more time feeling up than me, I get out of bed and begin clearing him out of my life. Tears are blinding me, and I am sobbing so hard my chest hurts. I look at my reflection in the mirror. My face is red where he gripped it and my eyes look like sunken, sad pools. I need to leave this part of my life behind. He has ruined me. My self-esteem is shattered, and I constantly doubt myself. I should have left the first time he hit me.

I didn't want to accept that there could be anything wrong until I visited my sister Charlie in Scotland after she had her baby. My super observant sibling knew as soon as she set eyes on me that something wasn't right, but it was a very short conversation with her friend Gina that forced me to admit to myself that this relationship was toxic.

As I picture Charlie giving me the evil eye when I told her I was fine, I smile. I'll be seeing her in a little over twenty-four hours and I'll never have to be back in South Africa again. It's the coward's way out, I know that, but I'm scared that if I tell him he'll kill me.

I don't even know how I ended up in this situation in the first place. I must have been so stupid and naive to even consider sleeping my way to a better position. My relationship with Mike started out as a casual fling. He was my immediate boss and was newly divorced at the time. He's also fifteen years older than me. I don't know why I listened to Mike when he said him getting a promotion would mean I would get to move up too. He said he'd make sure of that. I should have got out then, but I had stupidly fallen for the creep and by the time he started to show his true colours I was too scared to leave. Obviously, my career stalled while he got promotion after promotion.

The fact that he was so much higher up the chain of command than me made my work life unbearable. He picked on me all the time and pulled me up on trivial things. He always did it in front of other employees and told me it was to cover up that we were in a relationship. As time went on, he started to act the same in private. My hair was never right, I wore too much make-up, I didn't wear enough make-up, I was too fat, I was too skinny, I was stupid, I dressed like a tramp, I dressed like a hooker. The list goes on. I eventually got a job elsewhere, but I just couldn't seem to leave him. My bruises were always well hidden, I'd gotten good at that. And he did too. He knew where to hit so that no one could tell. So that no one would know what he really was.

When my parents decided they were moving back to the UK, I actually cried and begged them to take me with them. They thought I should stay since I had the 'perfect' job and a 'nice' boyfriend. *Little did they know!* I think if my dad found out what Mike has done to me, he would kill him.

Knowing that I can get away from here without him finding out where I am going makes me braver than I actually am. I gather up all my belongings into my backpack, get dressed and stop myself from making the bed. That's another one of the things I can never get right. I leave locking the door behind me. As I push the silver key through the letter-box, I feel scared and liberated all at once.

"Good riddance you bastard," I whisper as I walk away from the house without looking back. I try my best to convince myself that the tears falling from my eyes now are happy ones.

CHAPTER ONE

$\mathcal{I}$ never thought of Glasgow as being somewhere I would ever call home, but having been here for five weeks and, experiencing life on my own for the first time in my twenty-six years on this planet, I think I can safely say I do feel at home here. My sister Charlie was born here.

My days have been filled with getting to know this very cosmopolitan city, my nights spent fretting about the new job I am starting today. My interview was extremely short and sweet. I have a detailed work history and my former employer had put in a good word for me. It seemed as though the interview was purely a formality because I had an offer of employment in my inbox before I even got back to Johannesburg.

Holding up two different dresses, the last of about forty, in front of me, I try to decide which would fit with the feel of SecuriSoft. I'm going to be heading up a newly formed team working on brand new software. This is a major promotion for me and is the first time I'll be running a whole team of people. To say I'm nervous is an understatement; I'm petrified. I know how much first impressions matter, and if I don't get it right it'll show and it's all I'll be known for.

My phone pings with a text message and I'm startled since it's only four thirty in the morning. I see that the text is from my sister and my thoughts about who could be up at this time in the morning are sent packing.

Charlie says my niece is the spawn of the devil right now because she cries her little heart out at four every morning and as soon as she sees her mummy, she smiles like…and I am quoting my sister here…she has just shit out a rainbow. Charlie has a real way with words, but I love her dearly and I'm glad we are only forty miles apart now instead of almost six thousand. I put the dresses down on the bed and check the message.

Hey baby sis. Good luck today. I love you and I'm so proud of you. Devil baby loves you too.

C x

I laugh and hold the phone to my chest. My life has changed in more ways than I ever imagined it could, but I feel that had I waited any longer I may not be standing in front of this mirror debating what dress to wear.

I feel sick every time I think about my relationship with Mike: if you can even call it a relationship. The man is a controlling, nasty piece of work. I dread to think what his reaction was when he realised I had actually gone. When he realised he hadn't managed to break my spirit completely.

But he did ruin me. I have no self-confidence, no belief in anything. I look at myself in the mirror and I don't see the pretty, intelligent young woman Charlie tells me I am. I see a small insignificant shell of a person. Since I've been here, I've managed to keep my mask on. These people don't know me; they don't know that I almost die inside anytime a man speaks to me.

The shock of my phone ringing loudly in my hand makes me jump and I throw it at the bed as if it is on fire. The screen flashes and the caller ID says the number is unknown. I can't bring myself to answer an unknown number. I put my hands over my ears and shut my eyes until it stops. It takes me a moment but I realise I'm screaming when I take my hands from my ears.

"Pull yourself together you bloody idiot," I scold my reflection. There's no message.

This phone number I have is brand new, it's off the directory and I have my phone set to never share it when I call people except those in my contacts. It doesn't stop me worrying that someday, somehow, he will find me. I don't know how long I'll be looking over my shoulder when I'm walking alone or how long I'll stop and let some innocent person pass by me, when all they're doing is going about their business. I've lost count of the strange shops I've been in over the last few weeks that I'd never normally go into just so I could avoid someone walking directly behind me.

I look at the dresses on the bed and give myself a mental slap. I need to get ready to go into the office today and make the best first impression I possibly can.

---

*M*y taxi driver has been chatting away since I got in the back of his cab and, while I've been listening and nodding along, I've taken nothing in. I feel like my brain is about to explode and I should be tired, but I drank three cups of black coffee and a can of Red Bull for breakfast. I think I might have a heart attack at this rate.

As the taxi pulls up outside SecuriSoft's building, I steel

myself with a steadying breath, pay the driver and get out of the cab. *It's now or never.*

I take in the building, which looks taller today than it did the last time I was here. The mirror glass front reflects the cloud spattered blue sky and the April sunshine is pleasant, albeit about fifteen degrees lower than I'm used to at this time of year.

I settled on a navy-blue shift dress and jacket ensemble and a pair of nude heels. My brand-new tan leather handbag that mum and dad gave me, as a good luck present, looks amazing with it. My long blonde hair is in a soft ponytail and I look professional. I look like I should be heading up my own team. *I can do this.*

The elevator that will take me to the third floor is empty. I press number three and as the doors close, I shut my eyes and take in a deep calming breath.

The noise of the doors opening again startles me and I open my eyes as a scruffy looking, jeans and t-shirt clad guy gets in and presses number twelve. The top floor.

He's standing too close to me so I move away a little trying to be as inconspicuous as I can. I can't stand my personal space being invaded. He smells goddamn divine. *Damn it!*

I stare at the ceiling and hold my bag in front of me like some sort of Viking shield. I can feel him looking at me, but I can't make eye contact. I'm starting to feel closed in and I think I'm going to have a panic attack. This is bloody ridiculous; I'd be better off living like a hermit.

Thank goodness the lift has reached the third floor and the doors open into a huge open plan space completely bathed in beautiful warm light with empty computer stations dotted all around. Scruffy guy stands aside and allows me to get off. I'm forced to look at him and immediately wish I hadn't. He looks like he just walked off the cover of a rock album. He has tattoos on one of his tanned arms and my God are those arms ripped. His scruffy stubble and messy dark brown hair give him a carefree look but those eyes. Wow. They are the deepest chocolate brown eyes I've ever seen.

"Th-thanks," I stutter and hurry out of the lift as quickly as my heels will allow. I don't even know where I'm supposed to be going. All I was told was third floor, nine am.

I look back at the lift as the doors close. Rock star guy is gone. As I stand alone in the middle of the open area, I wonder what the hell I've let myself in for.

"Can I help you my love?" The voice from behind me makes me jump.

"Oh… ehm… sorry you startled me."

"Ooh you must be Nikki. I could tell by the South African accent. Nice to meet you I'm Damien Shaw but I prefer Damo." He holds out his hand.

"Eh, yeah I'm Nikki. It's nice to meet you Damien."

"Damo, please. I hate the name Damien it makes me feel like some sort of devil child. I think my daft mother was in some sort of cult when she had me." He puts his hands on his hips and I regard him for a second.

He's slim built with flawless skin and coiffed brown hair. The most beautiful eyelashes I've ever seen on a man frame his huge blue eyes and I don't know why but I instantly like him. I feel comfortable with him. "Thanks for getting my accent by the way. Most of the time I'm mistaken for Australian or a New Zealander."

"I'm good with accents and don't worry I've been mistaken for being Irish before, even English. I mean come on, listen to me."

"So, Damo, I don't actually know who I'm supposed to

be meeting here or what I'm doing. God I must sound ridiculous."

Damo waves his hand in the air. "No, you don't sound ridiculous. Astrid was supposed to call you on Friday and give you HR's contact name." Damo is interrupted by the click clack of heels. "Talk about shit and it hits you in the face." He whispers.

We both turn in the direction of the elevators and watch as a very tall, slim, blonde haired bombshell makes her way towards us. She walks like she's on a catwalk and must be almost six foot tall in the heels she's wearing. She stops in front of us.

"Nikki?"

I nod. "Yes. Nice to meet you." I hold my hand out.

"Astrid Laurent," she says her surname with a French accent. "As in Yves Saint." She shakes my hand like she's the queen.

"Astrid you were supposed to call Nikki and let her know where she was to go this morning."

"Damo for fuck sake you know I had a big weekend. Anyway, I tried to phone her this morning. Not my fault she never answered." She talks as if I am invisible.

"Well there's a surprise," Damo rolls his eyes. "Come Nikki I'll take you down to HR and get you set up with your passes and stuff."

Astrid tuts and tosses her hair over her shoulder and saunters away from us. I'm a little shocked at her total lack of professionalism and I hope to God I don't have to manage her on my team.

Damo and I get into the lift and when the doors are shut, he sighs and shakes his head. "I'm sorry about her Nikki. She's a nasty piece of work. I honestly don't know why she's even still here. We all think she's sleeping with the boss. I suppose that's one way to keep your job or get promoted for doing nothing."

His words make me want to run away. I feel tears surface in my eyes, and I can't stop them spilling over.

"God Nikki are you okay? I know she's a lot to take but you'll get used to ignoring her."

"I'm sorry Damo, I'm fine," I lie as I swipe the tears from my eyes and compose myself. "I'm just a little overwhelmed. I've never had a team of my own and I feel a little like a fish out of water here, but I'll get there honestly. Thanks for being so nice to me."

I'm taken aback when he hugs me. "We're going to be good pals you and me. I just know it Miss Nikki."

I smile as the doors open on the first floor and we make our way to HR. I'm glad I met Damo first and not Astrid.

---

*M*y time at HR was short and sweet. They already had my badge and I.D card ready for me and they've given me an access fob for the office doors. I also have a pass card for the car park but since I don't have a car it's pretty useless right now. I need to start making money so that I can pay my own rent and not have to rely on the bank of mum and dad much longer. And it turns out Damien is actually my PA.

Back on the third floor I have been shown to what is my office although the open plan nature of this place means it really is just a space in the area with a desk and chair. Thankfully, there is a small conference room that has walls and a door so at least it affords some privacy if needed.

Jed, my immediate line manager, has gathered the chatting, lively staff around my desk and I am about to be introduced to my team. I honestly hope I look composed because inside I'm dying.

"Right everyone." Jed raises his voice above the din, and they all fall silent. Eight pairs of eyes give him their fullest attention. Astrid's are not one of them and I breathe an internal sigh of relief. I wonder what her job is as she sits beside Jed taking notes.

Damo winks at me as Jed begins my introduction. "So, guys this is Nikki Olsson, your team leader." They all clap for me and I feel my cheeks heat. "Nikki you can get to know everyone over this week, get a feel for the company and what we do and make yourself at home. This is your floor, if you need to make changes please feel free to do so."

I'm really not sure what I was expecting with this job. I knew it was heading up a new team working on new security software, but I never imagined I'd have a whole floor of the building to myself. "Okay, um, thanks."

Jed asks everyone to give their name and their job title and they all smile at me as they each take it in turns to introduce themselves. The varying ages of the group is exciting to me. Many of the software companies I have known tend to favour very young people in their developer roles. I'm glad to see that this place challenges stereotypes. I think I'm going to be just fine here. I can't wait to get my teeth into this job, now that I have met my team, and this space I have to work in is excellent.

Jed leaves me to it, and I watch him head for the elevator quickly followed by Astrid. She towers over him, her backside swinging from side to side as she goes. She is extremely beautiful, unfortunately she knows it.

"Hey Miss Nikki, how you feeling?" Damo plonks himself down on the chair at the other side of my desk.

"Oh…I'm fine, a little overwhelmed, but fine. Can I ask you, what does Astrid do here?"

"She's Jed's PA."

"She's not sleeping with him, is she? He has a wedding ring on his finger."

Damo laughs. "No, not Jed. God no, he's so in love with his wife it's vom inducing. No, I heard she's sleeping with Dan King…The Big Boss."

"Oh. I haven't met Mr King yet. What's he like?"

Damo smiles. "He's a really great guy, don't know what the hell he sees in Astrid, and he doesn't like to be called Mr King. We don't really see him down here too often. His office is on the top floor, obviously. Wait till you see the view he has up there. Oh, and he's drop dead gorgeous. So, tell me Miss Nikki what's brought you to bonnie Scotland?"

I'm going to have to give him the edited version. I don't know him well enough to divulge my shameful existence. "Well, my mum and dad were moving back to the UK because of my dad's job, and my sister lives in Edinburgh, so I decided I didn't want to be the only one left on another continent."

"That's cool your sister lives here, you'll get to see her more often."

"Yeah and she's just had a baby, so I get to see my niece now too."

Damo claps his hands together. "Oh, I just love wee babies. They're so cute."

We are interrupted by the arrival of the elevator. It's Astrid and she's followed by Mr Rock Star. She makes her way to a desk at the far end of the floor.

"I'm going to make a coffee Nikki would you like one?"

"No thanks Damo." I shake my head, but I can't take my eyes off Mr Rock Star. I watch as he walks to the desk Astrid is sitting at. He has his back to me, but I can see from his body language that he is angry with her. They're too far away for me to hear what they are saying. I'm starting to feel a little uncomfortable as I watch the look on Astrid's face change from indignation to what looks like fear. When he shoves her chair back with his foot and scatters her papers off the desk I want to die inside. I should help her, but I can't. I look around the room at the rest of my team and see that every one of them is engrossed in their computer screens and they all have ear pods or headphones on so none of them can actually hear what's going on.

I watch in stunned silence as Mr Rock Star stalks off to the elevator. The doors open immediately, and he gets in. Still facing the back of the lift, he lifts his fist and bangs it on the wall as the doors close on him.

I can't believe what I've just witnessed. My opinion of this guy now has just taken a nosedive and I actually feel sorry for Astrid. She looks smaller and not so full of herself anymore. I get up and go over to her to make sure she is okay.

"Astrid are you okay?" I ask as I near her desk.

She looks up at me and I see tears in her eyes. She quickly composes herself. "I'm fine. Why do you care?"

"Well no man has a right to talk to any woman like that and what he did was verging on assault. You really should tell someone about it. Get him disciplined. It's not right."

"Oh, you think so?" She eyes me suspiciously. "You going to fight my battles little Miss Nikki? Just leave me alone. You don't know me, and I don't need you sticking your nose in my business."

She stands and walks towards the toilets, swiping tears from her eyes as she goes, and I decide I *need* to get my nose in her business. I could never live with myself if anything were to happen to her, as cold hearted as she is, and I had stood by and did nothing.

I head for the elevator feeling rather pleased with myself that I'm helping someone who is obviously going through the same mental torture I did at the hands of a man. I hit the twelfth-floor button and wonder to myself what Mr King is like.

CHAPTER TWO

*T*he seating area outside Mr King's office is plush and well equipped. There's a coffee machine, biscuits and a fridge stocked with almost any soft drink you could imagine. The whole building is beautiful but this floor reeks of sophistication.

"Dan is free to see you now Miss Olsson. Straight through that frosted door."

"Thank you." I nod to the secretary and make my way to the door. I stop for a second and compose myself. This is after all the first time I will be meeting the man whose company I now work for and my first thing to say to him is probably not going to go down well.

Pushing open the heavy door I'm greeted with a sight that shocks and confuses me at the same time.

Sitting behind the huge glossy white desk is Rock Star guy himself. I don't know what to do. All I am doing though is gawping at him. *Say something Nikki.* I will myself to talk but I just can't get the words out. I don't need to speak however as his voice cuts through the silence.

"Can I help you Miss Olsson?"

"Ehm… Mr King?"

He looks down at himself and nods. "Last time I checked yes." Oh God his smile is beautiful

"Shit," I whisper and bow my head. I have been royally had by that bloody nasty piece of work. I turn to leave. "I'm sorry to waste your time."

I don't know how, but I manage to move my feet and get out the door. I make my way to the elevator as quickly as I can in my heels and am thankful when the thing opens immediately. I get in and tap the button continuously until the doors close. I can't believe what just happened. I'm probably going to get sacked now because of that horrible woman. I let my guard down and it has backfired spectacularly.

The doors open on my floor, but I can't get out. I'm glued to the floor as I watch the doors close. When they ping open again Damo is there.

"Nikki are you okay? You're as white as a sheet."

I don't know what to say to him. I stare straight at him, but words fail me.

"Come with me." He grabs my arm and marches me to the conference room.

Taking a seat at the table I put my head in my hands.

"Nikki what happened? I came back from making my coffee and you were gone. Astrid said you'd probably gone to see Dan, but she was acting weird. She kept chuckling to herself. It was rather sinister actually."

"Oh, Damo I don't think I'm cut out for this place. I've just made a total fool of myself."

"Tell me what happened?"

I recount my tale to him and watch his expression go through a kaleidoscope of emotions, the last one being pure rage.

"That mean, nasty bitch. I swear the sooner that wee cow gets another job the better. I bloody hate her."

"What's her goal Damo? Does she think because she's fucking the boss she can get away with murder? What the hell did I do to her?" I am crying angry tears. I still can't believe someone would stoop so low as to humiliate a colleague like that, especially one they don't even know.

Damo comes to sit beside me. He puts a reassuring hand on my shoulder. "Nikki I honestly don't understand her sometimes. She's horrible to just about everyone she meets. You'll notice people giving her a wide berth just so they don't get a dose of her malice."

"I feel so stupid. I know she doesn't know anything about me, but I feel like she intentionally played on my biggest insecurity and sat back and enjoyed the fallout."

"What happened to you Miss Nikki?"

I look into his lovely warm eyes and I feel as though I can trust him, so I give him the heavily edited version of my horrid relationship.

When I'm finished and have a face full of tears and running mascara, Damo shakes his head. "I'm so sorry Nikki. Now I know why you got upset in the lift today. I really am sorry."

"No, please don't feel sorry for me Damo, honestly, you've been so nice to me today and I thank you from the bottom of my heart for that. In fact, you may be the only reason I come back tomorrow because right now I want to run for the hills and never show my face here again."

"Oh, darlin' thank you. I liked you the instant I met you. Now you go and get yourself cleaned up and then we can spend the afternoon sorting out how we are going to manage your calendar and staff rotas."

"Good idea. I'll never get any respect looking like Cruella de Ville."

The rest of the day has gone without a hitch and I haven't seen Astrid again, which has been a godsend. Damo and I managed to get loads of work done and I also got to know my staff a bit more too. They are a really interesting diverse group of people. Everyone but Damo and I are gone for the day.

"Right Miss Nikki, are we done for the day?"

"God yes Damo, I'm going home for a stiff drink tonight. It's been a bit of a mad day hasn't it?"

He laughs. "You don't say. I'll see you tomorrow then. Ciao."

"Bye." I watch as he leaves and get engulfed by the silence.

Sitting back in my chair, I survey my surroundings. I'm still extremely pissed at what happened today and I hope I won't bump into Astrid again for a long time. I don't even think I want to know what her problem is. Someone who can be so vindictive to a stranger is not a person I want to have anything to do with.

I get up and take a walk around the office space. The windows wrap right round three walls, the fourth being the wall housing the elevator. The lightly tinted glass gives a panoramic view of the River Clyde and the beautiful bridges that span it. The day is fading, and lights are starting to twinkle in the distance. This place is so far removed from my home city in every way possible but for some reason I don't feel homesick. I've made Glasgow my home and even though my parents are hundreds of miles away in London, I don't miss them as much as I thought I would.

The fire exit door next to the elevator leads onto a cold, bright white stairwell. I make a decision to use it every so often as some sort of exercise although I've heard a rumour of there being a gym somewhere in this building. I think I'll get Damo to give me a tour of the place tomorrow.

This is one of the best laid out and well-equipped offices I have ever worked in. This guy sure knows how to please his staff. I shudder at the thought as I think of Dan and Astrid together. I honestly can't see the attraction he has to her beyond the physical. I mean she is absolutely beautiful, but she has such an ugly soul. 'A black heart,' as my mother would say. I wonder if he is the same. Maybe they're kindred spirits in their own horrible way.

I gather up my bag and coat and turn off the lights. The ambient LED's around the room give the place a warm night-time glow. I nod to myself and call the lift. My phone pings with a text and as I check the message from my dad the lift doors open. I look up as I am about to step forward and stop dead as I see Dan and Astrid standing together inside.

"Oh... um... I'll get the next one. I forgot... um... yeah..." I'm a total mess. I really can't deal with her right now and seeing the two of them together cements in my mind Damo's assumptions that they are indeed an item. I turn and walk away from them as quickly as I can and head straight for the ladies toilet. I hear the lift doors close behind me.

Resting my bag on the side of the sink unit I shake my head at my reflection. "What's your problem Nikki?" My voice echoes round the room. I honestly have no clue what those two are up to, but I would have thought a man of Dan King's stature would behave a little more professionally in the workplace. My eye roll at my stupid hypocritical thoughts can probably be felt halfway down the River Clyde. Mike acted professionally in the workplace, but it had nothing to do with actually being professional; I was his dirty little secret and that's how he wanted me to stay.

I decide, as I leave the building for the night, that a bottle of wine, a big bag of popcorn and a rom-com are in order to wind down after this extremely stressful first day at work. I need to clear my head and will myself to come back tomorrow, I have to make my new life work.

CHAPTER THREE

*D*awn in Glasgow is something wonderful. The nightlife here is so energetic and fun and the bars and clubs are always full, but the early morning is my favourite. The sun rising over the river as I run along its banks gives me a huge sense of wellbeing. Each pull of cool morning air into my lungs makes me more determined to stick out my job and make a real go at this life changing opportunity I've been given. I'm under no illusion that it will be challenging, and I know I can't hide from Astrid forever, so I make a deal with myself that I'll cope with her through the day and scream into a pillow when I get home at night.

Pounding the streets before work has always been a great stress reliever for me, and I know I need it more than ever this morning if I'm to stand any chance of making it longer than a day at SecuriSoft. My recurring nightmares of Mike have started to become a little less frequent but the one I woke up from this morning has shaken me a little. It was all too real, and I woke up gasping for breath. Having somewhere to run and clear it all from my head is a godsend. As I reach the door of my apartment building, I feel almost ready to face the day and the hurricane that is Astrid.

I get into work earlier than anyone else this morning and I'm glad because it gives me a chance to compose myself before everyone arrives. I have a meeting scheduled today with Jed and Dan to discuss all the fine details of the software my team are working on. I'm a little apprehensive about it given my embarrassing moment last night at the elevator. I think I'm more nervous about Astrid being there though. Something about her doesn't sit right with me. She gives off a toxic energy and I noticed yesterday that people tense up when she's around. They don't even notice they're doing it, but I know I saw it. I could tell Damo has had his fair share of run-ins with her too.

As if he sensed me thinking about him, the man himself appears from the elevator.

"Morning Miss Nikki," he beams when he sees me at my desk.

"Good morning yourself. You're very happy this morning."

"Oh honey, I'm just happy to see you. I honestly thought after Astrid's shenanigans yesterday, you might not have come back."

I smile at him. I made the right choice in making a friend in Damo. He has a wonderful outlook on life. He's an optimistic person and I'm hoping some of that will rub off on me.

"Yeah, I had contemplated not coming back, but I couldn't leave you to fend her off yourself. We're a stronger force together. She needs to understand that she's an adult and adults don't act like that."

"Well I'm glad you came back. I like you Nikki and I think we'll be really good friends. Now what's the order of business today?" He pulls out his iPad and opens the diary.

"I've got a meeting with Jed and Dan at ten this morning, I know that much but I don't think there's anything else."

"Ooh calling him Dan now, that escalated quickly," he teases,

"Oh, stop that. I made a complete fool of myself last night in front of him. I was heading home and went to get the lift but when the doors opened Dan and Astrid were in there. I couldn't get in the lift with her after what she did but worse than that, I'm so unsure about Dan. Please don't laugh at me, but when I first got here yesterday, he was in the lift with me. You know before I knew who he was and being near him made my belly flutter. I felt like a silly schoolgirl."

Damo purses his lips and I know he's trying to stifle a laugh. "Were you making doe eyes at the boss Miss Nikki? Naughty girl."

"Stop. It was so embarrassing. He really is very good looking though, and from what I've heard, he's a genuinely nice person. It beggars belief that he'd be with someone like Astrid. She could turn milk sour simply by looking at it."

Damo laughs. "Yeah she's really one for watching. But don't you worry I've got your back."

"You're a total sweetheart Damo you know that."

We are interrupted by the elevator doors opening as the first of the workforce arrives. They have other projects they've been working on and all are due to wrap everything up by Friday so that we can get stuck into our project on Monday. I'm so excited by the prospects this job might bring me and the team I have to work with are so enthusiastic about bringing the concept to life. It makes me happy to see that there are some females on the team too. The last places I worked in weren't as diverse as this place. It was so male dominated with the only females being in receptionist or PA roles. It was very stereotypical of the industry and it used to make me feel uneasy at times. I was one of the exceptions, and I stuck out like a sore thumb.

As soon as everyone is in, I get on with getting to know them all a little better. Speaking to them all informally and individually, helps take my mind off the impending doom that is my first meeting with the big boss.

I watch Jed casually flicking through an industry magazine as we sit in the waiting area outside Dan's office and wonder how on earth he can work with Astrid every day and not want to strangle her.

"Okay folks you can go on through to the conference room." Dan's PA appears at the seating area and motions towards a door next to Dan's office.

"Cheers Tab," Jed says to her and I'm pretty sure I see a tiny eye roll from her as he turns his back to her.

"Thank you Tabitha," I say with a smile and she returns it warmly.

We head into the conference room, Jed with purpose and me with trepidation. In the two days I've been here there hasn't been one encounter with Dan where I haven't made a complete fool of myself. I have to pull myself together and show him that I'm a valuable asset to his firm if I ever stand a chance of keeping this job.

Dan is standing at the window with his back to us as we enter the room and turns at Jed's greeting. "Morning mate, how you doing?"

I take in Dan's appearance in the morning glow of the

sun. Gone is the scruffy rock-god look of yesterday and in its place is a suave and sophisticated businessman. His dark hair is styled and the suit he's wearing is obviously tailor made. It fits his form perfectly and my body tingles when he flashes a beautifully warm smile.

"Good as always Jed. Good morning Nikki, glad you could join us this morning."

"Morning Mr King."

He gives a little chuckle, as does Jed. "Please Nikki, call me Dan. I'm not into formalities from my staff, we're a family here. Isn't that right Jed?"

"Oh absolutely, all for one and one for all here Nikki. We've got each other's backs just like a real family would."

I'm starting to wonder if I'm in an office in Glasgow or some Italian mobster movie here. All this talk of family and having each other's backs feels more like a warning than a greeting and I'm starting to feel a little uneasy.

"Sorry, Dan it is then. It's nice to finally meet you properly. And I apologise for any confusion between us yesterday. I was a little overwhelmed by this place."

"No worries and It's nice to meet you too. I've heard great things about you, so you've got a lot to live up to."

I can't say I'm surprised he knows about me. Any business owner worth his salt would be diligent when it came to hiring someone new to work in their company.

"I can assure you I will give this job my everything. I'm so excited to be working for you. You have a wonderful company here."

Dan sits at the head of the table and motions for us to take a seat. We sit opposite each other at the top of the table and Dan hands us a folder each.

I watch as Jed opens his and frowns. "It's empty. Dan I

really need Astrid here if there's any note taking involved, you know I'm no good with that, it's why I hired her."

The mere mention of her name and the prospect that she may come to this meeting fills me with dread.

"No note taking necessary mate it's all in there. Tabitha has put together a comprehensive package for you both that should answer any and all questions you have on the project. It's nothing you haven't done before anyway. We just need to make sure it stays under wraps until the last minute. That's why only you two will have this information."

"Gotcha. My lips are sealed."

Dan turns his attention to me. "Nikki you will be responsible for delegating responsibilities to your team as you see fit. Your staff have been handpicked from the best of the company in order to deliver this project timeously and as confidentially as possible."

Wow this sounds like a higher profile project than I was expecting. "Absolutely Mr K… Dan." I laugh a little too nervously at my slip up, but he simply smiles at me and nods.

"Okay, let's read over this paperwork. I've had Non-Disclosure Agreements set up for both of you. As you'll appreciate in this business you can't be too careful." He hands us both a contract and I notice that Jed has gone a little pale.

"Um Dan I'm going to have to decline this. There will be stuff I'll need to discuss in front of Astrid. She is my PA and she does all my admin."

"There's nothing to worry about. Nikki will deal with collating her team's work and you'll come to me with it. I'm taking an active role in this one, and I know you understand why. Any other admin to be done will be carried out by Tabitha. She's already signed her NDA. Let's just say you're getting off lightly on this project for once Jed. Go with it. Enjoy the freedom."

"Hmm okay I suppose you have a point. So, signing this means that any leak on this comes down to four people?"

"Got it in one. Myself, you, Nikki and Tabitha."

Jed narrows his eyes a little and I get the feeling there's a sub conversation going on between them about something I'm not privy to. "I'm not trying to avoid signing this, but won't Nikki's staff know what's going on with the project too? I mean surely they'll have to sign these as well."

"That's the beauty of this one Jed. Each member of the team will have their own brief for each part they're going to be working on. Not one of them will have access to the whole project. That's why I need Nikki to delegate each part of this to the appropriate person. They are simply setting up the structure of the platform. The three of us will be fleshing it out."

For some reason Dan's explanation doesn't seem to be getting through to Jed and I'm starting to get frustrated by him. "It's quite simple really Jed is it not? I think Dan has explained as best he can. If anything is leaked about this project one of us is ultimately to blame."

Dan smiles and nods at me. "Couldn't have put it better myself Nikki. Thanks. So, let's read this over and get it out of the way. It's only a formality because, as Jed has already pointed out, we're like a family and family don't cross each other."

I look at Jed and realise I may have overstepped the mark when he narrows his eyes slightly at me. "Right I get it. Do you have a pen?" He asks Dan, his tone resigned but tinged with annoyance and his glare at me as he takes the proffered pen makes me recoil slightly. Great! It's my second day and I've already made an enemy of my line manager.

I've signed NDAs on a few occasions before. In this line of work, it's standard practice especially if the company stands to lose a lot of money due to a breach. Dan sits back as we both read over the agreements in silence. I take note of all the clauses, which seem pretty standard, and when I'm done and sit back in my chair, I realise Dan has been watching me. He smiles slightly at me then his gaze rests on Jed, who appears to be struggling with the wording of the document. I really don't understand why he's fighting this. It's not like he won't have done this before. He's in a senior management position after all, so it shouldn't be this hard.

"Everything good for you both?" Dan asks, looking at Jed with a smirk on his face.

"I'm fine with it," I say, closing the papers over.

Jed gives me a second of a stony glance and turns to Dan. "Suppose there's not much I can say about it, so I'm fine with it too."

"Excellent, let's get them signed and witnessed and get on with the day," says Dan in an almost too cheery voice, totally ignoring Jed's attitude.

Tabitha is called in to the conference room and is followed by Joyce, the manager from HR who both interviewed me and gave me my mini orientation meeting yesterday. Jed and I sign our agreements, then Dan, Tabitha and Joyce witness them, and we're done. It should all be painless, but Jed still has a bee in his bonnet for some reason.

"Right I have work to get on with. Catch you later." He turns and stalks out the door after Tabitha and Joyce, leaving Dan and I alone.

We stand in silence and I'm willing myself to speak and break it, but I don't know what to say. I'm so grateful when Dan speaks.

"So how did your first day go Nikki?"

"Hmm well… okay I suppose. I'll find my feet eventually, it's just a big change for me to be working in a senior role." I am not telling him about Astrid.

"You're talented Nikki. In fact, I'm very surprised you hadn't progressed further with your previous employers. Didn't you ever want to move up?"

"Ha!" I clamp my hand over my mouth. "Oh, I'm so sorry Dan," I mumble behind it.

"I take it you tried and were passed over?"

"The people I worked for weren't as forward thinking as you are. I was a rarity. A female in a developer role in those businesses wasn't the done thing. It took me a long time to establish myself. If I wasn't being asked to do other people's photocopying, I was given tea and coffee orders." As much as it's the truth in part, I can't tell him the real reason I never moved up the chain.

"Well I hope you'll find this place a welcome change. And for the record, if you'd done the type of work you did for them here, you'd have Jed's job."

"Yeah on that, what's the deal with him? I'm surprised you kept your cool."

Dan smiles. "Jed has his moments. I can deal with him."

Answered like a professional and giving nothing away. Typical of a big boss man.

"Okay Dan are we done here? I have a lot to get on with if we are going to get this project started on time."

"Absolutely. It's been a pleasure chatting with you Nikki. I'll be scheduling another meeting with you and Jed for Monday. We have some things to finalise before the project goes live." He reaches out and touches my elbow and I almost recoil into myself. "I'm looking forward to working with you Nikki."

I step back a little out of his touch. "I am too. Thanks

Dan, I'll catch you later." I leave the room, giving Tabitha a small wave as I pass her desk.

The elevator is already on the floor and as I step inside, I catch a glimpse of Dan leaning against the conference room door watching me. As the doors close and he winks at me, I stand there, open mouthed, the whole way back to the third floor. And damn it if that wink hasn't messed with my stupid body.

CHAPTER FOUR

"*H*ey girl, what you up to after work tonight then?" Damo asks as he spins circles in the office chair in front of me.

"Stop doing that you're making me feel sick."

He stops the chair in front of me and laughs. "Oh, hey I've done that before. When I was about three my dad put me on his chair and was spinning me round so fast, I puked everywhere. I did a full revolution before he managed to stop the chair. It was like a scene from The Exorcist. Dad was puking because I was and mum was screaming, it was all over when the dog…"

"Damo if you take this conversation any further, I swear I will throat punch you."

"Sorry honey. So, what are you doing then?"

"I'm actually meeting up with my sister. She's in the city visiting her friend Gina, so we're going for an early dinner this evening."

"How lovely. Is she bringing the wee one with her?"

"No, she's got the day off today. Her fiancé is coming to

pick her up later, so I'll get a quick cuddle before she goes home again. What are you up to tonight?"

"Oh, my mum's making me dinner tonight. It's a thing we do every Wednesday, have done since I moved out. I'm an only child and my da's been gone two years now so she gets lonely."

"I'm sorry Damo, I didn't know your dad had passed away."

Damo laughs. "Shit no Nikki, when I said he was gone I meant he left her. Shacked up with her best pal and moved to England. We've seen neither hide nor hair of him since. I couldn't care less to be honest, the guy's a piece of shit for hurting her like that. My mum's an angel of the highest order. You'd love her."

"Oh that's horrid. Your poor mum."

"Och she's better off without him."

I watch everyone start to pack up at four pm on the dot. You could set your watch by this lot. They all bid us goodnight as they pass by and within less than five minutes the office is quiet.

"Right I'm off Nikki, there's a steak pie calling my name. I'll see you in the morning."

"Night Damo, enjoy your dinner."

"Cheers honey you too," he says throwing his bag over his shoulder and disappearing into the waiting lift. He blows me a kiss as the doors close and it warms my heart.

Leaning back in my chair, I let the silence envelope me. A year ago, I had no life. I'd ended up down a hole I saw no way out of and as I take in my surroundings, I give a silent thank you. Granted I've had a little bit of a bumpy start, but I feel as though Astrid's bark may be worse than her bite. However, I've come across bitchy girls like her before and if they're not handled properly, they can be vindictive, dangerous even. Other than her, everyone else seems to be really pleasant.

The lift pinging startles me and my heart sinks when I see Astrid step out and strut her way over to me.

"Nikki, good you're still here. I've just come to hand these in." She holds out a slim white box to me. "Jed says you'll need them for providing your data every Friday."

I take it from her and look inside. It's filled with internal, confidential folders. "Okay thanks Astrid."

Hoping she'd simply leave when she was done is wishful thinking and I know this conversation isn't going to go well when she smiles slyly. "So, Jed tells me you've already been brown nosing the boss. Be careful there honey you'll make a name for yourself."

"Astrid, I'm really not in the mood to argue with you so if that's what Jed told you then so be it."

"Oh, I wasn't going to argue with you, it's just some friendly advice."

I'm at a disadvantage due to her height and the fact that I'm sitting down. "Consider it noted," I say trying my best to stay calm, but I can feel my bottom lip tremble slightly.

"Aw what's up dear have I upset you? Poor little you."

"Are you done? Please leave me alone Astrid, I've done nothing to you. What is your problem with me?"

She opens her mouth to answer but almost jumps out of her skin at the male voice behind her.

"Astrid, what are you doing here?" It's Dan and he looks pissed as he stalks towards her from the lift.

Astrid's eyes widen in shock and she turns to face him. "Oh, hi Dan I'm just dropping off Nikki's folders. We were just discussing what we are doing after work. I'm leaving now." Her sickly-sweet voice makes me shudder. She moves from nasty to butter wouldn't melt too easily, as though she's well practiced in it.

Dan narrows his eyes at her slightly, then turns his attention to me. "You okay Nikki?"

"Mmhm." I nod, thankful that he intercepted her before she was able to take it any further.

"Okay then let's allow Nikki to get on with her night." He nods towards the lift and Astrid turns to head out but not before giving me a final sneer.

"I came in on my way back upstairs to see if you were still here. I wanted to let you know that these were in." He taps the box. "Are you sure you're okay?"

I nod but I can't say anything because I know if I do, I'll start blubbering.

"Ok I'll see you at some point this week. Have a nice night Nikki."

I watch him walk away and as soon as he's far enough from me I make a beeline for the toilet. As soon as the door is closed, I let out a shuddering breath. "Shit," I shout and my voice echoes off the tiled walls.

I jump as the door opens and I find Dan standing there looking at me. "Why did you lie to me Nikki?" His voice is like silk and his smile makes him even better looking.

"Uh you shouldn't be in here. This is the ladies bathroom."

"It's my building. I'll go where I like."

"Well I'm going home." I grab my bag and walk towards the door. He doesn't move. "Excuse me please."

He still doesn't move. In fact, he straightens up so that he stands taller and becomes all at once rather intimidating. "You told me you were fine, but you lied. Why? What did Astrid really say to you?"

I back off quickly trying to put some space between us

but my heel slips on the tiled floor and my leg goes from under me. I crash to my knees and the contents of my bag scatter over the floor. I can feel panic rise in my chest and I'm becoming short of breath.

"My God are you okay?" Dan comes towards me and I scurry away like a frightened little mouse. I'm still on the floor but now I've backed myself into the corner between the sinks and the wall with the hand dryer. He comes closer to me and reaches out his hand.

"No!" I shout and put my hand up as if to defend myself. I've obviously put my hand up too high because the hand dryer turns itself on and I scream in shock at the loud noise. I think I'm having a heart attack. I feel like my heart is going to explode and I can't get a breath in. I'm so scared it feels like I might die.

"Nikki you have to calm down. Breathe." I realise he's sitting on the floor beside me rubbing my back, all the while soothing me with his voice.

I don't know how long we stay there but as the hand dryer turns itself off my breath evens out, and I start to realise I'm not going to die, my emotions quickly change from scared to utter embarrassment.

"Oh my God I'm so sorry," I whisper.

"Hey, what are you sorry for?" He leans back from me and moves my hair away from my tear stained face. "Are you okay to get up? This floor is freezing."

I nod and we get up off the floor. I watch as he gets down on his knees and starts picking up the contents of my bag. I want to curl up and die when he picks up the two tampons, but he doesn't utter a word or even make a face. He stands and hands my bag to me. "Thank you." My voice sounds feeble and pathetic.

"Are you okay? I'm sorry for startling you."

I shake my head. "No this is my own fault. I have... issues. I'm the one who's sorry. You did nothing wrong."

"Will you join me upstairs for a drink Nikki? I have some things I need to talk to you about."

My name rolling off his tongue sounds delicious and I have to look away so that he doesn't see what it has done to me. "Sure. Can you give me a minute?"

"Okay. Are you sure you're alright?"

I nod. "Yes, I promise I'll be fine."

"I don't know if I want to leave you like this."

"Honestly I'm fine. Go, I'll see you shortly."

He nods and leaves. I let out a long sigh and look at myself in the mirror. Well, if I didn't look ridiculous before I certainly do now. I get a makeup wipe from my bag and clean my face completely, fix my hair and head out the door. The floor is quiet and as I call the lift, I get a sinking feeling in the pit of my stomach. I can hear the lift car coming down from the floors above. I get in when the doors open and I can smell Dan, it's intoxicating. I'm about to press the twelfth-floor button but I can't do it. Instead I press the ground floor. I need to get out of here and meet with my sister, and I really don't want to have too much to do with a man that can see anything nice about someone like Astrid.

I leave the building as quickly as I can and manage to hail a black cab almost immediately. As the driver heads in the direction of the café I'm meeting Charlie at, that sinking feeling I had gets worse and I start to wonder what the fallout from my snub to Dan will be.

CHAPTER FIVE

I haven't seen Dan since I left on Wednesday. I've felt really bad about leaving without saying anything that night, but I've made my peace with myself. I have too many issues to work through right now and I really wasn't in the right frame of mind to be put on the spot by the boss.

We close at one o'clock on a Friday and Damo has invited me to go out with him and some friends. I'm looking forward to it. I haven't been on a night out since I got here, on account of having no friends. Well, I say no friends, I do have Gina and Steven, but they are my sister's friends. Damo is my first real friend and I intend to keep him.

I have my team assembled in the meeting room. I need to have a chat with them before we all leave for the weekend. We've already run through everyone's roles and responsibilities, talked over the main brief for the system we'll be working on and discussed the rota and holiday schedule Damo and I have been working on. Everyone has wrapped up all the other projects they were working on and they are all prepped and ready to get stuck right in on Monday.

"Now you guys are the backbone of this project so please feel free to question anything I put forward. We are a team after all. Is there anything you want to ask or add?"

Ben, an older, good looking guy, who was in the army before he came to work here, sticks up his hand. I nod to him.

"This is not so much a question but a statement. I just want to say on behalf of everyone on this team that we are so glad to have you here. I saw the other person they interviewed, and my God was he a sour faced bastard. You're a breath of fresh air."

I feel my cheeks redden, as there's a chorus of 'here here'. "Thanks guys… gosh I don't know what to say. I'm going to try and be the best team leader you've ever had, I promise." My smile gets wider as they all clap for me. "Right if there's nothing else you want to say get the hell out of here people, it's five past one. The weekend has already started."

I've hardly finished the last sentence, but they are all on their feet and making their way out the door. The office empties in a matter of minutes until there is only Damo and I left.

"God they were like rats deserting a sinking ship," Damo laughs. His smile soon fades and my heart hits the floor when the elevator doors open and Astrid saunters through the office holding a white folder in her hand. "Oh, shit what does she want?" He whispers.

She obviously hears him. "Shut it gay-boy," she says nonchalantly.

Poor Damo's face turns chalk white and he looks at me with such hurt in his eyes.

That's it; I've had enough of her now. She's a bully. I bang my fist on my desk. "Enough Astrid. Do you think you're in bloody school or something? This is a workplace;

we are grown-ups so you should start acting like one. God you're so disrespectful."

She takes a slight step back and narrows her eyes at me. "You better be fucking careful what you say to me. You should know by now, I have friends in high places here," she sneers as she points a skinny finger at me.

Is she for real? Is she seriously trying to threaten me? "Get out of my office," I shout at her. I want to crumble into a heap, but I can't let her know she has any power over me, it simply adds fuel to her fire.

She bites her bottom lip and smirks at me. "Okay don't have another fucking mental breakdown. Jed asked me to hand this in for you." She throws the folder down on the desk and walks away leaving me staring in utter shock.

As soon as the elevator doors close, I collapse into my seat and put my head in my hands. I can't stop the tears and before long I am a sobbing wreck. "How could he tell her?" I cry.

Damo wheels a chair over beside me and puts his arm round my shoulder. "Oh, Nikki please don't cry. You'll set me off. I'm so sorry your first week has been like this. I wish she would just fuck off."

"I'm starting to wonder why I bothered leaving South Africa you know that Damo. I really don't need this crap. I left enough of it behind."

"I know. Listen if you're not up to going out tonight I'll understand."

"No, I think I need it more than ever now. You head off, I'm going to clean up my face and head home myself."

He gives me a small smile. "By the way we are going to a gay bar tonight. She wasn't lying when she called me that. I just didn't want my sexual preference to cloud your judgement about me because, believe me, it does for some people."

41

"I don't care about that Damo. It's no one's business but yours and it doesn't have any bearing on the person you are. And I already knew. I'm not blind." I wipe my tears away from my face with a tissue.

He looks a little embarrassed. "Eh how?"

"Oh, for goodness sake Damo, I see the way you look at Ben. You've totally got a crush on him."

"Busted. Well he is handsome, and as straight as they come so all it will ever be is a crush."

His mock pining look makes me smile. "You'll find your Ben, I know it. You're a catch. Right get home, make yourself beautiful and come and pick me up at seven."

He kisses my cheek. "See you at seven then Miss Nikki."

I gather up my bag and jacket and wave to Damo as the lift doors close. I head for the toilet to clean up and make up my mind to get rat arsed tonight. Damo's saying not mine, but I found it funny so I'm adopting it.

Making sure the lights are off I get into the lift and press the ground floor. It takes me a moment to realise that the lift is in fact going up first. I hope against hope that it's anyone other than Dan on the other side.

The lift comes to a stop, the doors open and, just my luck, it's Dan who is waiting there. He's wearing navy blue suit trousers and a matching waistcoat. His white shirtsleeves are rolled to just below his elbows, showcasing his muscular forearms, and the collar is casually unbuttoned. I'm so taken aback by the sight in front of me that I momentarily forget I'm pissed at him.

We stare at each other until the doors start to close and he puts his hand between them opening them again. "Hi Nikki," he says. "Are you getting out?"

I shake my head. I can't seem to move. I back up to the wall when he steps inside. "You owe me a drink."

I reach up and push him back from me. "I don't think so. Get out of my personal space please."

He relents and steps back but stands in between the doors. I'm effectively trapped in this elevator. "You're very mysterious Nikki. What's your story?"

"I work here and you're my boss. I don't need to tell you my story. Now will you please let me go home?" I don't understand what's going on here but there is a certain tension in the air. I realise I'm clenching my jaw and I relax, drawing in a stuttered breath.

"Okay then. Nikki Olsson I would like to see you in my office right now please."

I sigh in defeat. "Excuse me please," I say as I move to exit the lift. He moves to the side and I stalk past him. Each step I take feels as though I'm walking into quicksand.

Dan catches up with me and walks beside me towards his office door. I can't look at him. I'm angry that he's using his authority over me to make me do as he wants. I wonder if that's how he controls Astrid. The thought does not sit easily with me.

He pushes the door open. "Take a seat Nikki," he says gesturing to one of the seats in front of the desk.

I sit on the one that's furthest away and watch Dan pour himself a whisky.

"Would you like a drink?"

"No. Please just get this over with and tell me why I'm here?" I can hear the anger in my voice, and I can see by his expression that he does too.

He takes his seat. "Are you mad at me for some reason Nikki?"

I shake my head and look at my hands. "Why did you tell her?" I ask, my voice low and full of defeat.

"Tell who, what?"

"Astrid. You told her about my breakdown in the toilet." I look at him and I feel tears surface at my lids. "How could you do that?"

"Nikki, I didn't tell her anything. I spoke to Jed about it. I asked him to keep an eye on you."

"Bullshit. You're sleeping with her so of course you told her. Please don't insult me."

He laughs and it only serves to boil my blood further. "Oh, you've just got to love the rumour mill, haven't you?"

I'm starting to feel less brave now and I can't believe I just spoke to my boss like that. "I'm sorry Mr King. I'll be more careful what I listen to in the future."

There is the tiniest glint in his eye but it's enough to make me notice. "You're a troubled young woman aren't you Nikki? Something's happened to you in the past and it's affecting how you treat people. Do you want to talk about it? Sometimes it helps. And call me Dan for goodness sake. Mr King makes me sound over the hill."

"I'm sorry *Dan* but I don't really know you, I don't think it's appropriate to air my dirty laundry right now," I bow my head, "and I wouldn't want you to think any less of me than you do already."

"Nikki."

I keep my head lowered.

"Nikki, look at me please."

I look up and see a sincere pair of warm brown eyes. Really taking in his beautiful face this time my breath catches slightly in my throat.

"I think very highly of you actually. You're an intelligent young woman. Do you think I'd hire someone who wasn't? How about we change tack here then? How has your first week been?"

I let out an over-exaggerated sigh. "Where do I start?"

"That bad Huh?"

"You could say that since the second person I met on Monday has taken an instant dislike to me for some reason."

"Hmm. Tell me what happened on Monday. You looked like you'd seen a ghost when you came in here. Did it have something to do with Astrid?"

"Yes, and it was then I knew I'd have to be wary of her." I tell him what she did, and how she's been talking to me since we first met, and when I'm done, he leans forward in his chair, clasping his hands on the desk.

"I'm going to let you in on something Nikki. I don't know what it is about you, but I feel like I can trust you and I think if you know more about the software project, you could really help me with what I have planned."

My brows knit together. I'm intrigued. "Okay."

"You have to promise to keep this quiet or it will blow everything."

I make a cross sign over my chest. "Cross my heart. I already signed that NDA though so I would never tell anyone anyway."

He nods. "What I want to tell you is more to do with the background to why the project is happening in the first place. That wasn't covered in the NDA, so I need your discretion on this."

"Oh, well carry on then."

"I met Astrid about seven years ago at a charity boxing match. She was one of those walk-on girls. You know those ones, all tits and teeth. Anyway, I got extremely drunk and ended up, well I think you can guess. Let's just say it wasn't one of my finer moments. We had a one-night stand and I didn't see her again until a year ago when she was hired as Jed's PA. It was a huge leap to go from a walk on girl to a PA but, apparently, she'd managed to get herself a PA diploma

45

from a distance learning college. Jed was impressed with her and her credentials stacked up. As much as she's not the nicest person to work with, she's good at her job. Doesn't make her the best though. I have that one.," He gets up and pours himself another whisky. "You sure you don't want one?" He holds an empty glass up.

"I've never tried it."

"Let's change that. You're not driving, are you?"

I shake my head. "No, I can't afford a car yet." Why I chose to tell him that I don't know.

He pours me a glass and places it on the desk in front of me. The golden liquid looks fiery in the clear crystal glass. He takes his seat behind the desk. "I'll show you how to drink it."

"Sorry?"

"There's a certain way to drink whisky, to really taste it. Have you ever done a wine tasting?"

"You do know I'm from South Africa, don't you?" I laugh.

"Ah yes excuse my oversight, of course you've been to a wine tasting." His smile lights up his eyes and I think he looks a little embarrassed, like he doesn't normally make slip ups like that.

"I've been to many wine tastings but, and don't tell anyone, I prefer Californian wine."

He laughs. "Your secret is safe with me. Well when tasting wine, you take air into your mouth right?" I nod. "But with whisky you don't. You take a sip, hold it in your closed mouth for a few seconds then swallow it. That's when you taste it. Like this."

I watch as he takes a sip and keeps his mouth closed. He swallows it and holds his glass up. "Cheers."

I lift the glass, which is remarkably heavy, and clink it

with his. "Cheers." I take a sip and hold my mouth closed. The liquid is instantly warming and when I swallow it, I feel as though my throat is on fire.

"You like?"

"Um it's interesting. I'm still tasting different things even though I've swallowed it."

"Yeah for four hundred pounds a bottle it should do that."

I cough and look at the glass. "Wow that's an expensive little glass full there."

"So anyway, back to my story." He takes another sip of his whisky and I do the same. This time my palate has a taste for it, and it goes down much easier. "I didn't remember Astrid at first, but she went out of her way to try and jog my memory. She did all sorts of crazy shit which I won't bore you with but let's just say I wasn't interested, and I'm still not interested." He says this pointedly making sure I heard him.

"Okay I get it. I was just saying what I've heard everyone else say."

"It's like bloody Chinese whispers in here sometimes. Now what I am going to tell you is strictly confidential. Got it?"

I nod.

"Jed is having an affair with Astrid."

"Really? Damo said he's happily married."

"Oh, it's not as simple as that. Right now, I'm conducting an internal investigation. In the last year I've had two different software products pulled out from under me, one of which was significant enough to cost me a lot of money, and I think Jed and Astrid are at the centre of it."

"Are you saying you think they are corporate spies?"

"That's exactly what I think. It pisses me off no end because Jed has been with me since the beginning. I'm worried he's involved in something he can't get out of, although unless someone kidnapped his wife and kids and forced him to do it, he's just as culpable as her. And that's where you come in. I set up your team to try and catch them out. The software you are working on will never do the job it's intended to do."

I'm seriously confused, and I really don't like to think where this is going. "What do you mean?"

"Your team and your project are a sting."

I'm shocked. "Do you mean to tell me I don't actually have a real job? My staff aren't actually my staff? Dan, I left South Africa and a good job for this." I stand on shaky legs; this news is like a punch to the gut. "If I hadn't been in here this afternoon would you even have told me?"

"Of course I would have. I was going to tell you on Wednesday, but you didn't come up. I've been in London since that evening. I only got back a couple of hours ago. I was actually coming down to see if I could catch you before you went home. I really felt like I needed to speak to you after what happened in the bathroom."

I sit back down. "Okay. Tell me exactly what you hope to achieve with this sting of yours."

"I think Jed is being paid by someone to steal concepts from me. The only way I'm going to catch him out is by feeding him bad information and getting him to pass it on. This is where you come in. Since Jed is your line manager everything your team does will have to go through him before it's given the go ahead to proceed."

"I think I see where this is going. You want me to doctor the code before I give it to him."

"Exactly. Your staff don't need to know. They will still be working on the real deal and you'll give that work directly to me, then you'll give Jed a bad copy of the same work. As you know the code only has to be a few characters off for it to fail. If my instincts are right, I'll have the proof to have him sacked and possibly prosecuted."

"Jed's a clever guy. He'll figure it out. I'm all for helping you, I hate thieves, but I also don't want anyone thinking I'm stupid or incompetent."

"Don't worry about that. I'll deal with that situation if it arises."

I frown at him. For such a clever man, he's putting a lot on the line. His plan doesn't seem fool proof, not in the slightest.

"What does Astrid have to do with it then?"

"She's the one who got him involved. I know more about her than she thinks, and I know she's involved with the company that has been stealing my work."

"This is a lot to take in."

"So, are you on board with this?"

"Do I really have a choice?"

He shakes his head. "No, not really."

"I still have a job though?"

"Of course you do."

"Okay then I'm in. If it means taking down that vapid, vindictive bitch then I'm in."

Dan holds his fist up. I bump it with my own. "Let's drink to that."

I lift my glass and drink the rest of the whisky and reflect on my first week at SecuriSoft. You couldn't make this shit up.

I really love that the office building is right on the banks of the river. If I take the walkway that starts across the road from the office, I end up at the part of the city centre I live in. It's a nice ten-minute walk and the breeze coming off the river is always refreshing. After everything I've had to process on this first week at SecuriSoft, it's a welcome walk this afternoon.

The only part of this walk I don't really like is the under-passes. They are created by the bridges that span the Clyde and on my walk home there are three of them, thankfully in quick succession. As I head under the first one and the light disappears, I have the horrible feeling that someone is following me. I pick up the pace a little and glance behind me. There's no one there, but there are shadows and my mind is playing tricks on me.

Exiting into the bright sunlight for a second or two before I head under the next darkened space, I walk faster still, a slight panic rising in my chest. I can sense someone behind me now and I start to run. I hear a mechanical noise at my back, and I stop still and flatten myself into the wall, a high-pitched scream coming from me as a cyclist whooshes past and comes to a screeching halt in front of me.

"I'm sorry Miss, are ye okay?" The man removes his cycle helmet and puts his hand on my shoulder, making me flinch.

"I… I… I'll…" I can't get my words out; my breath feels as though it's been stolen.

"Breathe, just breathe slowly, you'll be fine."

The man's voice is calming, and I manage to catch a breath. "Thank you," I whisper. "I'm so sorry."

"Are you going to be awright? Under these bridges can be a wee bit scary so I'm no surprised you got a fright."

"Yes, I'll be fine, thank you for your help."

I watch him get back on his bike and ride off and I sigh. "Fuck it," my voice echoes in the chasm.

I make my way out of the last of the darkened spaces and

decide I'm going to take the road from now on, at least until I get to the part past the tunnels. I'm already on edge anytime there's someone walking behind me, I really don't need my imagination helping with that.

I've been on edge since I got to Glasgow, constantly thinking I was being followed for the first couple of weeks I was here, but this is the first time I've had that feeling since I started my job. It's not sitting easily with me and I'm thankful that the part of the walkway along the river is quite busy today. I need to try and get over this. Mike doesn't know where I am, and I doubt he even cares. He's probably found another poor soul to torment by now, and that thought makes me feel wretched.

CHAPTER SIX

"*E*yelash curlers *then* mascara. You've pulled out half your lashes." Damo is trying his hardest not to laugh at me.

"Stop it. God this is so embarrassing. You'd think I'd know how to put makeup on. I don't know what possessed me to try curlers tonight. I've never used them before."

Damo grabs my shoulders. "It's okay I have a plan. What time is it?"

I check my phone. "Five to five."

"Excellent the Boots in the St Enoch centre is open till six. I'm going to get you some falsies. I'll be back in ten minutes."

Before I can say anything, he's hot footing it out the door. I look at the eyelash curler and cringe. Of all the nights for this to happen. I was trying to make myself look glam and ended up scalping my eyelid.

I'm about to head to the kitchen to get more wine when a text flashes up on my phone. It's from Gina, my landlady and Charlie's best friend.

Hey sweetheart. Hope your first week went well. I have

something I need to ask you. Are you free for a FaceTime right now? X

This sounds intriguing.

Yeah, sure. I'm just getting ready to go out with my new friend from work. X

I take the phone with me to the kitchen and I have just finished pouring a glass of wine when the phone rings. I press the answer icon and Gina's lovely face appears on the screen.

"Hi honey," she says and waves to me.

"Hi. Sorry about the mess of my face. I decided it would be a good idea to put on mascara then use eyelash curlers."

She winces. "Oh shit Nikki are you ok?"

"Yeah just lost a few lashes and a lot of pride. Damo, my friend, has gone to get me some false ones."

"Oh…he's a keeper. Right the reason I called. So, you know Steven asked me to marry him and this little baby is due in October?"

"Mhm. You're one lucky mama Gina."

"I count my blessings every day believe me. So, we have decided to get married in three weeks."

"God almighty that's quick. Will you have time to plan everything?"

"Hopefully. Dad has already managed to get us a venue. It's in the Hunter Halls at Glasgow Uni. Because we are both graduates of the university it was very easy and we got a cancellation."

"Oh, that will be beautiful."

"Well I need a bridesmaid now. I already have a chief bridesmaid, but I want two. Would you be the other?"

My breath catches in my throat and I feel tears come to my eyes. "Oh, Gina I'd be honoured. Thank you so much."

"Thank you sweetie and I'm sorry about ruining your makeup. You'll need to do it all over again."

I laugh and swipe the tears from my cheeks. "It probably looks better than it did."

"Okay, I'll let you go and get ready. Charlie will be in touch to arrange dress fittings. Enjoy your night out and thanks again Nikki, this means a lot to me."

"Thanks yourself, this has made me very happy. I'll see you later."

"Bye honey." She blows me a kiss and then she is gone.

Wow. I don't think this day could get any crazier. I lift my wine and take a huge gulp and at that very moment Damo decides to make an entrance that would wake the dead. I get such a fright that I breathe in the wine and I feel it go up my nose. It burns like all hell, but I can't help myself. I end up in hysterics, choking at the same time.

"Jesus Nikki are you okay?"

"I'm fine you gave me a fright that's all."

"I'm sorry. I got the falsies now let's get you dolled up. My friends are going to adore you."

We set about sorting my makeup malfunction and I tell Damo about my call with Gina.

---

*B*y the time Damo is done with me I look fabulous and my 'new' lashes are to die for.

"Mmm you look amazing Miss Nikki. I'm going to be the envy of the club tonight turning up with this on my arm."

He turns me to face the mirror. "Damo you're in the wrong job boy. You should be a bloody makeup artist. This is amazing." I turn my head from side to side admiring his handy work. I don't think I've ever felt so beautiful. My emerald green long-sleeved body-con dress shows off every curve and Damo has paired it with a pair of black ankle boots.

I'd never have put this outfit together, but it works. "Thank you." I grab him and kiss his cheek.

"Oh stop it. You're my friend it's what we do. Are you ready to go?"

"Ready as I'll ever be."

---

*T*he club we have gone to is literally on my doorstep and since we were here early, we managed to get a booth to sit at. Damo's friends, Jamie and Sandy, are lovely guys and I've been welcomed into their group with open arms. They're both straight and I've found out Jamie is a bit of a ladies man, although Damo has already warned him to leave me alone. He's a flight attendant who's back in Glasgow for a stopover for a few days. It explains a lot. He can have no strings company for a day or two and never has to be tied down. It's the perfect job for someone who wants a carefree life.

As the night has gone on the place has started to fill and become noisier. The music belting out is hugely upbeat and just what I need to clear my head after the week I've had.

"Oh my God I love this song. Let's dance Nikki," Damo shouts to me over the noise.

Since I'm now well on my way to being merrily drunk I take his hand and he leads me out to the dance floor to the slow, soulful voices of Barbara Streisand and Donna Summer. I know this song well and the fact that its lyrics resonate with my own life just a few weeks ago makes me want to dance to it.

We each sing a line as we belt out the anthem and dance round the floor. I'm in the middle of 'tell him to just get out' when someone at the bar catches my eye.

I grab Damo's arm. He's lost in his own little world dancing like there's no one else here. "Damo," I shout over the music.

Damo open's his eyes but keeps singing. "Enough is enough."

"Damo is that Dan at the bar?"

He trails off his line and looks at the bar. "Well yes I think it is. What's he doing in a gay bar?" He shouts over the music.

"Hmm yeah that's what I want to know." In my drunken state, I feel brave, so I head to the bar, ignoring Damo's pleas not to.

As I get closer to the bar, I can see he's sitting on a stool chatting to a guy next to him. He's a little thinner than Dan but good looking all the same. I'm stopped in my tracks when Dan turns and looks right at me. And it's at that moment that I realise how attracted to him I am. Not drunken beer goggle attracted to him. I mean literal panty ripping attracted. Wouldn't that be just my luck that he might be secretly gay. I shiver a little and I feel goose bumps rise all over my body.

I watch him get down from his stool and walk over to me. "Imagine bumping into you here my little spy."

"Hmm imagine. What are you doing in a gay bar?"

"I could ask you the same thing."

I sway a little on my feet, God I am drunk. "I'm here with my *gay* friend." I point at Damo who is eyeing me suspiciously.

"Well I'm here with my *gay* brother." He points to the guy still sitting at the bar who gives us a wave.

"Oh thank God." I realise I actually said that out loud as a smile spreads over his face.

"You're drunk young lady."

"Just how old do you think you are Dan?" I put my finger

on his chest. It's solid. "Dan the man. You're only six years older than me." I have to shout over the noise of the music.

Dan nods to his brother and takes my wrist leading me out into a quieter part of the club near the entrance. We stand in silence for what seems like an eternity until Dan breaks it.

"You look nice Nikki."

"Hmh nice, thanks I guess." I don't even hide the dejection in my voice.

Something in Dan's eyes flickers and he moves closer to me. "What do you want me to say Nikki?"

I shrug my shoulders. My instinct would normally have me backing away from him but right now, in this moment, all I want to do is grab him and kiss him.

He moves a little closer. "Do you want me to tell you how much your body is turning me on?" This time when he moves closer, I do back up so that my back is against the cold wall. He puts his hand on the wall next to my head and leans in close to me. "Do you want me to tell you that I want nothing more than to touch you?"

Oh God…I want him to touch me, more than I've ever wanted anyone to touch me. I shiver as he looks down the length of my body. This dress is so tight I've had to go braless, and it is leaving nothing to the imagination. When he sees my hard nipples, he sucks in a breath through his teeth. I jump when he slams his palm on the wall. "Fuck I can't do this Nikki. I'm sorry. It's not appropriate." He turns and walks away leaving me bereft and feeling rather stupid.

What the hell were you expecting you fool? He's your bloody boss. I make it my mission to get as drunk as I can tonight. I have a feeling Monday is going to be very awkward.

CHAPTER SEVEN

Oh my God...am I dead? The thought surfaces through a quagmire of pain, fatigue, nausea and dizziness. Tentatively I open my lids. *Oh shit!* This is not my bedroom. *WTF?!!!*

I sit up and look around. The room is bright white. It hurts my eyes. I close them and send up a prayer. No such luck. There's a guy lying next to me, asleep. He's young and not bad looking but I am mortified. I don't even know where I am or how I got here, and I certainly don't know who this guy is. I check my body and thank my lucky stars that I'm still fully clothed. I have never, in my life, been so stupid as to go home with a guy I don't know. I get out of the bed and, after finding my boots and bag, I leave as quietly as I can and find myself in a long corridor. It looks like it might be student accommodation. I fish in my bag for my phone and thankfully it's still there along with some money and my house keys.

As soon as I'm out the front door of the building, after spending ten minutes trying to find it, I take in a cleansing deep breath. My head is pounding, and my mouth is dry. It's still dusky outside so I know it must be early morning. When I check my phone, I see its *06:24* and find a million texts and missed calls from Damo and one from Charlie. *Fuck!* Where am I? I bring up my map and click to find my location. Thankfully I'm not too far away from home so my walk of shame will be short lived. I'm about to ask Siri to get me home when my phone decides to die. I want the ground to open up and swallow me. I feel ashamed and helpless and decide to start walking and see if I can catch a black cab on the main road. At least I know my address, so I know I'll get home eventually.

At this time on a Saturday morning the streets are eerily quiet and it's unsettling to say the least, when I see a cab approach with its hire light on, I almost run into the road to stop it. The driver smiles at me as I get in. I can tell he's judging me. I'm judging me. I can't believe how stupidly reckless I've been. I sit down in the back of the cab and give him my address. As the taxi pulls away from the kerb, I close my eyes and silently cry.

---

*M*y climb of the carpeted stairs in my building is like an uphill hike. As I reach my door, I get my keys out and, with shaking hands, unlock the door. I dump my bag in the kitchen next to the wine glasses that are still there from last night and head for the bathroom. I turn on the shower, kick off my boots and get in the shower still fully clothed. Letting the spray of the warm water run over me I cry loudly, huge heaving sobs wracking my body. I feel disgusting and dirty. I don't know what has happened to me. I used to be such a happy person until I met Mike. He has destroyed me and somehow, I don't think I'll ever recover from it. There will always be a part of me that thinks I'm no good for anyone.

As I strip out of my wet dress and knickers, I get a flashback to last night…being alone with Dan at the club. Oh good God that's why this happened. He walked away from me and I couldn't handle it. I dread to think how much I actually had to drink last night but I don't remember anything after Dan left me in the corridor.

---

*M*y shower has made me feel more human and I'm slowly going through my texts from last night. The ones from Damo started at about midnight so that must be when I lost touch with him.

Nikki where are you?

Nikki? I'm worried here can you call me?

Nikki will you please get in touch with me? We are going home now but I would really like to know you're ok. X

I'm going to call you in the morning. Whoever you're with better be worth my death. I'm having a heart attack here. X

The text from Charlie came in at half four.

Morning sis. Phone me when you get up we need to organise a dress shopping day. Love ya darling. Xx

I call Damo. I have to let him know I'm okay. His phone rings and rings and just as I think it's going to his voicemail, he answers it.

"Oh my freaking God Nikki!! Are you okay? I was frantic last night."

"Oh Damo, I'm so sorry," I say as I burst into tears.

"Nikki what happened last night?"

"I don't know. I woke up in some guy's bed this morning. I don't even know who he is. I totally fucked up Damo. I'm sorry."

"Stop apologising. I'm coming over okay. I'll be there in twenty minutes. Will you be okay till I get there?"

"Yeah."

"Hang in there, Miss Nikki."

We hang up and I lie down on the couch sobbing in shame.

The incessant knocking on the door and the constant ringing of the doorbell is not doing my delicate head any favours. As soon as I open the door and see Damo standing there, I break down again. He comes in and shuts the door and wraps me in a warm hug. "Hey, it's okay your bestie is here, and I've got the best hangover cure right here in this bag." He leans back from me and holds up a white plastic bag. I nod, swipe my tears from my face and we walk into the kitchen. Damo starts to empty the bag onto the kitchen counter. There's a large plastic bottle of transparent bright orange liquid. The label says Irn Bru. We had one called Iron Brew in South Africa, it may be a knock off of this. Ours looks more like cola though. I've heard of this one but I'm not sure what its healing properties may be. There are also two white bags filled with food, I'm guessing, since there are little spots of grease on the bags.

"What is this?"

"Irn Bru. *The* national drink of Scotland."

"I thought that was whisky?"

"Well, it is but this is a close contender. Although, for a hangover it has to be full sugar. None of that diet crap."

"Okay and this?" I point to the white bags.

"Ah…these are Scotland's national food."

"Oh, Damo I've tried haggis, I don't like it."

Damo laughs. "Not haggis, I hate that stuff it's just plain nasty. This my little darling is a roll and square sausage."

My mood is lifting with his enthusiasm and I smile. "My mum has talked about this. I've never tried it though."

"Well, prepare to be blown away. Where are your glasses?"

I point to the cupboard above the sink. The whoosh of the carbon dioxide as he opens the lid echoes in the quiet apartment. He pours us both a large glass and I take a seat on the couch with my orange elixir and food.

"Get stuck in, then we can talk about last night."

His words send a shiver up my spine. I take a bite of the roll and find that it's actually comfortingly tasty. The Irn Bru tastes like nothing I've ever had in my life. I expected it to taste like orange, but I just can't put my finger on the flavour. We eat and drink in silence and Damo is right, this is a good cure. Obviously, it is the combination of grease and sugar, but it has done the trick. I don't feel like I want to puke everywhere now.

"Feel better?" Damo smiles at me.

"Yeah."

"Right, what the hell happened last night?"

I bow my head in utter shame. "I honestly don't know. The last thing I can remember was being out in the corridor with Dan. After he left and I came back to get you I don't remember anything else."

"You don't remember getting us thrown out of the club?"

"Oh hell. What?"

"Well you tried to get up on the bar to dance and the bouncers threw us out. Sorry they threw you out, but I couldn't leave you on your own obviously, so I left with you."

"Where did we go?"

"I took you to a late-night coffee shop to get you sobered up a bit. You were seriously out of it. I went to the toilet after the coffees were made and when I came back you were gone. You hadn't even touched your drink. I tried phoning and texting you but got no reply. I even came here to see if you had come home. I swear if you hadn't called me this morning I was going to the police."

"I honestly don't remember any of this Damo. This is so bad. I know I had a lot to drink but I've had more and still remembered the night before. God anything could have happened to me."

"I think your drink might have been spiked."

The thought makes me want to be sick. "Oh no." I put my head in my hands. "How will I know?"

"The club opens at noon so we could go and speak to the manager and ask if we can have a look at the security footage. They take this sort of thing very seriously, so they'll want to know if it has happened."

"You know what this means though? If I don't remember anything, how could I have made a rational decision to go with the guy I ended up with?"

"Do you think you had sex with him?"

"Well, I woke up fully clothed in bed beside him so I don't know if something happened or if I passed out before it could."

"Are you on the pill?"

"God Damo, I met you less than a week ago. This is not a conversation I thought I'd be having with you."

He rubs my arm. "Look, I like you Miss Nikki. I like you a lot. I know this is the most embarrassing thing that could probably have happened. Believe me I feel entirely responsible for this. If I hadn't taken you out last night, we wouldn't be having this conversation."

"I don't blame you Damo. Yes, I'm on the pill."

"I suggest you get tested for STD's just to be safe but, by the sound of things you may have dodged a bullet. We'll check the cam footage at the club then you can put this all behind you."

"God, I feel like a stupid teenager. I've never done anything like this before. I think the whole thing with Dan has fucked with my brain."

"What thing with Dan?"

"Well, when we were in the corridor of the club there was... a... moment."

"Oh God Nikki. We'll fix this, I'll be here for you I promise."

"You're a good friend Damo. Can I trust you to keep this to yourself? I couldn't bear it if anyone found out."

He crosses his heart. "I promise."

---

*T*he club is quiet since it's only just after twelve noon. The manager has been more than obliging when we told him what we think happened last night. Right now, we are sitting in an office at the back of the club and the manager is flicking through all of the footage from last night.

"This looks promising. Is that you?" He asks.

I look closely at the screen and see Damo and I dancing.

Then I see myself heading to the bar and then Dan taking me out to the corridor. "Yeah that's us."

"Where was your drink?"

"At our table. We were sitting at a booth on the other side of the bar."

"Okay here's the footage from that side."

We watch our table which shows Damo and I leaving, obviously to go and dance. Jamie and Sandy turn their backs to the table to talk to people behind them. I am gobsmacked when I see a female come to the table and drop something into my glass. When she turns to leave the table, I am in shock. It's Astrid.

"What the fuck. Damo."

"I see her Nikki. My God that horrible cow. I'm going to the police about this."

"No." I say it almost too quickly, but I know Dan needs her to be able to prove what she and Jed are up to. "I'll deal with it."

The manager shakes his head. "Eh…darling if you know her, I have to call the police."

"No, I saw her earlier in the night, but I don't know her," I lie.

Damo shakes his head. "No, we don't know her." There is hurt in his eyes and I feel incredibly guilty that I've made him lie. The manager takes a screen shot of Astrid's face. "I'll circulate this to my door staff and if she comes back here, I'll report her to the police."

"Thanks for your help." We shake the manager's hand and head out into the sunny afternoon.

I lean against the wall and sigh.

"Are you going to tell me what just happened Nikki?"

"I can't."

"I thought we were friends."

"Damo we are. I'm sorry."

"Oh, Miss Nikki, I sure hope you know what you're doing." He takes my hand and rubs my knuckles.

I hate lying to him. He really has been a good friend to me. "I do and I'll be fine." My voice seems to do pretty well at hiding my inner turmoil.

CHAPTER EIGHT

*M*y sister and I look absolutely amazing in our fifties style light pink bridesmaid dresses. They sit just below the knee and are sleeveless. We look like two peas in a pod with our long blonde hair and blue eyes.

"These are the dresses," Gina says holding up her champagne flute filled with sparkling grape juice. This will be the fourth she's had; we have been all over Glasgow in different bridal shops looking for the perfect dresses. "Now I have my colour scheme."

My sister's best friend is such a beautiful person inside and out. She's been through so much in a short space of time and it's only right that she should finally be happy. It must have been awful to be widowed so young.

"They are perfect. And they fit." Charlie does a twirl and the tulle and chiffon skirt of her dress fans out then wraps itself round her legs. "Oh, I feel so elegant. And that's not happened in a long time."

My niece decides to let us know she's still here by letting out the loudest glass-shattering cry I've ever heard. We all jump and laugh.

"I'll get her. You two get changed and we can pay for these dresses." Gina lifts Georgie out of her pram and cradles her against her chest. She's going to be such a good mum.

Charlie and I get changed and head back out to find Gina. Before we get out of the dressing room Charlie stops me.

"Are you okay Nikki?"

"I'm fine. I've just got a lot on my mind with this new job. Honestly, it's nothing for you to worry about sis."

She looks at me in that way of hers that lets me know she doesn't believe me but that she's willing to let me off the hook. "Okay, but you know where I am if you need me. Don't be getting too stressed out at work it's not worth it."

Oh, if only you knew Charlie. "I'm not. It's actually really interesting." I can't even begin to tell her about Friday. She'd have a shit fit and I'd be promptly moved to Edinburgh.

"Are you guys ready?" Gina's voice echoes down the short corridor.

"Coming honey," Charlie shouts back.

We hand the dresses to the assistant who proceeds to package them carefully into garment boxes filled with tissue paper.

The assistant looks at us. "Okay that will be…" she stops as Gina waves her hand.

"I'm paying for these."

My sister tries to protest but Gina is having none of it. "Steven said I can buy whatever I want for this wedding and I want these."

Charlie shakes her head and laughs. She takes Georgie from Gina and straps her back into her pram. "You'll be the death of me, you rich bitch."

It still sounds strange to hear my sister's accent. She left Glasgow aged four, so she had a Scottish accent when she got to South Africa. Over time she developed a more local accent but as soon as she came back here the Scottish twang returned. Now it's a mixture of the two and it's quite funny sometimes. We leave the bridal boutique and Gina's driver, Gerry, is waiting at the kerb in a beautiful black Range Rover just like the ones the Royal Family drive around in. We put our dress boxes in the back so that Gina can take them home and I help Charlie get Georgie's pram folded.

"Do you want a lift home Nikki?"

"Thanks Gina but I'm going to do a little bit of food shopping before I go home. All my fridge has in it is a bottle of wine and some milk that's gone off."

We say our goodbyes and I head in the direction of the main shopping area wondering what my day will be like at SecuriSoft tomorrow.

I can't seem to function today. I'm still reeling from learning Astrid spiked my drink on Friday. Damo was right when he said I had dodged a bullet. Who knows what might have happened had it been anyone other than that nice student guy? I'll call him a nice guy since I woke up fully clothed although I'm sure that was probably only because I passed out before anything could happen. I take a seat on a backless bench facing the River Clyde. The Securi-Soft building looms over me from behind. I honestly don't know why I've come down here on a Sunday but here I am. My pitiful shopping trip managed to get me a pre-packed tasteless sandwich and a bottle of water. Since it's already almost five in the evening I suppose it'll do for dinner. The breeze coming off the water is chilly and I'm thankful for the warm jacket and scarf I have on. April was never this cold in South Africa and it's taking a little bit of adjusting. Watching the river flow, I contemplate how much my life has changed since I got to the UK.

I stayed in London for four weeks with my parents until it was time for me to fly the nest. My dad is doing a four-year stint at the foreign office in London and then he can retire on an amazing pension and mum can get her husband back. I love my dad and I know he loves us dearly, but he's always been married to his work. I remember once listening to him and mum having an argument about it and she said something that has stuck with me all these years later. *"You're never here. Even when you're home, you're never here."* His job was, and still is, extremely important and we all knew that. I think that's why he got away with it. I know my dad thinks this move was his decision, but I have a sneaking suspicion that mum had been planting the seeds for a long time. As soon as this job opportunity came up, he jumped at it and I know it was a huge relief to mum. She always wanted to come back home and if London was as close as she could get, that would do.

Deciding I should really get off this cold bench I swing my legs over the other side so that I'm now facing the Securi-Soft building. My heart falls into my feet as I see two very familiar people leaving through the front doors. I quickly pull my hood up and put my scarf over my face. I watch as Dan turns to Astrid and touches her arm in a way that looks more familiar than a working relationship. As they walk off in opposite directions, I turn to face the water again. I'm left with the horrible feeling that I've been used. That I've intentionally been put in danger, for what gain I have no idea, I just know that tomorrow may be my last day working there.

CHAPTER NINE

*T*he radio host on my alarm clock sounds far too happy for my mood this morning. I reach my hand out and almost smash the thing putting it on snooze. I lie staring into space for the nine minutes it takes to sound again. This time I turn it off and decide I really need to get up. I'm going to need to start this day as strong as I can.

My sleep was extremely restless. My dreams took me on a strange tour of all my insecurities. I let my guard down with Dan and he used it to his advantage. I don't honestly know what my purpose is in this little game he's got going on but I sure as hell won't have my life put at risk for it. I decide to do a bit of job hunting before I get ready. At least I will if this piece of shit laptop will ever connect to the WiFi. The MacBook I used to have had been part of my job, so I had to hand it back when I left. This antiquated thing I am using is one of my dad's old ones. As soon as I can afford it, I'll be buying myself a new one. Although I may end up homeless first, if I don't find another job.

There's not a lot on offer in my sector in Glasgow, in Scotland for that matter. Dan has very much cornered the market here, which explains why he is one of only a handful of billionaires in Scotland, albeit the poorest one. It makes me feel a little uneasy when I realise I don't know much about this man. I grabbed this job as soon as it was offered to me, probably before it was offered, no questions asked, because I was in a bad place and it was my way out. I had control over that decision; it was mine to make. I should have made the decision sooner. But now I'm in the middle of something I have no control over, and it's already cost me too much. Dan King can get some other patsy to piss all over.

*T*he building is quiet since it is only ten past eight in the morning. I take the elevator to the third floor and when I get off, I stop to take in the office. My heart pains at the thought of leaving this job. I thought this was going to be where I would find my fit. As much as my first week was filled with drama, I was really looking forward to hitting the ground running with this project, but I can't stay. I know it's not in my best interest and I've done too much of putting other people first or taking other people's crap because I thought I wasn't worth anything better. Taking a deep breath, I head for my desk and start clearing out the little bits and pieces I have managed to accumulate over the last week. I almost want to die inside when I look at what is in the box on the desk. Two pens my dad gave me, a mug that my sister gave me with a Superman logo on it and a welcome card that Damo gave me. That's it. That's what my week has been. It's pathetic.

I know what needs to be done today and there's no point holding it off any longer. I know Dan is in, I saw his car outside, so before I can overthink things I get back in the lift and push the button for the twelfth floor with more confidence than I'm feeling. The higher the car goes the less sure I am of myself and by the time it reaches its destination I'm all but ready to give in and take whatever shit they want to throw at me. The doors opening startles me slightly. I step out and find the floor empty. Dan's secretary isn't at her desk and the place is eerily quiet.

I take a look around the place. Everything is pristine and shiny. I didn't really take it in the last time I was up here. Dan's office walls are made of windows and I'm pretty sure when I was here before they were opaque. Now they are transparent, and I can see why he has his office up here. The view is to die for. I peek my head in his office door and find it empty, so I venture in. His space is lovely and bright and airy. The art on the walls are bursts of colour but not overpowering. They are a cross between Picasso and Jackson Pollock. Very surreal. The white leather sofa and chairs are luxurious but don't look like they've been used.

I'm busy looking out the window at the river when a slight creak from behind makes me jump and I whip around to find Dan standing in the doorway. Damn him he looks amazing. I can feel my resolve slipping with every second that goes by. We stand, staring at each other.

"Can I help you Nikki?"

"Um…" I can't think what to say and as I watch him walk to his desk and sit down, I wonder if I'm making a mistake. Maybe I should just call him out but keep my job. There's a phrase my mum uses: '*Don't cut your nose off to spite your face.*'

"Um… what?" He flicks a switch on the wall behind him and the wall of windows frost over.

"I quit." The words are out of my mouth before I even realise.

Dan raises an eyebrow and smiles at me. "Really? You quit. Can I ask why?" His mocking tone is pissing me off.

"I don't want to be a part of this game anymore. I won't be put at risk again."

"What are you talking about…put at risk? I never put you at risk Nikki. What you're doing for me isn't dangerous."

I turn away from him. "You're dangerous," I say under my breath.

"Look at me when you're talking to me Nikki." He sounds angry. I can't look at him right now because if I do, I know my resolve will crumble. "Look at me!" He shouts this time and bangs his fists on the desk.

Startled I turn and look at him and his face is like thunder. I can't help but start to cry. I came up here with a plan of what I was going to say and now I look like a scared little girl. "You're fucking dangerous," I spit the words at him.

He stands up. "You don't fucking know me. How the hell can you say I'm dangerous?"

"I saw you yesterday… leaving here with Astrid… the way you… you touched her, you're more than her boss. I could see it." I talk between sobs. God almighty I don't know if I'm this upset because I've been used or because deep down I'm jealous.

"Nikki you don't know what you saw." He rounds the desk and comes towards me, his tall strong frame looming over me and I back away from him. "For fuck sake will you stop flinching every time I come near you. Do you think I'm going to hit you or something?" He steps back from me as realisation spreads over his face. "That's what happened to you isn't it?"

"What would you know about it? You used me and you don't even care what happened to me after what your girl-friend did to me."

"Oh my God," he runs his hand down his face in exasperation, "you are going to have to tell me what the hell is going on here Nikki. I'm at a total loss. Will you sit down so we can talk about it?"

I relent when I realise that he isn't pretending. He really doesn't know what I'm talking about. "Okay."

I sit down on one end of the white couch and he sits on the other. "So?"

I don't know where the hell to start. I should just tell him about what happened on Friday, but my stupid mouth has other ideas. "My ex abused me."

"Fuck. I knew it." He clenches and unclenches his fists a few times. "Nikki I'm sorry."

"Why? You didn't know. My bloody sister doesn't even know. I've never told anyone."

"No, I'm sorry for what happened on Friday night. I wasn't professional and I should never have spoken to you like that much less invaded your personal space."

"Why was she here on a Sunday?"

"I met her in the foyer when I was heading out for dinner. She had been here using the gym. It was a complete coincidence that we left at the same time. And the touch? I have to keep things exactly as they are while I get all the evidence I need. I was only saying goodbye."

"You didn't look friendly to her the first day I was here. You were downright nasty to her on my floor. That's why I came up here that day. I was going to report you."

"Hmm. Yeah not the best thing for you to see but she had cornered me in the lift. It was a warning. I'm not interested. And now I know why she got out on the third floor. She wanted you to see that. She obviously feels threatened by you Nikki."

"Did you know Astrid spiked my drink on Friday while I was in the corridor with you? Did you tell her to do it?"

"Fucking what? I didn't even know she was at that club. You think I put her up to it? I can't believe you'd think I would do that."

I've started now so I have to finish. "I woke up in some guy's bed on Saturday morning. I don't know how I got there, and I didn't know where I was. I was fucking terrified Dan."

His eyes are like fire. "Did you…?" He shakes his head and I know what he wants to ask.

"I don't think so. I woke up fully clothed so chances are I passed out before anything could happen." I shut my eyes and bow my head. "She took away my right to consent Dan."

"Hey." He puts his finger under my chin and makes me look at him. "I'm going to have her fucking arrested Nikki. She's more than crossed a line here."

"No."

"No? Why? She could have killed you. Anything could have happened to you."

"You need her."

"No, I can't let you do this. I'll get Jed some other way."

"I want to help Dan."

He puts his elbows on his knees and clasps his hands in front of him. I notice the tattoo he has on his left wrist. It's a soundwave with a series of ones and zeros below it. Binary. I calculate it in my head. "Two Thousand and One." My voice is merely a whisper, but he hears me because he covers it with his other hand.

"Okay I'll let it go, but please, don't feel as though you have to put yourself at risk for this. There are other ways."

"I won't and I promise, I'll stay vigilant when it comes to Astrid. I have a feeling this isn't the last thing in her repertoire."

"Good and I promise to remain professional around you Nikki. The last thing I want is for you to feel uncomfortable around me."

"Thank you, Dan. All I want is to do my job. I've had more than enough drama in my life, I need this to be where I finally fit in."

I stand and hold out my hand to him. He rises too and shakes my hand, his touch lingering a little longer than is customary for a boss and employee.

He takes in a sharp breath and, as if remembering himself, lets go of my hand. "Thank you Nikki. For everything. I'm glad we can still work together; I'd hate to lose you."

I smile as I leave the office, Dan's parting words playing over in my head. *I'd hate to lose you.* Not lose you as an employee, lose *you.* I shake my head and sigh at myself. I have got to stop this. It's not healthy. But I have been left a little bit more intrigued by Dan's story. That tattoo he so quickly covered when I worked it out. I leave with a plan to research a little more about Dan. I feel as though I may be able to understand him a little better if I know what makes him tick.

I watch my staff all working away quietly at their desks, totally engrossed in their tasks. Damo has the afternoon off for a dental appointment and there's an air of calm over the office today.

Pulling my phone from my bag, I decide now is as good a time as any to look into Dan's background. I already know about his career and his fortune, but I know nothing about his personal life. I hope against hope that he isn't attached. Not for my own personal gain, I can't go down that road again. I simply want to make sure he's a good guy if I'm going to be working so closely with him.

I type his name into my Safari app and watch as page links start to appear. Wikipedia is always a good one to start with, albeit not always completely accurate, it's mostly a decent source of information. I tap it and start to read through the information.

Born: Daniel King, Age 32, Glasgow, Scotland
Occupation: Entrepreneur
Parents: Marcus King and Stephanie King
Siblings: Jason King
Net Worth: £1.05bn

I already know he's a billionaire but seeing it actually written in front of me makes it all the more real. I was born into a little money, my dad was and still is paid very handsomely for his diplomatic work, and we were always around people with money when I was young. Dan's wealth is colossal compared to what we had.

As I read through his personal life details I gasp in shock. A sub-title brings tears to my eyes. *Murder/Suicide of Parents.* It makes sobering reading.

On Monday 16th of July 2001, a housekeeper working for the King family arrived for work, having been given the weekend off by her employers, and found the bodies of Marcus and Stephanie King. It has been widely reported that Marcus King was indebted to a notorious Glasgow gangland figure and that the murder of his wife and his subsequent suicide were as a result of a hit being placed on him by said gangster.

The couple's two children, Daniel who was seventeen at the time and Jason who was twelve were not at home at the time of the incident.

I feel physically sick at the thought of those poor boys

losing their parents like that. Closing my phone and placing it face down on the desk, I sit back in my chair and sigh. Now I understand Dan's need for his business to be above board. It makes more sense to me now that Jed's betrayal runs a lot deeper than simply his theft of intellectual property. He probably saw Jed as family and to be let down by anyone is bad enough, but family, that's a blow too low.

Two thousand and one. Dan's tattoo. I wonder why he'd want to be reminded of such a terrible time but then everyone grieves differently. Maybe he uses it as a tool to make sure he never ends up like his father. My research has me intrigued about Dan. I want to know about his life and how he and his brother coped after their parents were gone. A traumatic experience like that can have such a negative effect on some people and it warms my heart slightly to know that he did okay given his tragic past.

CHAPTER TEN

*T*he rest of the week has been normal and every time I have seen Dan, he has been nothing but respectful and professional, just as he promised he would. I've also managed to be civil to Astrid although I almost wanted to knock her out on Tuesday when she asked how my weekend had been. I countered her smug smile with one of my own. I'm going to take great pleasure in bringing that bitch down.

I feel like I'm in a spy novel right now. My little team are doing great work on this new project at the moment but, being that it's only in the planning stage, there's not a lot I can do to doctor the work they're doing. I'm on my way to Dan's office to hand in the weeks work and discuss what he wants me to give to Jed. The elevator opens on the twelfth floor and as I step off, I see the walls in Dan's office are frosted. I've come to realise that means he's with someone. I've also learned this week that when he had this place built, he had his apartment put in so that he could crash here if he needed to, which happens quite a lot. He has a home outside the city, but he spends most of his time working so he's usually always here.

Tabitha nods to me. "Afternoon Nikki."

"Hi Tabitha. I take it he's busy."

"Yeah take a seat. Would you like a coffee?"

"No, I'm good thanks."

I'm seated less than a minute when the office door opens, and Jed emerges. He nods to me as he strides towards the elevator. It's five past one on a Friday so he obviously thinks he's been kept too late. I'm about to stand when Astrid comes to the door with Dan at her back. As soon as she sees me, she puts on a little show.

"Bye Danny, have a nice weekend darling." She turns and runs a red polished fingernail down his cheek. I see his jaw tense. God she's nasty and I hate to admit it but I'm jealous.

"Bye Astrid." His tone is dismissive, and it makes me happy.

She walks past the seating area and looks at me. "Oh, hi Nikki, I didn't see you there."

The fucking hell you didn't. "Hi Astrid."

"He's all yours." She flicks her hair behind her and swings her hips as she walks to the elevator.

Dan rolls his eyes and smiles at me. "Hi Nikki." My name sounds like honey rolling off his tongue.

"I'll just be a second."

He nods and walks back into his office. I pull my phone out of my bag and send a quick text to Charlie.

Hey sis. I'll be as quick as I can. If you don't hear from me in 20 mins phone me. X

I need this weekend to start as soon as possible and the more time I spend with Dan the more I'm falling for him. I just want to get out of here and enjoy Gina's hen weekend without any complications or thoughts of tattooed, handsome as fuck men.

"So that was a nice little show Astrid was putting on for me there," I say as I enter Dan's office and take a seat in front of his desk.

"Hmm, she's close to crossing so many lines it's unreal. I have to keep her onside though, so I'll just have to try and avoid her as much as possible."

"I think there's something seriously wrong with that girl Dan, she's twisted."

"You're not wrong there. So down to business. I don't want to keep you here longer than you need to be. How has the first week working on the software gone?"

I nod enthusiastically. "It's going brilliantly. Your plan to have different people working on their own little piece of it was genius. I got everyone's initial plans back this morning and I can see how good they are at their jobs already. When you read it all together, it's as though it was put together by a full team working as one."

Dan smiles. "Excellent. That's exactly the feedback I wanted. I'll get Tabitha to switch some things around in this and type up the final draft and your team can get to work with the bones of the project from next week. Great work Nikki, thank you."

I smile back at him, pleased at myself for holding it together and sticking the job out. I really think it could be great working here, as long as I can keep my relationship with Dan professional. I can't put myself through that type of misery again.

"*Y*ay. My little sis is here." Charlie grabs me and squashes me right into her body in a tight hug.

"Charlie you're suffocating the poor lassie," Gina laughs as she walks over to us and I get out of Charlie's hold and give her a hug and a kiss on the cheek.

"Thanks Gina. How much has she had to drink? It's only three o'clock."

"Oh, honey I think it's a combination of not drinking for so long when she was pregnant and missing her baba. She hasn't really had that much to be fair."

"I'm not drunk, I'm just excited and a wee bit tipsy," Charlie says pointing her finger at me. "Come on, I don't get to spend much time alone these days, so I'll enjoy two nights away. Yes, I'll miss Georgie, but she'll be there when I get back."

Gina raises her voice over the chatter. "Right I think that's us all here so let's get going."

Gina's Hen weekend is in a spa resort at an old stately home between Glasgow and Edinburgh. Apparently, a Baron used to live there so I'm expecting it to be very grand indeed. As we all pile into the waiting minibus, I smile genuinely for the first time in ages. It's as though my life is being realigned and I'm getting what I deserve out of it. I'm having fun with my friends and work is going well now that I've found my feet. I bat down the little voice that tells me it's too good to be true as I take my seat on the bus. *Shut up stupid voice!*

---

*W*hen Gina said this place was a country house, she didn't let on that it was like a castle. What better way to spend a weekend than getting pampered and relaxing in a Scottish castle? It's sprawling gardens and beautiful architecture look magnificent and imposing, even in the drizzling rain.

We are met at the door by some staff who take our bags, check us in and show us to our rooms. Since we are a party of eleven, I've managed to bag myself a single room. Everyone else is sharing twin rooms, with Gina and Charlie sharing a suite. I'm pleased. A little down time to rest is exactly what I need. I have to try and get over my attraction to Dan. I know it could never possibly work and I vowed when I walked away from Mike that I'd never get into a work relationship situation like that again. It's too complicated and I have to convince myself that he feels the same way. An instant attraction to someone is only natural, it's how we are built to find a mate in life, but it doesn't mean we have to act on it. Dan is a good looking guy, there was no way I wasn't going to be attracted to him on sight.

I've been given a package of beauty treatments to have over the weekend. I see Gina has spared no expense on this trip as I take in the bottle of champagne cooling in an ice bucket on a small table in the middle of the room.

I'm about to open my little wheelie case when a message makes my phone buzz. Damo told me to FaceTime as soon as I got here to show him the place.

Did you get there ok? I'm dying to see the place. X

I select his number from my FaceTime app and when he appears on the screen before the end of the first ring I laugh.

"You're keen."

"I'm on tent hooks here woman."

"Tent hooks?"

"Och it's something my ma always said, she could never get it right. Who cares, show me the place." He's like a child at Christmas waiting to get stuck into his presents.

"Okay, you ready? This place is stunning."

He squeals with delight and by the time I'm finished showing him the beauty of the castle and its grounds he's suitably impressed and as we hang up, I'm left wishing he'd been able to come here too. I'm grateful to have him as a friend. He's never once judged me or wanted anything from me other than friendship. I've definitely found a friend for life in him.

CHAPTER ELEVEN

"Charlie, I don't want to go home. I want to win the lottery and live here," I say lazily as we lie on loungers by the indoor pool. I've had the best weekend of pampering and relaxation, but it feels like only five minutes ago we got here.

"Ugh, I know. I mean I've missed Georgie and Mark but oh man am I relaxed. I've forgotten what this felt like. Do you know I've slept more over this weekend than I have since my little cherub was born? So, tell me how the job is going then. Are you adjusting to your new life yet?"

I sit up and turn to her, crossing my legs in front of me and leaning forward. "It was hard to start with, but I really feel as though this could be a great opportunity. Dan says he knows how talented I am, and he thinks I'll do well in the job."

"Ooh look at you all excited. I'm so pleased for you. I've missed this. Us, talking and knowing we're not too far away from each other now. You know I hated to leave you, but I hated South Africa even more. I never felt as though it was ever my home."

"I know you had your reasons; you don't need to keep apologising for following your dream. I wish I'd done it sooner, then maybe I wouldn't have got involved with…" I trail off, having forgotten myself and who I'm talking to. I know I've said too much when she narrows her eyes at me.

"Involved with what?" She sits up mirroring me on her lounger.

"Oh, it's nothing really," I lie. And she sees right through me.

"Liar. Spill. Now."

On a sigh, I decide now is as good a time as any to tell my sister about Mike.

"I was in a relationship with a man I met at work for around a year and he was horrible to me."

"Did he hit you?" Her eyes are like fire and I fear if I tell her the whole truth, she will be furious at me for not telling her in the first place, so I lie again.

"No. No, it wasn't like that."

"Oh, thank God. If he'd laid a finger on you, I'd have hunted him down and cut his balls off and fed them to him."

Yeah, I don't doubt that for a second Charlie.

"He was very controlling. He wouldn't acknowledge that we were in a relationship when we were at work. Granted, there were rules against employees dating but there were disclaimers you could sign for it. He wouldn't do it. He said it was best if we appeared as colleagues only because it would stop us getting promotions."

"And how did that work out for you because I know you never got promoted? Bastard used you, didn't he?"

"Yeah that's exactly what happened. He got promoted and I stayed where I was. The higher up he went the worse his behaviour got. He started checking my phone and telling me who I could see. He only let me stay at his place on certain nights too and when I wasn't with him, I had to be constantly within reach. So help me if I missed his calls. When mum and dad said they were moving back here I was never so glad. I left and didn't tell him I was going."

Charlie opens her mouth in shock and laughs. "You Dear John'd him?"

"No, I didn't even leave him a note, I just left."

"I'm proud of you baby girl. That took balls." Her eyes shine with pride and my stomach twists.

"No Charlie, it was the coward's way out, but it was the only option I had. Anyway, that's my story and now that you know I'd like to put him out of my mind."

"Fucking bastard is lucky you don't like to share your personal life freely. Who knows what dad would have done to him?"

I roll my eyes at her, mostly because I know dad wouldn't have done anything. It's what he would have *had* done to him that would have had me worried.

"Why didn't you tell someone, me even?"

"I was ashamed. I mean come on; I'm supposed to be intelligent. I should never have got involved with him at all."

"Come here you," Charlie says, her eyes filling with tears.

I sit beside her, and she pulls me into a tight, reassuring, big sister hug.

"You're incredibly intelligent but matters of the heart makes us crazy and sometimes we forget ourselves. Hopefully you've come away from it stronger and now you know what you're not looking for in a partner, maybe you'll find the perfect guy for you."

I think I already found him!

"Thanks Charlie I needed this. Not just this conversation, but this whole move and making new friends. I really feel as though I've finally found somewhere I can call home. South

Africa never felt like home to me. I think we both knew it was never going to be permanent anyway. I don't think there was a day that went by that mum didn't wish she was back in the UK. It's possible it rubbed off on us after a while."

"Well it's the very reason I came back here as soon as I could. I wish you'd been able to come too. I really missed you. But you're here now and that's all that matters. And mum and dad are only an hour's flight away now, so I feel much better knowing we are all in the same country again."

"Yeah I remember mum's reaction when she found out you were pregnant. I'm pretty sure she had someone kidnapped and held to ransom until they gave dad a new job back here."

"Wouldn't surprise me", Charlie laughs, her prosecco sloshing in her champagne flute. "Mum always gets what she wants in the end. I like to think she's the reason our family stayed together. If I had a husband who was as married to his job as dad, I'd have been long gone. She's a tough cookie for sticking it out."

"Hmm, yeah she is that."

Our last afternoon at the spa is so relaxing and, for a few hours at least, I put thoughts of Dan and my shitty former life out of my mind and enjoy my time with my sister. My beautiful, strong sister, who's shadow I've always been grateful to walk in. I never wanted to be better than her. If I had turned out to be anything like her, I would have been grateful, but she is a million times the woman I am. She'd never have let a man treat her how I did, and I never want her to know what really happened because I could never bear to see her disappointment in me.

CHAPTER TWELVE

y weekend at the spa certainly had a
wonderful effect on me and has led to my
week being rather subdued and uneventful. My team have
been busy beavering away on their project and Jed has been
quieter than usual, mostly due to the fact that his little cohort
has been away on a secondment to the London office. I don't
even care why she was sent there. I'm simply thankful of the
peace and quiet. It's been an absolute dream to get up and
come to work every morning knowing there wouldn't be any
drama from her. I'd liken it to an old Disney animation where
the birds all tweet, mice make dresses and the princess goes
about her day singing.

"So, Miss Nikki, are you all set for the big day tomorrow?" Damo plants himself in the seat in front of my desk as
we start to wind down for the weekend.

"Oh Damo I can't wait but I swear I'm looking forward to
this all being over. It's made my sister insane. Since we came
back from the hen weekend, she's been unbearable."

"Aw you know she's just stressed out. She wants her

friend's big day to go without a hitch and from what you've told me about Gina, that's understandable."

"I wish you could come with me tomorrow."

"I do too, I love weddings, but my mum doesn't turn fifty every day. I hope she still has no clue about her surprise party but knowing her she'll have got it out of someone in the know. She's a bloody nightmare with things like this." Damo looks at his watch. "Right it's tidy-up time. I have a buffet to help out with. You have the best weekend and no kissing the groomsmen okay." He stands and throws his bag over his shoulder, blowing me a kiss as he leaves.

"I promise, no kissing. Enjoy your mum's party."

As the last of the office leaves to start their weekends and I'm left alone, I take a deep breath. I'm really excited about Gina's wedding but at the same time all I can think about is the fact that Astrid will be back on Monday. I love my job, but she's tainted everything for me since the day I walked through that door. I'll never understand the maliciousness of people sometimes.

The lift sounding its arrival on the third floor makes me jump slightly and as I watch the doors open a smile spreads across my face. Dan smiles back and I watch him walk towards me full of purpose. He looks so handsome in his suit and casually laid back with no tie and open collar.

"Hey Nikki, I'm glad you're still here."

"I'm usually last to leave Dan, you know that. As soon as it hits one on Friday, that lot all forget I exist. What brings you down here? I was just getting ready to leave myself."

He stalls slightly, his eyes looking right into mine and I sit back slightly, feeling a little self-conscious.

As if my movement made him remember what his purpose was, he shakes his head slightly and takes the seat

Damo vacated earlier. "Yeah um, I came down give you these." He hands me a slim, white envelope.

"Okay what is it?"

"It's two tickets to a software conference at the exhibition centre next week. I was thinking you could give them to two members of your team. Conferences aren't for everyone, but they can be good for networking. These guys won't always be at this company and they'll want to climb higher than the roles they have now. I'd never stand in their way and I'll always encourage anyone to spread their wings and move on if it's what they want to do. If I can help them in any way while they're here, then at least I'll know I've made a difference in someone's life."

This guy is forever full of surprises. "You're a good person Dan. There's not many company owners who'd ensure their employees were well enough trained for someone else to poach them."

"Everyone should end up where they want to be in their lives, and no one should ever be able to keep them from achieving their full potential, even if it means me losing them. I know there are many employers in my position who want to keep their best employees for themselves but all they manage to do is oppress them. When you oppress people, they rise up in a fiery anger."

I hold my hand up, stifling a laugh. "Did you seriously just quote Step Brothers?"

"Damn I thought you were too refined to watch that sort of film Nikki." His smile is wide and lights up his beautiful brown eyes.

I smile back. "Ah Mr King there's a lot you don't know about me."

He regards me for a second longer than necessary before he speaks again. "Yeah, there is."

His tone has turned a little contemplative and I don't fully understand why I choose this moment, when I know I need to be out of this office sharp today, to ask about his parents.

"Dan, I told you I took this job without doing any research on you or your business right?"

"Mhm," he answers giving me a suspicious look.

"Well I did some research the other day and I know why you have that tattoo."

He holds his wrist, shielding it from me, protecting himself almost. "Well it is public knowledge."

"Is it true? Was your dad involved with gangsters?"

Dan sighs. "My dad's name was Marcus King. He had his fingers in so many pies I don't even think he knew which business was which. He was filthy stinking rich, but it was always at the expense of other people. He was ruthless, dangerous even. I think he thought he was a fucking gangster himself. That was until he crossed the wrong people."

I watch him as he talks. I can feel the pain behind his words.

"He scammed someone who wasn't a patsy like his other victims, and they put a hit out on him. It turns out they had connections to real gangsters. People who didn't care who they killed because it was a pay check at the end of the day. These were people who always managed to stay out of jail no matter what they did because they were clever."

"Where were you and Jason when it happened?"

"Dad sent my brother off to a holiday camp in France for two weeks during the summer. We said goodbye at the airport, I went on holiday to Spain with my girlfriend and that was the last time we were ever a family." He sits back and clasps is hands, twiddling his thumbs nervously as he talks.

"You don't have to tell me this if it's making you feel uncomfortable Dan."

"You've already read most of it anyway, so I'll fill in the blanks that Wikipedia has left out. Anyway," he looks at me and smiles, "I want to tell you. I don't like to talk about it much but with you, it feels okay."

I nod and smile. "Okay."

"We were gone a week when we were both summoned home. Jason, my brother, had no clue about any of dad's dodgy dealings but I had picked things up, I wasn't stupid. I had heard whispered conversations, arguments between my parents and even people at school had talked about how my family was corrupt. I knew something terrible had happened and Jase could see that I was worried. When I met him at the airport he was as white as a sheet. We were taken to a police station as soon as we were back in Glasgow and were met there by a social worker. It turns out that, rather than be caught by these gangsters, my dad decided to off himself. I could have lived with that, but the bastard took our mother with him. We lived on a huge secluded estate just outside Glasgow, so no one knew what had happened until the housekeeper came on the Monday, three days later. He had shot mum in the head with a shotgun then hung himself."

I can't believe what I'm hearing. I can't even begin to imagine how terrible that must have been for those two poor boys. "Christ."

"I don't know what was gained from him shooting mum. I'll never know, but he was a twisted son-of-a-bitch, so it was probably justified in his own mind. Maybe she knew too much. Or maybe he just hated us so much that he wanted us to suffer for the rest of our lives. It made me realise that the only way to conduct business is legally and beyond reproach. Every asset my dad had was seized because the police linked it all to being gained through fraudulent activity and money laundering. Jase and I were put in foster care and as soon as I turned eighteen, I became his legal guardian."

"Two Thousand and One. That's what that tattoo is for then."

"Yeah, well done on that one. Having the date in binary saves me having to explain it to too many people."

My heart is breaking for him but, as I look into his dark eyes, I don't see sadness, instead his resigned look makes the story that much more tragic. Losing one parent must be bad enough but to lose both and in such tragic circumstances must have had a huge impact on both Dan and his brother.

"Thank you for telling me Dan."

He regards me with a tiny smile pulling at the corners of his mouth and as I'm anticipating what he might say next he stands abruptly and nods to me, breaking whatever was happening between us. "Right get out of here Nikki. Go and enjoy your weekend. See you Monday." He tips his head to me and makes long, forceful strides to the waiting elevator.

He gets in but doesn't turn around. Instead I watch as he pushes the button for his floor and pulls his phone out of his pocket. As soon as the doors close, I breathe out and slump back in my chair. *What the hell was that?* I can see trying to think about Dan in any way other than as my boss is going to be harder than I expected.

As I leave the building my phone rings with the now familiar strains of The Imperial March. I changed my ring tone for my sister when she started bugging me with her attitude over this wedding. Anyone would think it was her getting married. Darth Vader has nothing on her this week. It's not as though she hasn't done this before, she was Gina's chief maid when she got married the first time. I understand that this time it's different given Gina's history but still, there's no need to be such a bitch to everyone. I roll my eyes as I pull my phone from my bag and answer the call.

"Where are you?"

"Hi Charlie."

"Well, where are you? I thought you finished at one on a Friday. I'm at your flat right now and you're not here."

I sigh louder than I mean to and I know she hears me. "Charlie, I had some stuff to do before I left but I'm out now and on my way. Give me ten minutes."

"Okay but hurry up we need to be at Gina's soon. She's freaking out because Steven is having his stag do tonight."

"Doesn't she trust him?"

"She trusts him, she just doesn't trust his pals. She's got herself all worked up thinking he's going to end up in another country tonight, tarred and feathered, and not make the wedding tomorrow."

Poor Gina. She's been through so much already, she doesn't need the stress, especially in her condition.

"Okay I won't be long. I'm packed anyway so I just need to get changed and I'm good to go."

We hang up and I make my way home promising myself that I'm going to ignore Charlie's tantrums and enjoy my weekend.

CHAPTER THIRTEEN

"There you are." Charlie's voice comes from behind me. I turn to her and stifle a smile at the harassed look on her face.

"I've been here for ages. I didn't know you were looking for me."

"The cars will be here soon. I need to help Gina down the stairs, so I'll need you to take Georgie." She hands the baby to me and disappears.

It's Gina's wedding day and my sister is in full on chief-bridesmaid-from-hell mode. I can't wait till later when she can relax, she's doing my head in right now. I look down at the beautiful little girl in my arms. We managed to get her a dress made from the same material as ours. She's like a little mini-me of Charlie. I can't believe she's already almost four months old. How time flies.

Charlie's voice booming from upstairs makes me sigh. "Nikki the cars are here."

"Let's go Georgie before your mummy has a breakdown."

Georgie gurgles and shoves her hand in her mouth. She couldn't give two hoots about what's going on today. I walk out into the hall just as Gina and her dad get to the bottom of the stairs, followed by Charlie. The sight of Gina in her wedding dress takes my breath away.

"Oh, Gina, you look absolutely beautiful."

"Thanks honey, so do you two." Her smile could light a million candles.

$\mathcal{T}$he place Gina and Steven are getting married is absolutely beautiful. It's at Glasgow University and apparently you can only get married here if you are a student, graduate or the son or daughter of a graduate or member of staff so it's very exclusive. Gina is both a graduate and the daughter of a former faculty member. As the entrance music starts Gina looks back at us and my sister ends up in tears. I'm so glad the make-up artist who did our faces used waterproof mascara. We make our way in and down the aisle and I try to keep my head forward but a face in the congregation catches my eye. It's Dan. He sees me and looks at me with the same bemused look as I do him. For the last few weeks we have chatted easily with each other although there's always an underlying, unspoken tension between us. I can't believe he's here and my God does he look good. I can tell from the upper half of him, that I can see, he's wearing what every other man at this wedding is wearing. You don't go to a Scottish wedding and not wear a kilt.

Dan winks at me and mouths the word hi. I give him a little wave and face forward again, with a huge smile on my face. When we reach the altar, I give a last glance at him and a flutter rises in my belly when he smiles at me. *Oh Dan what are you doing to me?* Smiling back, I turn my attention back to my bridesmaid duties.

Gina and Steven take their places at the altar in front of each other. Anyone looking at them can see they're so in love with each other. Their nervous smiles and tender looks evoke such a feeling of longing in me. It's every woman's dream to be looked at with as much love and pride as Steven looks at her. He truly loves her, cares for her, would never hurt her.

I look out over the congregation and take note of how many people love and cherish this couple. Steven doesn't have any family to speak of, but he has been taken right to the heart of Gina's family and theirs is a beautiful story.

As the minister starts with his "Dearly Beloved," I smile and catch Dan's eye again and he smiles back at me. I turn away to listen to the minister, my mind a whirl of emotions.

Steven takes Gina's hand at the minister's announcement of the vows. I watch as they look into each other's eyes, their smiles lighting up their faces. The sun shining against the stained-glass windows creates a stunningly colourful display of tiny dancing lights and every time Gina moves, the crystals on her dress pick them up. It's as though I'm in a real-life fairy tale and for the next few hours I allow myself to be enchanted, pretending as I catch Dan staring at me, that my own prince charming is waiting for me.

The reception is in the same place just a different hall. The meal we've just had was absolutely amazing and I was impressed by the efficiency of the staff and by the speeches that were given. Gina's dad was hilarious regaling us with tales of both Gina and Steven and getting some great laughs at his jokes. He made his daughter blush a few times and had us all in tears at the end when he told them both how proud he was of them and that he couldn't wait to meet his first grandchild, who we have now been informed is a boy.

I'm sitting feeding Georgie her bottle of milk while Charlie is off organising her sitter. I know as soon as she's with Mark's mum they'll both be able to relax and let their hair down. I'm seriously dreading Charlie's wedding; she's going to be insufferable.

"Imagine meeting you here."

I turn and look up into Dan's beautiful dark eyes. "Yeah imagine."

"So you're the chief bridesmaid's sister then?" He sits down beside me.

"Mhm. Bridesmaidzilla."

His hearty laugh startles Georgie who lets out a cry and almost chokes on her milk. "Oh I'm sorry baby," he says and rubs her little hand. It looks so tiny in his. We look at each other and the air is thick with a feeling I'm finding hard to resist.

"Oh, here she comes. Look at her, she's like a woman on a mission." I watch Charlie stride towards us.

"Anne's outside. Let's get this little one handed over and then we can party. Hi there." She nods at Dan as she lifts Georgie out of my arms.

"Charlie this is Dan my boss."

She looks at me and nods her approval. "Nice to meet you Dan. You a friend of Steven's?" She asks him and I can see her narrowing her suspicious eyes at him.

"Yeah we've known each other a while. He's a great guy."

"I know he is; I wouldn't want anything less for my best friend." She turns to me and smiles, and I know what she's thinking. "I'll catch up with you later sis."

We watch her walk away and I sit staring at my French manicured nails.

"You look beautiful Nikki."

"Thanks," I reply and when I look at him, I'm done. My damn body is sent into a free-fall.

"Danny boy." We both turn and find Steven standing behind us. "Hey Nikki, sorry to interrupt, do you mind if I steal him a minute?"

"Not at all, I'm going to get a drink before the dancing starts. Need to get in the party mood."

"I want you to meet my wife man, she's fucking amazing."

Dan stands and gives me a nod. "I'll catch you later Nikki," he leans down and whispers in my ear, "save a dance for me."

As I watch him walk away with Steven, I wonder just what this night has in store for me. Whatever is going on between us is getting harder and harder to fight. And I've realised now that I really don't want to fight it.

---

*T*he dance floor is lit from below and all round and the lights in the hall have been changed to a muted setting. Tiny LED lights sparkle all around and the atmosphere is buzzing as we await the arrival of the bride and groom to take their first dance. I have chosen a table at the back of the room and it appears I have managed to bag myself an empty one.

The DJ makes his announcement. "Ladies and gentlemen please be upstanding as we welcome your bride and groom Mr & Mrs Parker."

The whole place erupts in applause and whistling as Gina and Steven take to the floor. They stand facing each other and it's clear to see how in love they are. Steven kisses Gina to whoops and applause and they start to dance as the music plays. The song is '*At Last*' and I know it's fitting to both of them. They deserve this, to be happy at last and I feel tears well up. I watch as Gina's mum and dad get up to join them. Then Charlie and Steven's best man Gerry take to the floor. At this point it would be customary for me being the other bridesmaid to dance with another of the males from the groom's wedding party but Steven doesn't have anyone else, so I'm sat here like the proverbial wallflower, alone at the back, in the dark, scared to talk to anyone.

"Why aren't you up there dancing?" Dan's soft voice just about melts my bones.

"I don't have anyone to dance with. Anyway, I'm quite happy to stay here."

"I told you to save a dance for me. Next song we're dancing okay?"

I nod at him and take a large drink of my champagne. We sit in silence watching everyone dancing and as the song nears the end, I get nervous. I honestly don't know why, I want to dance with him, hell I want to do a lot more with him, but I'm scared. I swore that I'd never let myself get into another relationship with a colleague let alone my boss. I don't know if my fragile heart can take another beating. I lost a year of my life and a lot of self-worth to Mike and I don't know Dan well enough to know he won't do the same to me. The song finishes and Gina and Steven kiss each other to jubilant applause and as the next song starts, Dan and I look at each other and burst out laughing.

"Well I did say I would dance with you. Do you know the moves to the Y.M.C.A?"

"It's my favourite." He stands and holds out his hand.

"Come on then."

I roll my eyes and take his hand. "God this is so embarrassing."

What's even more embarrassing is that we appear to be the only ones on the dance floor. Dan doesn't seem to care as the singing starts and he gets his groove on. I'm relieved when other people start to join us, and I let myself go a little and mirror Dan's moves. By the time the track is almost done I'm thoroughly enjoying myself and when the song changes, I'm a little breathless.

This one is slower and soulful and, if I'm not mistaken, is the song that plays a pivotal role in Dirty Dancing. Dan takes my hand and pulls me close to him.

"Now this is dancing," he says over the music.

I barely have time to register how close he is holding me as he starts to sway me from side to side. Now, I can dance but this guy is seriously good. He leads me around the floor like a professional and his moves are so fluid and effortless that it's easy for me to follow him. He has me pulled in close enough to feel the heat of his body. I'm amazed at how every step we take seems to give me more and more confidence. At the bridge of the song he runs his hand up my back and tips me back. As he brings me up slowly and I look into his eyes I forget we are in a room full of people. It's like we are the only ones here and the heat between us is intense. Dan pulls me in close again and we sway together until the song finishes.

I try to move to get off the floor, but Dan's arms are strong, and he holds me firm.

"What are you doing?"

"What are *you* doing?" He whispers and brings his face so close to mine that our noses almost touch. I swear I feel a spark move between them. I swallow hard and am about to speak when a hand on my shoulder startles me and I push back from Dan who at last releases me.

"Nikki sorry to interrupt your little love-in here," Charlie waves her hand between us, "but I need you to take the guest book round the tables to get signed."

"Um okay. Sorry Dan… I… have to go." I turn and stride across the dance floor before he can say anything else. The high I was feeling as we danced has been shot down in flames and I feel like my old stupid, pathetic self again. *Fuck you Charlie.* I'm about to leave the hall when Dan catches me by the wrist and pulls me into the corridor. He pins me against the wall with his strong, hard body.

"Dan I…"

"No." He puts his finger on my lips. "Nikki there's something between us, I know you feel it." His voice is low and raspy. "I know you've felt it too."

"Dan I'm sorry, we can't do this."

"Says who?"

"You're my boss."

"It's my company, I don't care that I'm your boss." Every time he speaks his mouth gets closer to mine until our lips are almost touching.

I hate the thought of being in another hushed relationship for fear of what 'people might think'. "I can't be a secret," I whisper and saying those words means I am giving over that last unbroken piece of me. I know if I get my heart broken this time, I'll never come back from it.

"Never," he says, and his lips are on mine.

His kiss feels right. More than any other I've ever had. It's soft and sensual and filled with all sorts of delicious promises. I feel a complete sense of abandonment and I let go, my body moulding into his as we both give in to the tension that has been building between us for weeks.

"For God sake Nikki," Charlie's screeching voice makes my eyes shoot open, but Dan doesn't let go of my lips. Instead I feel him smile and see his eyes sparkle. I can't help but smile too.

"I'm in the middle of something here," I laugh against Dan's mouth.

"So I see." I can hear the smile in her voice. "I'll do the guest book myself; you carry on."

As soon as she's gone, he lets me go and we both burst out laughing.

"Oh my God, I'm so sorry Dan. She is really pushing it today I swear."

"Go and do your bridesmaid duties but come and find me later. I'd like to take you home with me tonight. We need to finish this."

"Oh… ehm… okay. To your apartment?"

"No home. Just come and find me okay."

I nod and he plants a chaste kiss on my lips and walks away holding my hand until only our fingertips touch and then he is gone. I take a deep breath and sink against the wall with what I can only imagine looks like the smile of a twelve-year-old girl at a One Direction concert.

CHAPTER FOURTEEN

I have come to realise that there are many traditions in Scottish weddings that don't make sense unless you are Scottish. I have to say the one I have found to be my favourite at this wedding reception tonight was the last dance of the evening while Gina and Steven were still here. It was a rendition of Loch Lomond and the dancing ended in carnage. They put the bride and groom in the middle of a massive circle of people and everyone just goes completely mental. I decided to watch it from the back standing on a chair and I'm so glad I did, it looked bloody dangerous. There were body parts flying in all directions and the fast-paced part of the music coupled with the drunkenness of the guests made for the most hilarious spectacle I've ever seen.

We said goodbye to Gina and Steven a while ago and the reception is winding down now. The lights are up a little more than earlier and the guests have started thinning out. I'm staring at the tiny bottle of Chanel No.5 that we got from Gina as part of our wedding favours, the lower volume soul music playing in the background is soothing and I'm completely lost in my own head.

"Penny for your thoughts sis?" Charlie comes and sits beside me.

"Hey."

"You okay honey?"

"Yeah I'm fine I'm just tired, it's been a long day."

She puts her hand on mine. "I'm sorry, I've been a complete bitch today. I honestly think this wedding has sent me insane."

I laugh at her. "Oh Charlie if this is how you are as a bridesmaid, I might be washing my hair when you get married."

She slaps my arm. "Don't be cheeky to your elders."

"What are you and Mark doing tonight?"

She claps her hands together. "Baby free tonight, me and my man are going to *get it on.*"

"Ugh too much info Charlie, God."

She laughs a little too hard at herself. "We're staying in Gina and Steven's apartment tonight, there's plenty of room if you want to crash there too. They're going to a swanky hotel."

I shake my head and feel a warm blush spread over my face. "No, I'm good thanks."

Charlie narrows her eyes at me and a sly smile twitches at her lips. "Hmm, going home with Dan are you?"

"Charlie come on." I shake my head in embarrassment. I don't really know what to say to her. She saw us kissing after all.

"Honey you're a grown ass woman, do what and who you want, just be careful. I don't want my baby sister getting hurt again."

"Charlie I'll be fine." I look away from her because I'm lying. I don't know that I'll be fine. I don't know that I won't end up in a situation I can't get out of this time. I don't know what happens from here on out and if I'm honest with myself I'm scared.

"Nikki," Charlie squeezes my hand, "you'd tell me if there was something wrong, wouldn't you? I really don't want you to feel as though you have to deal with anything on your own again."

I plaster on a fake smile and look back at her and lie through my teeth. "Of course I would, you're my sister."

I can tell by her expression that she doesn't believe a word I've said but in her big sisterly fashion she nods as if everything is okay.

"Hey sweetheart are we about ready to go?" Mark puts his hand on Charlie's shoulder as he appears behind her.

"Yeah can you get my coat from the cloakroom honey?"

"Okay. Nikki are you coming with us?" My sister's handsome and ever so sweet fiancé asks, rubbing her shoulders.

"Nikki has other plans tonight." She winks at me.

"Yeah I'm fine Mark thanks."

"Okay I'll get you by the doors. See you later Nikki."

We both watch him walk away and Charlie turns back to me. "I'll have my phone by me all night, if you need anything call me okay."

I nod and pull her into a hug that's tighter than I mean it to be but that speaks volumes to her. "Love you big sis."

"I love you too," she says against my hair.

I let her go and as she stands, I see the glint of tears in her eyes. I know she's worried about me and I know she's not stupid. She knows there are things I'm not telling her about. I don't know if I'll ever be able to tell her everything that happened with Mike. God help me if she ever finds out the whole truth. I've never wanted to look like a failure to anyone especially not the one person in my life that I idolise.

"Right I'm off. Enjoy the rest of your night." She walks

away, her pink dress swishing as she goes, and I smile when I look at her feet. She's wearing a pair of pink fluffy slippers. The woman is as mad as a hatter and my heart bursts with love for my big sister.

My phone vibrates on the table and when I turn it over, I see it's a text from Dan.

I meant what I said Nikki. We will finish what we started. X

I slump back in my chair and watch as the hall starts to gradually empty. I want so much to carry on where we left off. I think about Dan's lips on mine, the exquisite feeling of his tongue touching mine, how happy it made me in the moment. I realise I haven't seen him since our little rendezvous earlier and I wonder where he is now.

Ok.

I can't think of anything else to say. I don't know if I'm ready for this. Dan's reply comes through almost immediately.

Your enthusiasm is inspiring Nikki. Stop playing with that bottle and put some of the perfume on. I want to smell it on your skin.

I sit bolt upright and look around the room. I can't see him and it's making me nervous knowing that he's watching me.

Put the perfume on.

I open the bottle and run the opening against my neck, transferring a little of the beautiful scent to my skin. My phone buzzes again.

Perfect. Your neck is delectable.

I'm becoming increasingly aware of the heat radiating over my body and I'm glad there aren't many people left in the hall or near me. Another text comes in.

Do you trust me?

I bloody better if I'm even contemplating going home with him.

I do

His reply makes me blush and gasp at the same time.

Take off your knickers

I've never even contemplated doing something so brazen and I'm all at once embarrassed and turned on. I stand to head for the toilets to do as he told me when he sends another text.

Stay where you are. I want to watch.

Where the hell is he? I scan the room again, but I still can't see him. I sit back down and lift my glass. Finishing the last of my gin and tonic, I take a steadying breath. Thankfully the layers of my dress are such that they will hide what I am about to do and my position at the back of the hall against the wall is an advantage too. Manoeuvring myself to the edge of my seat I put my hands under the skirt of my dress and hook my fingers over the top of my knickers and pull them down and off, scooping them up before someone sees. I force them into my bag and adjust myself back to a normal seated position. I can't help the smile on my face, and I have to squeeze my thighs together to keep from losing control of my senses.

Take an ice cube out of that glass and put it inside yourself.

I have to read the words a couple more times to really grasp what he's asking me to do. He's rather forward and very presumptuous. My God my cheeks must be bright red right now. *Can I do this? Do I want to do this?* Of course I want it. I've wanted it since the moment he got in that damn lift with me. I don't know why I'm trying to convince myself otherwise. I'm obviously taking too long to do anything as another text comes in.

Do it now and meet me outside

I look at the glass and contemplate how the hell I'm going

to do this. I put my bag on the floor and wait a few moments. Lifting my glass I tip it to my mouth and three small cubes of ice fall into my mouth. I put the glass down and duck my head under the table as if to reach for my bag. Spitting the cubes into my hand and shivering at their slippery coldness I gather up the front of my skirt as far as I need to and push them inside me. The instant cold inside my heat makes me gasp and my fingers fist in the tulle of my dress. *God this is the hottest thing I've ever done in my life.*

Steadying my breathing I stand, and the cool sensation intensifies as I feel the ice move around. I honestly don't know how I make it to the doors, but I do and when I see Dan standing outside my body responds independently of me. My insides clench at the sight of him in a pair of dark jeans and bright white t-shirt. That's where he's been, getting changed. His muscular forearms are bare, and he has that rock star look about him again. His smile would set fire to my knickers if I were still wearing any.

"Hi," he says as I get close to him. "How are you feeling?"

"Cold."

He laughs and opens the back door of the black Range Rover he's standing beside. "After you."

I take his hand to help me climb in and the action of opening my legs to step up sends a little water running down my inner thigh. "Oh shit." I gasp and look back at Dan.

"Fuck. This is going to be the longest half hour of my life."

His deep voice vibrates through me and I can't do anything else but get in and sit down on the cream leather seat. The leaking water makes my thighs stick together and I sit back in the seat, thankful it's dark and the guy in the driver seat can't see my embarrassment.

Dan gets in beside me and shuts the door. "Clyde View Jim. Thanks."

Jim nods and we pull away from the kerb. He presses a button on the car stereo and puts on some music. It's loud enough so that we have some privacy but not overbearing. I'm finding it hard to look at Dan right now. I honestly am starting to wonder what I'm getting into here.

"Nikki?" He whispers my name.

"Mhm." I still don't look at him.

"Look at me Nikki."

I turn to face him, and he beckons me closer with his finger. I slide into the middle seat and am taken by surprise when he grabs my right knee and pulls my leg over his lap. The cool air travelling up under the skirt of my dress and hitting the wetness of the melted ice makes me shiver.

Dan leans in and I can feel his lips at my ear as his hand moves achingly slowly up my leg and under my skirt. "If this is too much, tell me to stop," he whispers moving his hand ever higher.

I have to bite my lip to keep from whimpering at the feel of his hot hand on my bare cool skin, but I say nothing. I'm in this car with him. God, I stuffed ice cubes inside myself for him. I think I'm past the point of telling him to stop.

His hand is right under my skirt now and he pulls the front of the dress down so that it covers what he's doing. As his hand skims my inner thigh, I take a shaky breath knowing that the next time he moves higher he is going to be past the point of no return.

"Are you okay Nikki?" Dan's breath against my ear sends shivers up my spine.

I nod. I think I've lost the ability to speak. His hand brushes lightly over my sex and I feel goose bumps rise all over my skin, hardening my nipples to the point that they hurt.

"I'm going to make you come now Nikki. Don't make a sound, understood?" He whispers.

"Oh my God," I say under my breath.

"Understood?" He whispers again.

I nod and as soon as I do, he runs his finger slowly up my sex and rubs my clit softly. My body bucks under his touch and I try as hard as I can to keep quiet. I grab hold of Dan's forearm to try and anchor myself. His muscles ripple as his finger moves round and round over the sensitive swollen bud. In one swift move his finger is replaced with the soft pad of his thumb and he slides a fingertip inside me. I dig my nails into his arm and bite my lip hard as he eases his finger deeper inside me. I feel like my body might explode into a million pieces any minute now as my hips writhe against his hand of their own accord. He has found a part of me that I never knew existed and within seconds I am so close to coming that I have to bury my head in his chest to keep from crying out as my orgasm takes hold of me. The music in the background has faded against the rush of blood in my ears as my inner muscles contract and relax on his finger over and over. I have never had an orgasm like it and right now I don't want it to end.

My body softens against Dan's as I come to my senses again and he kisses the top of my head. "Well this is going to be one interesting night," he whispers, his words telling me that was just a preview.

CHAPTER FIFTEEN

*W*hen Dan told me he had a home outside Glasgow I pictured a huge mansion in a posh suburb. The road we have taken has become very rural and we have passed through a couple of tiny quaint villages on the way. Now the Range Rover pulls off the main road and travels across a bridge that looks like a mini viaduct spanning a river. Jim comes to a stop at a set of huge wrought iron gates attached to a gatehouse with an archway and a turret on it. It is lit from below and looks striking against the dark sky. The gates swing open and we continue up a long gravel driveway lined with trees also lit from below. We stop at another set of gates and the sight beyond them takes my breath away. This isn't a mansion; this looks more like a castle with its turrets and large panelled windows.

As the gates open, I gasp. "Wow."

Dan squeezes my hand as Jim makes his way through the gates and stops outside the most magnificent oak door. It must be about twelve feet high and is arched at the top. Jim gets out and opens the door for us. Dan climbs out first and then helps me out.

"Thanks Jim, I'll see you in the morning."

"No problem," Jim nods to us. "Mr King. Miss Olsson. Have a nice night."

Jim drives away back down the driveway and we watch the gates close behind him. As the car lights disappear out of sight, all is quiet, and I mean *really* quiet. The only noise is the breeze rustling through the trees and I know that if it weren't for the lights on the front of this huge house it would be pitch black out here too.

"Are you sure you're okay being here Nikki?"

I look at his face illuminated by the beautiful lights around us. "It's a little late to be asking me that Dan. After what you just did to me, I'm more than happy to be here."

He places his hand at the nape of my neck and pulls me in to him. His lips cover mine in a soft lingering kiss that speaks more to what this night will entail than words ever could.

I whimper softly when he breaks the connection and the fire in his eyes lets me know he heard it. "Get in here." He turns and leads us up the sandstone steps to the enormous wooden door.

As we step inside my breath is taken away yet again by the entrance hallway. The floor is a highly polished grey marble that carries on up the huge grand staircase. The glass panels on either side of the stairs create a beautiful contemporary contrast to the traditional marble and the façade outside. I stop on the huge grey rug and take off my shoes. Dan looks at me questioningly.

"I don't want to scratch your floor," I say quietly.

"The floor will be fine, now come on I want you in my bed." He takes my hand and I'm surprised as I step onto the marble floor in my bare feet and find it warm.

We make our way upstairs and through a couple of corridors, but Dan is moving us so fast I don't think I'd be able to make my way back even if I wanted to. He takes us through the bedroom door and no sooner is it closed than I am pulled up and into his arms as if I weigh less than a feather, which I can safely say is not the case. I throw my arms round his neck and drop my shoes behind him as he crushes me against the wall kissing me as if I might disappear. His hands are on my bare bum cheeks and his fingers knead them gently as we continue to kiss. Dan groans into my mouth and moves us away from the wall setting me back on my feet as he breaks the connection between our lips. He reaches behind my head and starts to undo my hair clips. One by one and achingly slowly he takes out the pins and tendrils of my blonde hair fall to my shoulders. When they are all out, he pushes his hands into my hair and massages my scalp. I shut my eyes against the delicious feeling and melt into his grip.

"You're so beautiful Nikki, has anyone ever told you that?"

I open my eyes, but I can't look at him. I'm ashamed. I know I did nothing wrong and yet I can't help but feel it was my own fault that I was treated like a piece of shit. I don't recall Mike ever telling me I was beautiful, or that he loved me. I can't even say I was ever happy with him. I was constantly on edge around him and when I wasn't with him, I was always wondering what he was up to. He made me think about him all the time and that I needed him to exist. Like I was nothing on my own. I shake my head and the wonderful feeling of being in Dan's arms and being worshipped by him disappears in a heartbeat. I move to push away from him, but his strong hands hold me still.

"Look at me Nikki."

"I'm sorry Dan I shouldn't be here. You know you can do so much better than me. I'm not what you want."

"Come here." He takes my hand and leads me to the bed. "Sit."

I do as he says and sit with my hands in my lap feeling even more stupid than I did before. "Sorry," I whisper my voice on the edge of breaking.

Dan puts his hand under my chin and makes me look at him. "What are you sorry for Nikki?"

"For allowing things to get this far. I'm broken Dan. You can't fix that, no one can."

"I don't want to fix you Nikki, you don't need to be fixed and you wouldn't be here if you didn't want to be. You have your own mind, no one can ever make you do something you don't want to."

"He did and I let him."

"He played on your insecurities Nikki, there's a difference. You wanted to be loved, to make your life better and he knew it. It made him feel powerful. What did you say to him when you left?"

I smile a little. "I didn't say anything, I just left. He didn't even know I had a new job. As far as he was concerned, I was going to be there when he got back from work."

Dan laughs. "Ooh you little badass. Now you tell me that's not a strong-willed woman?"

"It was the coward's way out. I was scared of him Dan." I avert my eyes as I remember being pinned to the bed, his nasty, sweaty hands on my jaw squeezing hard. "I thought he'd kill me if I stood up to him, but I saw a change in him that day. It was as though he finally realised he had succeeded in breaking me down and it excited him. He got off on it."

"Do you think in some way he saw that you were maybe changing? You might not have noticed you were doing anything differently, but people can sense these things. If he even had an inkling that he was losing his power over you it would have scared him shitless. You see Nikki, guys like him are the cowards. They see women as objects, as something to own." He reaches out and strokes my jawline softly with his fingers, resting his index finger on my bottom lip.

I close my eyes and breathe in deeply savouring his touch.

"Women are not our possessions Nikki." He moves his hand down my neck to my shoulder. "A man should never take what a woman isn't willing to give." His fingers skim over the top of my dress and I see the question in his eyes. I nod and his finger slips inside slightly grazing my nipple and shooting sparks down my body. "A man should worship a woman's body like she is Aphrodite herself."

His words make my insides somersault and his touch seems to be doing exactly what he wants it to. I feel powerful when I'm with him, like I don't owe him anything. I know he'll take what he wants from me but now I know it'll only be if I give it willingly.

"Tell me to stop and I will Nikki?"

I know I want this; I want it more than air. I stand up from the bed and move in front of him. Reaching behind me I unzip my dress and let it fall to the floor so that I'm left completely naked. Dan leans back on the bed propping himself up on his elbows and stares at me. His eyes rake over my body, but he says nothing. I'm starting to feel a little self-conscious now and move my arms to cover myself.

He quickly sits up and grabs my wrists. "Never be ashamed of your body Nikki, never." He pulls me down so that I'm straddling his lap. "You are beautiful."

He runs his hands down my sides brushing the sides of my breasts with his thumbs making my body shiver and my nipples harden to stiff points. He takes one in his mouth and rolls his hot tongue over it making my body buck. I'm a mass of sensation as my clit hits his erection straining through his jeans.

"Ah," I breathe out the word in a sigh.

He grabs my bum and pulls my hips in closer. He bites gently on my nipple and I writhe against his hard heat. Before I can react to the sensations rushing through my body, he stands with me and turns putting me down on my back on the cool cotton sheets. He pulls his t-shirt over his head and I giggle as I'm reminded of a line in a film, '*Fuck. Seriously. It's like you're Photo Shopped?*' His torso is ripped beyond belief and there is a tribal tattoo over his right shoulder snaking its way down to his dark nipple. The other shoulder is bare and it's only now I realise all his tattoos seem to be on the right-hand side except the binary one on his left wrist. He strips down to his boxers and now I get an even better picture of what lies beneath them. I cross my legs together to keep my greedy body from overreacting. He smiles and takes off his boxers and I gasp at the sight of his cock standing proud almost touching his abdomen.

"Touch yourself Nikki." His voice is low and desire blooms low in my belly.

I've never been asked to do anything like that before. I'm nervous. It's not something I wouldn't do, I'm a woman, I have needs, but it's a private thing.

"Do it Nikki. Make yourself come. Let me watch." He leans over me and whispers in my ear, "When you're done, I want to taste you."

That's all the convincing I need. I look up into his dark eyes as he moves back slightly to get a better view of me. I start slowly, letting my hand linger for a few seconds just above my pubic bone. I want to close my eyes to try and shut out some of the embarrassment I'm feeling but I can't. It's as though Dan has hypnotised me with his gaze. I watch his face as I move my hand slowly down towards my now very swollen and wet sex. His expression is like steel except for the tiniest tick of his jaw muscle. I want to make him as needy as me, so I run my finger through the warm honeyed wetness and bring it to my mouth. I see his stoic expression falter when I take my finger in my mouth and suck long and slow on it, tasting my own arousal and becoming wetter still. I don't break eye contact with him as I run my finger slowly back down the middle of my body and push a finger, then two inside me. I press the heel of my hand down over my clit, giving some weight to it with the other as my fingers go in deeper. Dan opens his mouth and sucks in a huge breath, which tips me over the edge, and I feel my inner muscles spasm against my fingers.

"Oh my fucking God Nikki." Dan launches himself at me and I take my hands away so that he can lap up all that sweet nectar. And he does, licking and sucking and moaning against my sex like he's a vampire and needs to feed. "You taste divine."

I push my hands into his hair willing him to lick me harder. He stops and rises up over me taking my mouth in his and I can taste myself on his lips and feel his hot, heavy cock on my belly. This is the single most erotic experience I've had in my life and he hasn't even fucked me yet. He reaches into a drawer in the bedside table and pulls out a condom. Even watching the act of him rolling it over himself is hot.

He pulls me up onto his thighs and up further so that I'm positioned above him. "Are you ready Nikki?"

I nod and he pulls me down onto him so hard that I gasp at the intrusion. It hurts but it's not painful and I can't help but want more. I slide myself up and down his hot shaft and he bucks his hips to meet me. Before too long we have a rhythm going and as I arch my back, he takes my nipple into his mouth and bites. And that does it; all sense of reality goes as every nerve ending in my body shoots for the stars. He hits me on that sweet spot once more and I come around him shouting his name. He follows suit after a few more thrusts and I cling to his body, both of us hot and sticky and panting for breath. As our breathing returns to normal and we sit staring into each other's eyes I wonder to myself what the hell sex was before this, or what *I* was before him.

CHAPTER SIXTEEN

"*O*oh," I groan as I stretch my body out. My muscles ache and when I remember why I smile. I can hear water running, a shower, and I sit up and take in my surroundings. I didn't get a good look at this room in the muted light last night and now, in the rising light of dawn, I can see it for the opulent space it is.

This bed is huge and in any other room would look too big, but I think this one bedroom has more square footage than my entire apartment. The wall behind the bed is entirely made of light grey leather padded panels that could rival a modern art installation, but also acts as a kind of headboard. All the furnishings in the room are light grey and the walls stark white although it doesn't feel cold. The huge windows are draped with a light grey sheer fabric and heavy dark grey velvet curtains on either side. I'm about to get out of the bed and check out that lovely specimen of a man in the shower when the bedroom door flies open and a little girl, I would guess about two or three years old, runs in.

"Daddy, daddy, daddy." She stops when she sees me

sitting in the bed and cocks her head to the side like a little puppy, her light brown curls bouncing around. "Hi."

I know I look like a deer in headlights right now and I can't answer her. I also can't take my eyes off her beautiful face. She's like a little doll and her eyes... my God her eyes. Those dark brown pools are hard to mistake. I looked into eyes just like that last night.

"Olivia. Olivia King, where are you?" The high-pitched female voice echoing up the corridor is getting closer and the little girl giggles and puts her hands to her mouth. She's so fucking cute it's making me want to cry.

"OLIVIA." That voice is like the high-pitched whine of a teapot on a stove. The owner of the voice appears in the doorway. She's young, maybe a little younger than me and she has her long brown hair scraped back in an Ariana Grande style ponytail, not a strand out of place. Her tight sweater and skinny jeans look like they've been painted on. "Olivia what have I told you about running away from me?"

Olivia stamps her feet. "I want my daddy."

The young woman eyes me suspiciously. "It appears your daddy's busy, now come on." She grabs Olivia's wrist and drags her from the room slamming the door behind her.

I listen to the little girl's cries and protestations until they disappear, and I let out the breath I didn't even know I was holding on to. It comes out stuttered and brings a wave of tears with it. I've done it again. I can't believe I've done it again. He has a fucking kid. I researched him and nowhere, in any bio I read, did it say he had a bloody kid. Now I'm in the middle of nowhere with no way to get home. I don't even know where this place is. I hear the shower stop and I jump out of the bed and grab my dress. Pulling it up I fumble for the zip. I'm in the process of trying to pull a piece of caught chiffon out of the zip when the bathroom door opens. I look up and see Dan standing in the doorway with a towel wrapped round his waist and one in his hand rubbing at his hair. I have to turn away from him. I want to run away but I have nowhere to go.

"I want to go home." It's all I can manage, and I know he can hear the tears in my voice.

"Nikki what's up?"

I shake my head. "I just want to go home Dan please." My hot salty tears are free flowing down my face as I stand in the middle of the room half dressed in my bridesmaid dress, which looked so beautiful yesterday, but now reminds me that I am about to do yet another walk of shame.

"Nikki will you look at me please?"

I shake my head.

"Nikki look at me." It's not a request this time and I turn to face him, still holding the zip of the dress closed against my front. "What's wrong?"

"Why didn't you tell me you had a kid Dan?" My voice cracks on the last word and I stare at the floor.

"Shit," he mutters under his breath.

I feel rage boil up inside me. I have a right to be angry. "Shit. Is that all you have to say? You knew what it took for me to trust you Dan, why didn't you tell me?"

"What the fuck would it have mattered if I had told you Nikki? Would you not have come home with me? Would you not have admitted how you felt about me just because I have a daughter? What sort of person would that have made you?"

"How dare you question the kind of person I am Dan, how fucking dare you." I don't know what possesses me, but I pick up my bag and launch it across the room at him and in the process let go of my dress, which falls to the floor leaving me naked again. Dan moves out of the way and the bag hits the wall and falls onto a grey velvet sofa emptying the contents, one of which being the knickers I was wearing last night, over the cushions.

Dan looks from my naked body to the couch and back again and his eyes are like fire. He laughs and shakes his head. "Is this how it's going to be Nikki? Are you going to get spooked every time something pops up?"

I pull my dress back up and sit down on the bed. I shake my head and look at the door as tears fall from my eyes. I know I've made a big mistake here and I don't know how to take it back. Dan comes and sits beside me.

"Nikki, I don't know why I didn't tell you about Olivia. She's the most important thing in my life and I'm lucky she's even here at all." He takes my hand and rubs my knuckles. "I like you Nikki, I really do but I love her. I think I didn't tell you because I was worried this is what would happen. Women don't tend to take the fact that a man has baggage very well and if I have to choose my daughter over a woman who can't accept her, she will win every time."

"Dan I'm sorry. I'm an idiot. I just thought since you told me about your family that you had told me everything."

"Nikki, I didn't tell you anything you couldn't have found out yourself."

"I told you I needed a way out, if your company hadn't offered me that job I'd have gone with the next best thing. It didn't even occur to me to check you or the company out, I was just happy to be getting away. Please don't get me wrong Dan I love my job and I'm glad I have it but at the time I was in a terrible place. I dread to think what may have become of me if I hadn't come here."

"This isn't how I imagined this morning going Nikki." He lets go of my hand and leans forward, his forearms on his thighs. "I swear I would have told you about Olivia, I just... I didn't want you to run."

I place my hand on his shoulder. "Dan I wouldn't have run. I just wish you had trusted me enough to tell me. God I've agreed to be your spy I think I could've handled this." I put my hand on his jaw and turn his face to me. "She is absolutely beautiful by the way."

The pride in his eyes makes me smile. "Yes, she is. I'm sorry Nikki; I should have given you more credit I know. Please tell me I haven't fucked this up."

I lean in and kiss him softly. "You haven't fucked this up," I whisper against his lips, "just trust me next time okay."

He crashes his lips down on mine and I can feel the relief in his kiss. He stands us up and I let my dress fall to the floor again. He lifts me off my feet and I wrap my legs round his waist kissing him back, reassuring him that I'm going nowhere.

"*D*an, where's Olivia's mum?" I run my fingers up and down his arm as we lie on the bed.

He sighs and I lean up on my elbow so that I'm looking at him. "It's a long story Nikki are you sure you want to hear it?"

"Of course I do."

He sits up so that he's mirroring me, and we lie face to face. "She's in prison."

"Oh wow. I wasn't expecting that… wow."

"Irena is a scumbag drug dealer. I met her five years ago when she was apparently here from Latvia on a student exchange programme. I thought she was the one. I got suckered right in, but it turned out she was using my status and wealth to hide her drug outfit."

"That's disgusting."

"It crushed me when I found out. I loved her, but I loved a lie. She could have won a fucking Oscar for the performance she put in. I found out about everything when she was pregnant with Olivia. I was going to propose to her, so I had her checked out. I don't even know why; I had already made up my mind that she was going to be my wife. I suppose paranoia comes with the territory." He turns onto his stomach and I keep quiet, letting him continue. "The information that came up about her almost killed me. She had set up businesses, using my surname, to launder her money. She wasn't just *a* dealer she was *the* dealer. She was top of the fucking chain."

I'm utterly shocked at his story and knowing about the stuff he went through because of drugs and his dad makes it all even more sad. "Did she have Olivia in prison?"

"Fuck no. I was never going to let her bring my child into the world behind bars. No, I waited till Olivia was born then I made sure the police got every bit of information I had on her. Her court case would turn your hair grey. She was eventually found guilty of supplying and distributing Class A drugs, extortion and fraud, here's the biggest kicker that even I didn't know, arms dealing. There was also talk of murders but that couldn't be proved."

This is starting to sound like some crazy Netflix show. "Weren't you worried for Olivia's safety? Surely she would have other people who would do something to hurt the person that took her down."

"That's why very few people know about Olivia. When Irena went down it brought down an entire network not only here but in other parts of Europe too. It was a massive operation and I'll tell you right now, if you had seen her, you would think butter wouldn't melt in her mouth. She got the maximum the judge could give her, life with a thirty year minimum. She's wanted all over Europe, so I doubt she'll ever get out of prison."

"Oh, Dan I'm so sorry."

He holds up his hand. "No don't be, I'm not. I got my beautiful little girl out of it. She's my saving grace, my reason for getting up every day. You're the first woman I've brought home since Irena."

I reach up and touch his face. "Thank you. Not for bringing me here but for telling me that. I know it wasn't easy. You're a good guy Dan and I bet you're an excellent dad."

He smiles. "On that note, would you like to meet my little cherub?"

CHAPTER SEVENTEEN

*T*he table in this breakfast nook off the kitchen is big enough to seat about forty people and I feel like Jack at the giant's table.

"Would you like some breakfast Nikki?" An older woman dressed impeccably asks with a smile as she places a pot of tea and a cafetiere of coffee on the table in front of us.

"Uhm… yes please." The fact that she knows my name, and I have no idea who she is, throws me. "What do you have?"

She gives a little laugh and looks at Dan, who answers my question. "We have whatever you want."

"Oh okay. Could I get some French toast and syrup?"

"Of course. My name is Valerie. If you need anything else, please let me know."

I watch her walk away and turn back to Dan. "I feel like I'm in a restaurant. Your house is stunning by the way."

"Thanks. I like it. Steven Parker, your friend's new husband, was the architect on the project. That's how I met him. He let me have significant input on the design. I wanted it to be luxury but to still feel like a home. This place was finished just before Olivia was born."

"Well she certainly has a beautiful place to grow up in." No sooner have those words left my mouth than the little lady in question makes an appearance.

"Daddy," she shouts as she runs through the kitchen and into Dan's outstretched arms, her beautiful curls bouncing like springs.

The young woman I saw earlier follows her and her face is just as stern as it was then. I assume she's the nanny although, by the way she looks at Dan, I think she'd like to be more. I watch as Olivia wraps her little arms round his neck, and he kisses her forehead. She turns in his arms and looks at me.

"That's my daddy's jumper," she says as she points at the ensemble I'm wearing.

Dan gave me the smallest clothes of his he has, and they still drown me. "Yes, it is. Your daddy let me borrow these."

I'm almost floored by the cuteness when she puts her hands to her mouth and gasps in mock shock. "What's your name?" She asks.

"I'm Nikki and what's yours?" I ask

"My name is Olivia King, I'm three." Her smile is so cute, and her voice is even cuter. She's very articulate for her age.

"Nessa take the rest of the morning off. I'll keep Olivia with me until Nikki goes home."

Nessa looks at me with frosty eyes then nods at Dan. "Okay. I'll be at home if you need me." She turns and disappears from our view.

Olivia squirms in Dan's arms and he relents and lets her down. She giggles at me then runs off into the next room.

"Nessa doesn't like me," I whisper to Dan.

He laughs and shakes his head. "Nessa doesn't really like anyone, but she is an amazing nanny and Olivia adores her. She has a lot of issues. She's actually very nice once you get to know her."

"Nessa likes *you*," and my words are unintentionally tinged with jealousy.

"It's something I've already dealt with. She's here to do her job and that's it. If she steps out of line or crosses that boundary, she'll lose her job. She's an employee, nothing more."

I lower my eyes to the table. "That's what I was supposed to be." My words are mumbled but I know he heard me.

"Nikki," my name is said in a sigh. "Nikki look at me please."

I do as he asks and the internal conflict he is feeling is visible in those chocolate eyes of his. He is about to say something else to me when Valerie appears beside the table with a huge tray of food.

"Sorry folks, breakfast is ready. I've put some bacon on there too because…well, it's bacon…you can't have too much of that. You're not veggie are you Nikki? I'm sorry I should have checked."

I shake my head and give her a small smile. "No I'm not Valerie, this looks great, thank you."

"Phew," she runs her hand over her forehead, "thank God for that. Well enjoy." She turns to Dan. "I'm going into town today to pick up some books I ordered is there anything I can get you."

"No thanks love, I'm good. I'm heading into the office later anyway. Enjoy your afternoon, I'll probably see you tomorrow night."

"No problem. I've left next week's schedules on your

desk for approval and the menus for the month are ready. I'll need them signed off by Wednesday at the latest."

Dan salutes her, "Yes sir."

Valerie slaps him on the back of the head. "Don't be cheeky to your elders," she scolds him.

I smile at their interaction. She seems like a bit of a mother figure to him, which is nice considering his past.

"It was really nice to meet you Nikki." She emphasises the word *really* and I know it's because I'm the first woman he's had here since Irena.

"And you Valerie, thanks again for breakfast."

She gives my shoulder a little squeeze. There are more words in that small action than she could ever say, and I can't deny that it worries me a little. I watch her walk away and turn back to Dan who has a slightly pensive look on his face.

I decide to break the silence. "So, Valerie is your cook then? She's good." I take a bite of salty, smoky bacon and I feel like my mouth has just exploded. "Oh my, this is nice."

Dan laughs. "She's more than that. I like to call her my chief of staff because… well she is. She runs the household and grounds staff and takes care of the day-to-day running of the house. I honestly don't know what I'd do without her."

I get the feeling he means in more ways than in just a professional capacity.

"She is lovely." I sigh as I break off a piece of French toast and push it into my mouth.

"What's up Nikki?" Dan asks softly.

I shake my head and swallow my food. "Dan, I like you I really do, but…"

He narrows his eyes ever so slightly. "But what?"

"I don't know how a relationship between us is ever going to work. Not right now anyway. Not with everything you've asked me to do."

He's about to say something when Olivia comes back to the table carrying two Barbie dolls who should be embarrassed at their state of undress. "Nikki, want to play dollies?"

I smile at her and wonder how much interaction she has with other kids. She's three so she must go to kindergarten or some sort of pre-school. The education system in the UK is very different to what is on offer in state schools in South Africa but, because my sister and I were private schooled, we went from age three. "Sure sweetheart. I'll come and play with you as soon as I've had my breakfast, okay?"

"Okay," she says in her little voice and goes off again running at breakneck speed, her bare feet slapping on the tiled floor.

"She likes you Nikki. So do I. We can make this work I promise we can." Dan puts his hand on mine.

"I think we need to take this slowly. If I'm at all honest I don't think it's a good idea to take our relationship any further right now. Not until you have all your evidence about what Astrid and Jed are up to."

He lets go of my hand and sits back in his chair. He sighs and bows his head. "How can I see you every day and not want to touch you? Last night was... I honestly don't know what to do."

Standing up in front of him, I run my hand through his hair. He grabs me by the waist and pulls me into his lap, laying his head against my chest.

"Will you wait for me?" I ask.

"You know I will."

CHAPTER EIGHTEEN

I thought work was going to be a nightmare today, but it has been okay. Now past the planning stage, we've started to generate some decent output on our project, and I have actually had some concrete work that Dan and I have already been able to alter the data on to give to Jed. I had to talk to Jed at length today and it was a little uncomfortable knowing what I know. Don't get me wrong he was pleasant enough but simply knowing what he has been doing to Dan's business makes me want to slap some sense into him. I get the feeling that Astrid is using him but he's a man, he won't be thinking with his brain. That being said I know this industry well and it does leave itself open to all sorts of intellectual theft. Astrid and Jed are merely exploiting that. I'm sure I saw an ounce of glee in Jed's eyes when I handed him our work today.

I feel for Dan. He wanted to run his business legitimately since he's seen more criminal activity than a whole season of Law and Order. Jed has been with Dan from the start, so he obviously knows about Dan's dad. It makes me angry to know of the opportunities afforded to him by Dan. It's like that old saying; 'don't bite the hand that feeds you'. I make my way up in the lift to Dan's office and halfway there my phone vibrates in my pocket. I check it and see a message from Damo.

Sorry about not coming in today Miss Nikki. I will be in tomorrow I promise. x

I smile, *little shit.* He phoned in sick this morning saying he wasn't feeling very well and thought he may have a bug. I know otherwise because I received an after-midnight phone call from a very drunk Damo telling me I was his bestie and that he loved me. I'm going to kick his ass tomorrow and take great pleasure in reminding him about the phone call.

Dan and I are in complete agreement about taking things very slowly. Not only so that we don't have to keep it a secret but also for the fact that I need to stay on the trust side of Jed at least. Astrid is a lost cause; she already hates me, and I know that will never change but it would only be worse if she knew about us. It was nice to be able to talk about it with him instead of doing a Nikki special and simply running away. I even got to play dollies with Olivia before I left.

The lift pings as it reaches the twelfth floor and I step out to complete silence. Tabitha's seat is empty and her computer screen dark. She's definitely gone for the day. Dan's window wall is clear, and I can't see him in there either. It's like the Mary Celeste up here. I know Dan will probably be in the apartment, but I decide not to bother him. I slip into his office quietly and place my folder on his desk. I'm about to leave when I hear movement from the back of the office. I stop still and close my eyes. It's going to be hard to be around Dan and resist the urge to touch him. Oh, who the hell am I kidding, I want to do so much more than bloody touch him.

"Afternoon." His voice sends a shiver down my spine and I take a deep breath to counter it, my mind taking me right back to his bed.

"Hi," I say as I turn to face him. *Holy what!* He's standing behind me with a fucking towel wrapped round his waist and the remnants of a shower beading on his skin. I mean come on, how the hell am I supposed to stay away from him when he does that.

"Sorry, I have a dinner thing this evening, I was just getting changed and I heard a noise in here."

"It-its' okay. I was just dropping off this work from today. Jed now has the first doctored data, so we'll see how that one pans out. I'm heading home now if that's okay."

Dan nods at me and smiles. "Well it is after five, I would have thought you'd have been away ages ago."

"Yeah I had a couple of things to finish off and the office was too loud earlier. The team are really excited about this project, I think it's going to be a really good system when it's done."

"I know it will and that's why I don't want Jed and Astrid to get hold of it. It stands to make us a lot of money and they have already stolen enough from me. As soon as we have enough evidence, I'm going to ruin them."

I can't believe I'm standing here having this conversation with him while he's more or less naked. *Get your head together Nikki.* I give myself a mental shake.

"Okay, so I should go." I turn as quickly as I can and leave the office and thankfully, since the building is more or less empty, the lift is still here.

As the doors close, I make a deal with myself to try and stay away from Dan unless it's absolutely necessary. I can't trust myself around him.

I should have gone straight home after work tonight yet, here I find myself sitting at a table at the back of a little bar I found nearby the office. I run my finger up the side of my glass and watch the condensation bead and run down to the table. I'm in a contemplative mood after seeing Dan. I want so much to be with him, but I know this is for the best right now. He could lose too much if we went public. I'm caught off guard when the screen of my phone flashes and I see I have a text from my sister.

Hey Nikki, how would you like some auntie duties? X

I know the only auntie duties she could want right now would be babysitting. My other auntie duties will come when Georgie's older and falls out with her mum.

Sure, you need a babysitter?

Her answer is so quick it's like she had already typed out her reply.

Yeah tomorrow night. We managed to get a couple of Ed Sheeran tickets this morning. I'm so excited. X

I sigh as I reply. Lucky bitch, I'd love to go and see Ed.

Of course. What time? x

We want to go for dinner first so could you have her from 4? x

I assume it's in Glasgow so just drop her off at my work she'll be fine until I'm finished. x

Thanks sis. Hope I'm not disrupting any plans with Dan the man. Hope you had as much fun on Saturday night as I did. Lol x

Ugh. Why Charlie? I know her question is completely innocent, but that fact doesn't make me feel any better about the situation.

See you tomorrow. Xx

It's a short and sweet reply but it puts an end to the conversation. If it had carried on all it would have done is made me realise how stupid and pathetic I am. I down what's left of my gin and tonic and head for home. I need to put a little space between Dan and me and hanging around in a bar near work isn't the way to do that. I wonder if I subconsciously chose to come here because it *is* close by and I know he's still there. Since it's a nice night I decide to walk home and I'm there in no time at all. As I reach the top of the communal stairs and step onto the landing that leads to my front door, I stop dead at the sight that greets me.

There, leaning against the door, is a bouquet of red roses. There must be over a dozen of them and they are pretty stunning, the long stems standing proud and tall against the doorframe. I don't know why but those red petals against the stark white door is a little unsettling and instinctively I look around to see if there is anyone there. I make my way to the door and lift the flowers and frown as I let myself into my apartment. Dan must have had these sent for me and it makes me feel a little uneasy. Since we've made a mutual decision to take things no further right now, I find it strange that he'd send me flowers. There's a card attached to the flowers and I put them down and open the little envelope. The card is printed and seems to be a poem or a quote.

*Y*ou say you love the rain,
    But you open your umbrella.
    You say you love the sun,
But you find a shadow spot.
You say you love the wind,
But you close your windows.
This is why I am afraid,

You say that you love me too.

*W*hat the hell is this? I never told him I loved him. I wouldn't have. Did I? Oh God, *did* I? I drop the card onto the counter and head for the shower with a million thoughts running wild in my mind.

CHAPTER NINETEEN

I've kept a low profile since I got in to work at eight thirty this morning. I really don't want to see Dan today, not after getting that note. It had me in a bit of a state last night. I honestly don't know what it means, and I know I wasn't that drunk on Saturday night that I didn't know what I was saying. I remember everything about that night, so much so that I have replayed it constantly since.

"Hey Miss Nikki."

My eyes snap open at Damo's voice. "Hi. Nice of you to make an appearance today."

He looks rather sheepishly at me and bites his lip. "Hmm sorry about that."

"Yeah you should be you little shit. You bloody woke me up on Sunday night drunk-calling me telling me you loved me, and I was your bestie."

He holds up his hands in defeat. "I know and I'm so embarrassed."

I smile at him. "It's just as well I like you or you'd be in big trouble."

He puts his hands together as if he's praying and mouths a thank you to me. "So how did the wedding go?"

He's getting the edited version and right now I'm glad he wasn't here yesterday because I may have spilled my guts to him.

"It was lovely, yeah. Gina was beautiful. I know they'll be so happy especially since their baby will be here in a few months too. Oh, and talking of babies my niece will be here later today. I'm babysitting tonight."

Damo's eyes light up. "Oh I love babies; I can't wait to meet this little lady." He dumps his bag at his desk. "Coffee sweetie?"

"I could murder one thanks."

"That's a bit violent," he says as he walks away.

The smile I have on my face drops as the lift doors open and Astrid walks out. The fake smile she has plastered on makes me want to be sick. She swans around this place like she's invincible and it's only as she makes her way towards me that I realise I have my hands in fists, my nails leaving half-moon dents in my palms.

"Nikki darling, how are you?" Her condescending voice is like scraping nails down a blackboard and the way she talks to me makes me shudder.

"I'm fine Astrid, what can I do for you?"

"Jed wants to see you at some point today. He says there's something not quite right with the work you handed in yesterday."

My stomach takes a nosedive. This shouldn't be an issue right now. The work I've handed in should still add up at the moment but will taint the bigger picture when it is all put together. *How the hell does he know?*

"I'll go and see him when the rest of my staff are in and we've had our morning briefing."

"I'll let him know. Caio." She turns and struts off leaving me a little shaken.

I don't know what to do now. I could blow this whole thing if I talk to Jed. I find it hard to handle confrontation, especially when I know so much is at stake.

"You okay Nikki? You look like you've seen a ghost." Damo puts my mug down in front of me and sits opposite.

"Astrid was just here."

He rolls his eyes.

"Yeah that's enough to give anyone the heebie jeebies. She is without doubt the vilest piece of shit I've ever had the displeasure of working beside and, believe me I've worked with some belters in my time." He takes a sip of his coffee. "Before I came to work here, I did a four-week stint at a lawyer's office. The fuckwit I had the displeasure of working with thought she was amazing. In reality she was what I would call an educated idiot. When it came to the law, she could rhyme off anything without having to look it up, but she used to come out with all sorts of stupid things. She really was a fool but harmless. Astrid, well she's fucking dangerous if you ask me."

I nod in agreement. "Damo will you excuse me? I need to head upstairs to speak to Dan if you don't mind."

"Of course."

*T*abitha is on the phone when I get out of the lift and she smiles at me while ushering me into Dan's office as if he's been expecting me. I suppose he probably has been expecting me to appear at some point since he sent me those flowers yesterday. I nod to Tabitha and push open the door to Dan's office. He's at his desk looking at some paperwork and has a slight frown on his face. As soon as he sees me his frown turns to a lovely warm smile. He looks genuinely pleased to see me and I have to say it feels nice.

"Nikki hi."

"Hi."

"What can I do for you?"

I hate the way we talk to each other now as though nothing has happened between us. I know it's my own fault. I could make it right, but I would feel like a total hypocrite and it would only serve to show how weak willed I truly am.

"Jed knows." I get straight to the point because I really need to put some distance between us. If words are how I have to do it then so be it. I take a seat in front of him.

He narrows his eyes at me. "Knows what?"

"Astrid came to me this morning and said Jed wants to see me because my data didn't add up. You told me this wouldn't be a problem but yet here we are at the first hurdle and already I want to throw in the towel."

"Hmm…this is a problem."

I shake my head. "What do I do here? And how the fuck does he know?"

"He must be running it by someone from the get-go. I underestimated them."

"You don't say. Will you tell me more about this Dan? What company has Astrid got ties to?"

He shakes his head. "I already told you the less you know the less you can be held accountable for."

"Then I'm sorry Dan but I can't do this." *Where the hell did that come from?*

"If that's how you really feel then so be it. I'll have HR sort out a severance package for you. I assure you it will be generous given the work you've already done."

Fuck, he's firing me. I look at him in disbelief. "Oh…

um… okay." I feel tears welling in my eyes. I don't under-stand what's happening here. What the hell have I done?

"What did you think I was going to say Nikki? I already told you that there was only so much you needed to know. It's safer for you this way."

I stand and head for the door but stop before I get there. I wasn't going to mention the flowers but now I need answers. If this is how things have to end, then I want to know what that note was about. I turn back to him.

"Why did you send me those roses Dan?"

His look of puzzlement shocks me slightly and I realise I've made a huge mistake.

"I didn't send you roses Nikki. I fucking hate roses so I'd never send them to someone I…" He shakes his head. "Any-way, why did you think I had sent them?"

I sit back down in the chair and put my head in my hands. "I guess I… hoped it was you." And then a horrible realisa-tion crosses my mind. *Astrid.* I won't say anything about the note. "It must have been a thank you from Gina for being her bridesmaid." I'm astonished at how plausible I just made that sound.

"Nikki look at me." I lift my head. "Do you have any idea how hard it's been to be normal around you since the week-end? How much I've wanted to touch you, kiss you, and feel you under me again?"

"I know. I've felt the same." I'm not lying; I have felt the same. I want nothing more than to feel his hands on my body again, to feel his lips on mine, to be held in his arms.

"Then why are we doing this Nikki?"

"I honestly don't know Dan, my fucked up stupid pride, I guess. This is hard for me. Mike has ruined me. I don't know what to do. What we did at the weekend, it… well it made me feel like a real person for the first time in as long as I can remember. It felt… right."

He sighs and leans back in his chair.

"Do you think we could start over? I don't want to lose you at this company, but I also don't want to lose *you.*"

"Dan are you sure you want to do this? I'm not exactly the most stable female on the planet."

"I think I know how to change that stupid label you've given yourself. How about a compromise that might benefit both of us? You tell me what happened to you and I'll give you as much information on Astrid and Jed as I have."

This makes me feel good and scared all at once. It means he trusts me enough to let me in, but I don't know what he'll think of me when I tell him how I ended up in the situation I did with Mike. "Okay."

His smile is genuine and beautiful. "Good, then let's do it right this time."

He gets up from his chair and rounds the desk until he is standing next to me. I take his outstretched hand and stand so that I am facing him. "Nikki, how would you like to go for dinner on Friday with me?"

"I would love to go for dinner with you." All of a sudden, I feel rather shy. *Good God he's seen me naked and now I'm shy.*

"Okay, I know a great place to eat. We can leave straight from here since there's an hour or so of travelling."

"Hmm…I'm intrigued." I'm genuinely happy that we can work through this and I can tell from his smile that he is too. I was stupid to think I could stay away from him. "Okay, as much as I'd love to stay here with you, I have a job to do, or not do or… well you know." I laugh at the strange situation we have going on here and it actually feels real, not a fake laugh put on to hide my shame.

"Yes, you do have a job to do and by the end of the week you'll be fully informed about it all."

"Till Friday then," I say as I start to head for the door.

Dan gets there before me and holds the door open for me in such a gentlemanly manner that it makes me chuckle. He takes my hand and kisses my knuckles. "Till Friday."

I leave and head for the lift, passing Tabitha who is staring at her computer screen but has a knowing smile on her face. The smile on my own face could rival the Cheshire cat's, but as I step into the lift, I remember the flowers and my good mood disappears. If it was Astrid, the worst thing I could do is draw attention to it with her. It would only make her feel good about herself and she'd know she's succeeded in getting under my skin. And she has done just that. It seems every office has one of these bitchy women, but it's not every day you get to silently have the upper hand over a horror like her. That's what keeps me going whenever she rears her nasty head.

---

*A*t four o'clock on the dot my phone rings and the girl on reception lets me know my sister is here with Georgie. There is no one on this earth that is more punctual than Charlie. It has always been a running joke in my family that if Charlie is ever late then something terrible has happened to her. Even Georgie has followed in her footsteps since she decided to come into the world a few weeks early. The office is quiet, and everyone is busy beavering away at their computers so it's the perfect opportunity to slip out. I make my way down to the reception area and find Charlie and Mark admiring the artwork on the walls.

"Hey guys." They both turn in unison as I near them.

"Hey sis," Charlie says as she hugs me.

They are both dressed up and they remind me of a couple of teenagers going out on a date. It's so nice to see my sister so happy.

"You two look like you're more than ready to rock out tonight. I won't lie to you; I am extremely jealous, and I do hate you a tiny bit right now."

Mark laughs. "This is one of those 'in the right place at the right time' things. I got these tickets from a friend who I wouldn't actually have seen if I hadn't missed my train, and the reason I missed the train was because I was buying Charlie flowers."

"Yeah, we had a little heated discussion that morning and he was going to try grovelling with flowers. Well, for Ed Sheeran tickets I'd forgive anyone kicking my granny, so he was more than forgiven."

Yes, my sister has a weird sense of humour.

"Oh, Charlie you are awful. Now I'll take this little one and let you two get on. My staff are going to love meeting her. Damo is especially looking forward to it."

"Listen to you, 'my staff'. The girl done good and by the way it's nice to see you with a real smile on your face. You look happy today sweetie."

I really am happy today, so much so that I would say I feel like I'm glowing.

"Yeah I really am happy Charlie. I'm so glad I came here."

"Yeah and not just for the job," Charlie leans in and whispers. "Right Marky Mark lets go before she changes her mind. We'll pick her up when the concert is done. Hopefully before midnight." She plants a kiss on Georgie's head.

Mark hands the pram over to me and they both disappear out the doors, giggling as they go. I look down at my niece who has decided to see how much of her fist she can fit in her mouth. Charlie has her dressed in the cutest little pair of dungarees and a marshmallow pink T-shirt. She is such a stunning little baby and I know my colleagues are going to love her.

CHAPTER TWENTY

"*R*ight Miss Nikki you ready?" Damo arrives at my desk, chirpy as ever. I, on the other hand, look and feel like I've been dragged through a hedge backwards. My sister seriously has a lot to answer for, and so does the clock since it feels like it has been going backwards all day.

"Oh God Damo I'm not sure this is going to be such a good idea today, I'm bloody exhausted."

He puts his hands on his hips and gives me a suspicious look. "Well what did you get up to last night that's got you so tired? Spill."

"Oh not what you think, get your mind out the gutter *Damien*."

"Ooh I've touched a nerve. What's up my little chicken?"

I can't help but laugh at his mother hen act. "Well you know I was babysitting Georgie last night." I talk as I tidy up my desk.

"Mhm that sweet bundle of gorgeousness."

"Ah not so sweet at two, three, half-three, four and five this morning. My God that girl has a set of lungs on her. I thought I was going to get arrested for anti-social behaviour at one point through the night."

"I thought you only had her while the concert was on."

"That was the plan, but little did I know Charlie had packed enough stuff for an overnight, so they decided they were going to a hotel for the night. '*She's a great baby*' she said. '*She doesn't really wake through the night*' she said. Well these," I point at my eyes, "are proof that she does wake through the night. I swear I actually wanted to murder my sister at four this morning. The poor little soul just wanted her mum."

"Oh dear, well hopefully you won't fall asleep in this class today. I've heard it's very intense."

"Oh, I thought you'd done this before."

"No, I've done normal yoga, but I had heard this Bikram Yoga is supposed to be good for inflexible people. Like me."

"Oh God I don't know if I'll make it out alive."

"Don't be a wuss. Let's go we need to be there fifteen minutes before it starts." Damo swings his yoga mat over his shoulder, and I gather my stuff and follow him as he heads for the lift.

---

*T*he studio we are going to is only a minute walk from the office. I love how everything is within walking distance in the city centre. Everything I need, I can find between home and work. When I lived in South Africa my office was outside the city so there wasn't much to do before, during and after work that wasn't a half hour drive away. The building housing the studio is much like many of the older buildings in Glasgow, made from old sandstone with ornate stone carvings on the walls and beautiful large sash windows. We make our way through the front door and stop at the reception. The girl behind the desk is slim and flawless and I wonder for a moment if she actually does this class or if they are just using her as an advert.

"Hi there, we're booked for the next class. Damien Shaw and Nikki Olsson." Damo takes the lead and I'm happy to let him.

The receptionist looks at her computer screen and smiles as she looks back at us. "So, you're booked in for the introductory class. Let me just show you the full list of monthly and yearly options we have..."

Damo holds his hand up stopping advert-girl in mid sell. "Why don't we try the class first, *then* we'll look at the price list sweetie."

"O-kay." She looks a little perplexed. Obviously, people don't normally argue with her. "That'll be thirty-two pounds fifty each then."

"Christ," I say under my breath. That's more than I was expecting, and this is only the introductory class. I dread to think how much a monthly membership is let alone a yearly one.

"I'll get it honey," Damo whispers as he pushes his card into the machine. The advert hands him his receipt and directs us towards the studio.

"Thanks for that. I'll pay you back I promise." I push open the door and instantly feel like I've been hit by the fires of hell. "Holy shit that's hot." I look back at Damo who is giving off a '*what have I gotten us into*' look.

"Oh, it smells ripe in here doesn't it?"

He is not kidding. The heat and humidity mixed with the smell of classes past are not a nice mixture and I wonder how I am going to make it through ninety minutes without dying. There's a large digital thermometer on the wall, which is reading 95°F. I was wrong; it's hotter than the fires of hell. The class looks rather full and unfortunately the only spaces are right at the front. If this heat doesn't kill me the embarrassment will. We take our spots and as I unroll my mat, I feel the need to shed some clothes. I strip out of my t-shirt so that I am only in my sports bra. It's still too hot but it helps slightly. The yoga pants I'm wearing are a little too thick and I feel like I'm in an oven being cooked in foil.

"I am actually going to die in here Damo." I look over at him and he's standing there in a pair of *really* short shorts and apart from them he's effectively naked.

"I'm fine," he smiles, and I actually want to do him some harm.

"Why didn't you tell me I was over dressed you little shit?"

"Hey dumbass the name hot yoga should have given it away."

"You said it was called Bikram Yoga not hot yoga."

He laughs, a hearty sarcastic laugh. "You can use a computer; you should have Googled it."

I'm about to hit back with something equally cheeky when the door opens and what I can only describe as the tiniest hippie woman enters. Her dreadlocks reach her backside and she has a tie-dyed scarf round the top of her head. She is also in an incredibly short pair of shorts and as I scan the room it appears that everyone else is too. Now I feel like an idiot. Who the hell takes on something new like this without researching it? I just thought it was another name for a different type of yoga.

"Okay everyone, I'm Suzie, and welcome to the class. I see we have some newbies here today." She looks right at Damo and I and the whole class turns to look at us too. I feel my face blush and right now I would gladly slink out the door and never return.

"Hi," Damo says loudly and waves to everyone.

Rolling my eyes at him I turn and give a small smile to the forty pairs of eyes on us.

"Nice to welcome you both. Why don't you introduce yourselves?"

Damo, who I have come to realise is something of an extrovert, goes first. "Damien Shaw, Glasgow born and bred. Call me Damo I don't like being associated with The Omen."

The class laughs in unison and Suzie gives him a huge smile. "Nice to meet you Damo. And you my love?"

I sigh and all at once feel my body recoil into itself, trying to make me as small and inconspicuous as possible. "Nikki Olsson."

"Nice to meet you Nikki. Now that's not a Scottish accent is it?"

I answer her only because I want to get on with the class and get out of this extremely uncomfortable situation. "South Africa."

"Well it's always great to have some fresh blood and we welcome you with open arms, both of you." Suzie turns and addresses the class as a whole and I'm thankful for the reprieve as everyone turns their attention from us to her. As I do the same, the digital thermostat catches my attention and I notice that it shows a temperature of 98°F. Holy hell-balls, how bloody hot is this place going to get?

"*N*amaste," says Suzie and the class repeats it back to her. I open my eyes as a bead of sweat drips off my nose. The class has ended on a temperature of 108°F and I think I may have lost about a stone in water. Thankfully, I brought a towel with me because there may have been some slipping and sliding on the mat if I hadn't.

"Let's hit the showers Miss Nikki and then we can go to the juice bar for a power smoothie."

"Okay but I think I'd rather hit a real bar for a power G&T."

Damo leans in close to me. "That's what I meant," he whispers. "I just didn't want Suzie to think we were taking the piss. Come on we'll get ready and head out. Let's see where the night takes us."

---

*A*s we make our way out of the building, I'm thankful for the cool breeze coming off the river. That class was bloody hot, but I actually enjoyed it. It was nice to have an hour or so concentrating on something other than all the crap in my life.

"Did you have any plans tonight Miss Nikki?"

I shake my head. "No not especially. I was just going to go home and sit in front of the TV with a ready meal."

"Well instead of a bar, how do you fancy coming out to dinner with me tonight. I was thinking something casual though I'm not into anything fancy after all that sweating."

"I'd love to Damo thanks."

Damo hooks his arm through mine and we walk and chat for the next ten minutes until we reach the doors of the little café in the same block as my apartment.

"Well it looks like you've basically walked me home. How do you fancy grabbing some food to go and taking it upstairs?"

"That sounds cool. Do they do takeaway?"

I smile at Damo and wink. "The manager knows me. I get my coffee here every morning before I go to work so I'm sure he won't mind."

"Ah I love knowing people who *know* people."

I laugh at him. "You make me sound like I know a hit-man or something."

"Well you are the daughter of a diplomat, so you do *know* people. I bet you could have me murdered and never bat an eyelid." Damo elbows my arm and winks at me.

I pull a serious face and lean in close. "Yes," I whisper, "I could, so watch it matey."

---

*L*oaded sandwiches and a bottle of rosé in hand, Damo and I head for my apartment. Luckily, we got to the café just before it closed so we have ended up with much more food than we paid for. As we step onto the landing, we both stop and take in the red heart foil balloon tied to my door handle.

"What's this Miss Nikki? Do you have an admirer?"

"I am getting fucking fed up with this shit now," I shout as I stomp to the door and try to pull the damn thing off the handle. But pulling at it only makes the red ribbon knot tighter. "Arrggh," I scream and kick the door in frustration.

"Hey honey are you ok?"

"No, I'm not ok. I think that bitch Astrid is really trying her hardest to get me to leave SecuriSoft. This is the last straw I'm telling you I've had about as much as I can take from her."

Damo frowns at me. "Right let's get in and you can fill me in."

It's at this moment I realise I haven't told Damo about the

roses but most of all I haven't told him about Dan. I think now might be as good a time as any to confide in the only person I would consider a friend here. And hell do I need to have someone on my side right now.

"Good idea, I have a lot to tell you." I get my keys out and let us both in.

"Where's your scissors."

I point to the cutlery drawer as I set about putting out the food and pouring some wine for us both. Damo comes back to the kitchen with the scissors in one hand and the limp deflated balloon in the other. We smile at each other, mine saying thanks, and his saying you're welcome. He bins the balloon and we take our food and drinks through to the living room and plonk ourselves down on the sofa.

"So, spill. What the hell has been happening to you?" Damo asks taking a big sip of his wine.

"Oh God where to start."

"The beginning is usually the best."

I shake my head and do just that, and in the process of pouring my heart out to Damo I am hit by a sense of relief as I feel my whole body relax.

"*O*h. My. God. Miss Nikki you wee dark horse." Damo's eyes are like saucers as he takes in everything I've just told him.

Everything except the theft. That needs to remain confidential, but I did tell him about Astrid and Jed's affair.

"Please Damo you have to promise me you won't tell anyone. I really don't fancy Astrid getting wind of this. It would play right into her hands."

"I will not tell a soul I promise. Why did you tell me all this anyway?"

I reach out and take his hand. "You were really nice to me on my first day and you didn't need to be. I feel like we've become good friends, don't you?"

"Oh hell of course we have."

"Well apart from my sister's friend Gina I literally have no other people I would call friends in this city. You've done nothing but be kind to me since I started at SecuriSoft and I feel like I could probably trust you with my life. I suppose it's my way of saying thank you and showing you that I trust you."

"Oh, come here you." He grabs me and pulls me in to a tight hug. He sniffs on my shoulder.

"Damo?"

"Mhm," he sniffs again.

"Are you crying?" I ask, as I break free from his hold.

"No, it's my hay fever." He swipes at his eyes and smiles. "Oh shit, okay I'm crying. You happy? I've never had someone confide in me like that before, it made me emotional."

"Oh honey." I pat his knee.

"I have totally become a stereotype, haven't I? Drama Queen," he sings as he fans his face with his hand.

"I wouldn't have you any other way."

Damo composes himself before he speaks again. "So, where is he taking you tomorrow then?"

"I have no clue. He said there was about an hour or so of travelling so I doubt it will be anywhere too far."

"God Nikki I still can't believe this. I think Jed has gotten himself involved in something over his head. I honestly thought he was madly in love with his wife. I suppose the dick rules the heart in this one eh?"

"Nice analogy Damo but I don't think you're wrong. Astrid obviously knows how to get what she wants, and you have to admit she is very beautiful. It wouldn't be hard for her to get under a man's skin."

"I know but she's nasty. I just hope he sees sense before his wife finds out or he's going to seriously regret ever meeting her."

I shake my head. "I feel like it might be too late for him. If he even tried to break it off with Astrid, she'd only have to threaten him that she would tell his wife and he'd have no choice but to stay with her."

Damo sighs. "Poor Jed. Makes me glad I'm a singleton." He stands and finishes his glass of wine. "Right honey I'm going to make a move, I have work in the morning and my boss is a total dragon lady."

"Cheeky little shit," I throw a cushion at him. "And after I just poured my heart out to you too."

He laughs and kisses my cheek. "You know I love you Nikki." He drops his glass off at the breakfast bar and picks up his stuff. "Ciao," he says as he saunters to the door Astrid style, swiping his imaginary hair over his shoulder, and leaving me in hysterics.

I smile as I close the door behind him and laugh as I hear him still chuckling to himself going down the stairs.

CHAPTER TWENTY-ONE

*I*t's Friday. My first official date with Dan will take place in less than three hours. I've already been at work since eight am and in those two hours I have thought about nothing else. Even when everyone started to arrive, I couldn't hold much of a conversation with any of them. Every time I think about Dan, I get a rush of butterflies, which is ridiculous considering what we've already done together. I'm still a little uncomfortable with our relationship being kept a secret but I've come to terms with the reason why. Dan's whole life revolves around his daughter and I can see that he strives to be a better father than his own was.

"Nikki do you have the weeks reports ready for Jed yet?" The voice that sounds like nails scraping on a blackboard startles me and I look up to find Astrid standing in front of my desk. I really want to stick my foot out under the desk and kick her hard in the shin. My patience is seriously wearing thin with her.

"No Astrid, I don't, because it's only ten thirty and we are still working." I can hear the exasperation in my voice, and I can tell by the wry smile on her face that it pleases her to know she's annoying me.

"Well Jed needs them in an hour. He has a meeting to attend this afternoon and he needs everything wrapped up before the weekend."

I sigh. I just want her away from me, so I relent. "Okay, come back in an hour and they'll be ready."

"Thanks Nikki, you're a star." She turns, throws her hair over her shoulder and struts away.

I turn to Damo, whose face is puce as he tries to stifle a laugh, and I smile. As soon as the elevator doors close, we both end up laughing so loud that the whole office stops to stare at us.

I hold up my hand, "I'm sorry folks, we didn't mean to put you off your work. Although while I have your attention, Jed wants the reports early this week so finish what you're working on before his foot soldier comes back in an hour for them."

I am met with a collective groan and I give them all an apologetic nod as they return to their work. I swear one o'clock is not going to come quick enough.

*N*o sooner had I finished collating all our reports than Astrid was back to collect them. I handed them over without much conversation. I really didn't want her spoiling my good mood and now, as I watch everyone leave for the day, my mood is turning anxious. I know it's all about what I have to reveal to Dan, and I'm worried about what he'll think of me. I think very little of myself as it is, if he ends up feeling the same way it will destroy whatever there is left of me.

"Right Miss Nikki, I'm done for the day. You make sure you have the best time tonight okay."

"I'll try Damo."

"Oh, honey you'll be okay, just be yourself and it will all work out fine." He throws his bag over his shoulder, kisses my cheek and walks off, whistling as he goes.

I sit down at my desk and am about to shut down my computer when a memo notification comes through. I open my email and see it's from HR. It's only addressed to me and the title says First Month Appraisal. An appraisal already? Good grief that's quick. I don't really feel like I've had time to breathe since I started here let alone done enough to be appraised on. As soon as I click on the invitation my calendar pops up on my screen and the date is slotted in for Monday morning. Oh, that's wonderful, now I can think about it all weekend. I hope whatever Dan has planned for tonight is good enough to take my mind off it for a few hours. With a sigh I shut down my computer and grab my bags. Dan and I are leaving straight from the office so I'm on my way up to his apartment to get ready. I'm feeling all kinds of emotions right now, the most prominent being gut wrenching fear.

I take a steeling breath as I get in the lift and check out my appearance in the mirrors. As the doors close and the car starts to move, giving me that familiar whoosh in my belly, I know it's now or never. This is my chance to put the past behind me and move on. To be the normal person I should be, not the frightened little girl Mike made me. The doors opening again makes me jump a little. I step out of the lift and am surprised to see Tabitha still sitting at her desk. I stop and check my watch. She looks up and smiles at me.

"Yes, I'm still here," says Tabitha with a smile on her face that speaks volumes about the fact that she knows exactly why I'm here. I suppose being a PA to a man as powerful as

Dan means that she must be privy to a lot more than just what goes on his business.

"Don't worry my love, I'll be out of here in ten minutes. I just have an appointment to arrange for Dan for tomorrow." The smile she gives me makes her eyes sparkle and I can sense that she's happy for him.

It's only now that I wonder about his dating history after Irena. I know about what happened with Astrid and I wonder if that's what he did right after having his heart broken. Did he just sleep with every woman that threw herself at him? Good Lord is that what I've done? Since I left South Africa, he's the only man who's shown me any interest. This could have more to do with the fact that the only places I've really been to socialise have been a tiny deli in my building and a gay bar. My almost brush with a one-night stand shall remain at the back of my mind and will forever be locked up in the cabinet marked '*What the fuck?*'

"Is he with someone Tabitha?" I ask gesturing to the frosted office walls.

"Nope, just waiting for you." She bites her lower lip and can't help herself but smile at me.

Feeling extremely self-conscious, I give her a tentative smile back. "Thanks," I say as I make my way through the office door and as I turn to close it, I see Tabitha's smile widen as she stares at her computer screen.

I turn to face the office and find it empty. Dan's apartment door is slightly ajar, so I make my way in, slipping off my heels as I go.

"Hello," I call, my voice echoing along the white hallway.

"In the living room," Dan shouts, his voice sending goose bumps up my bare arms.

I walk through to the open plan living room / kitchen to find him sitting on one of the brown leather chairs surrounding the coffee table. "Oh." I stop abruptly and take in the sight in front of me. His dark hair is wet, obviously from a recent shower. The only thing he's wearing is a pair of washed out grey jeans and his tattooed skin is bathed in the early afternoon sunlight shining through the massive windows.

"Hi," he says, his smile as bright as the sunshine behind him.

I don't really understand why I feel so awkward in front of him. I've seen him naked; he's touched almost every inch of my body. For God sake his mouth has been on most of my body.

"Hi," I say back but I can't seem to make myself say anything else.

This is bloody pathetic. Dan stands and takes my overnight bag from my hand. It's rather large but a girl needs to be prepared. Okay so two sets of straighteners, three makeup bags and every bobby pin I own is a bit overkill, but you never know.

"Christ woman have you got a body in here?" Dan laughs and it immediately lightens the mood, swiping away most of my awkwardness.

"Just essentials for making me beautiful."

"Follow me," Dan says as he turns towards the bedroom, stopping beside me to whisper in my ear, "you won't be needing this then."

His breath on my face makes me want to turn and kiss him. I smile as I follow him, watching his muscled back as he pads barefoot to the bedroom.

"You can get ready in here. Feel free to use the shower, and if you need it there's a hairdryer in there. We need to leave here for three thirty, so I'll let you get on."

I walk in and put my shoulder bag on the bed and turn to

see Dan close the door behind him. I sit down on the bed and take a look around the stark white room. This apartment is as far removed from Dan's country house as you could get. Everything in here is white and minimalistic. The country house is opulent and charming and looks lived in, like a home should. It's like he lives two different lives. I get up and walk into the adjoining bathroom that is just as white as everything else. Turning on the shower, I watch the plumes of steam rise from the shower tray and sigh deeply as I contemplate the night ahead of me.

---

*A*s I sit in the familiar back of the Range Rover, I'm reminded of what went on the last time I was in here. I shiver slightly at the delicious feelings the memory conjures. However, when I look at Dan, the memory disappears in an instant. He's looking anywhere but at me. Why? It dawns on me that we've been in each other's company for almost three hours and he hasn't touched me once.

"So, um, where are we going then?" I ask, trying to lighten the mood.

It takes Dan a second longer than it should have to turn to me. He smiles and I'm relieved to see that it's a genuine smile. "London," he says.

My eyes widen and I can only imagine what my face looks like. "Oh…uh…okay then".

CHAPTER TWENTY-TWO

I can't seem to take in my surroundings or actually believe what's happening tonight. I had left my flat this morning with a completely different idea of dinner to Dan's. He told me it would take an hour or so to get where we were going. Silly me, to think it was an hour or so drive outside Glasgow. Nah it was an hour's flight on a huge private plane to London City Airport. And now we are sitting sipping champagne in a beautiful restaurant in The Shard with the twinkling lights of early evening London spread out below us. A waiter comes to the table and clears our starter plates.

"How was it?" Asks Dan.

"Very nice indeed," I say and then I can't help myself but laugh.

"What?" Asks Dan, slightly bemused.

"I'm sorry Dan but this is a little overwhelming. I really wasn't expecting this when you said we were going out for dinner." I smile and gesture at the restaurant.

"A most beautiful restaurant for a most beautiful woman," he says smiling as he reaches across the table taking my hand

and rubbing my knuckles. It's the first time he's touched me all evening.

I feel my cheeks redden and my hand is set on fire.

"So, does the plane just wait for us while we have our dinner?" I ask.

"Well," he says with that sound in his voice that tells me there's more to this evening than meets the eye. "We're not going home until Sunday."

"Sorry?" I'm a little taken aback.

"We are staying in London for the weekend," he says with a proud smile on his face.

"Dan, I haven't got anything with me for a weekend. All I have is my phone and my purse and what I'm wearing. I left everything back at your apartment." I know my voice is a little higher than it should be for such a swanky restaurant, but I hate being surprised.

"Honestly, Nikki don't worry. We'll stay at my place and I've made sure there's plenty of clothes and toiletries there for you. I really hope you don't mind me organising this. I hoped it would be a nice surprise." His voice sounds a little hurt and I instantly feel terrible.

"Oh, Dan it's a lovely surprise it's just…" I stop talking as our main courses of Seared Sea Bass for me and Saddle of Welsh Lamb for Dan are delivered to the table along with all their sides. The food is exquisitely presented and if the starters were anything to go by, I know this will be delicious too.

"Nikki, I don't really know how to handle you."

Handle me? "Why would you need to *handle* me Dan?" I can hear the dejection in my voice.

Dan holds up his hand. "Sorry, that came out wrong. I didn't mean handle *you*, I meant I don't know how to do things *for* you without appearing... I don't know, controlling."

I shake my head and stare at the food on my plate. Food that looked so delicious when it arrived at the table but now makes me want to puke. Closing my eyes, I feel tears fall down my cheek and a soft sob rise from my chest. "I'm sorry," I whisper.

"Let's get out of here. Dinner can wait," Dan says. He holds out his hand and I take it, getting up from the chair.

Dan nods to the maître d', who nods back to him, as we leave the restaurant and I realise the men know each other. As soon as we are in the empty lift, which didn't take long to arrive at the 31st floor, Dan pulls me into his chest and in that safe place I let go. I've totally ruined what should have been a wonderful surprise and I feel terrible for him. He's absolutely trying his best and it's lovely and sweet and everything I want, everything I need.

"Hey," Dan whispers, stroking my hair.

I look up at him, the air cool as it hits my tear stained cheeks.

"You okay?" He asks softly.

I nod, unable to answer for fear of starting to cry again. Dan hands me a linen napkin from the restaurant. I smile at his blatant theft from a swanky establishment and dab at my eyes as the lift doors open on the ground floor.

"I've got a car waiting outside," Dan says, smiling at me as he leads me out of the lift and through the marble tiled lobby.

Outside, waiting at the kerb, is a black Porsche SUV. I will admit that sometimes I forget he has more money than a small country. Sometimes, when we talk, it's as though he's just a normal guy, then I see a car like this, hear him take a call or, shit, remember he's my boss and I'm pulled back to reality. I watch as Dan opens the door and I climb into the back of the sumptuous tan leather interior of the Porsche. He closes the door and gets in on the other side. The person driving is a woman this time. For some reason it makes me feel awkward. This is the third person I've seen driving Dan around. I wonder if he ever drives himself anywhere. I jump slightly when Dan puts his hand over mine on the seat. I'm still holding the poor linen napkin that will never be with its friends in the restaurant again.

"Are you alright Nikki?" He asks.

I look at him as the driver takes the car away from the kerbside. "Yes I am. I'm so sorry I ruined our dinner Dan. I'm an absolute head-case, aren't I?"

"Nope, you're not. Come here." He tugs on my hand and I loosen my seatbelt, sliding across the back seat to snuggle into his warm, inviting body.

I stay in his safe, quiet embrace the entire car ride through London. Over one of the bridges spanning the Thames, past Buckingham Palace and Hyde Park coming to a stop outside an apartment building on the opposite side of the road to a lovely park. We get out of the car and head into the building still in silence and with an air of trepidation hanging between us. I know what's to come tonight and I'm not looking forward to it.

CHAPTER TWENTY-THREE

I'm pleasantly surprised at the normality of the inside of Dan's apartment. Sure, it's huge as I expected it would be, but it isn't what I would have expected of an apartment in one of the most expensive areas of London. Dan is in the kitchen pouring us some drinks and I'm standing out on the balcony overlooking the park. It's huge and wraps around three sides of the apartment which incidentally takes up the entire top of the building. It's a little chilly up here as a slight breeze brushes past me pulling little wisps of hair over my cheeks. I'm surprised when I feel those wisps being pulled back from my face by warm fingers, a radiating heat forming at my back.

I close my eyes as Dan kisses my neck. "Come inside," he murmurs against my skin. "We need to talk."

A cold sweat overcomes me. I nod, turning and following Dan through the doors and through the dining room to the living room. He sits on one of the large, pale blue sofas and I take the opposite one. I notice two glasses with a finger of whisky in each and a bottle in the middle. He obviously realises we are in this for the long haul tonight. I lean forward and lift one of the glasses. I down the whisky and pour myself another, more than the first and down that one too. The glass clinks as I rest it back down on the glass table top. I close my eyes against the burning in my throat and feel my eyes water behind my lids.

"No. No more," Dan says softly as I go to pick up the bottle again.

I sit back slowly and look at my hands. I feel as though I'm going to throw up and I know it's not just the whisky. There's a horrible silence between us.

"Nikki."

As I look up, the tears pooling in my eyes tumble down my cheeks. I feel so pathetic. When I think back to the person I was when I graduated from university, there's a pain in my heart. I was so confident in myself. I knew I was clever. I have a thing for numbers and knew I deserved the job I landed after I got my degree in Computing Science. In fact the cocky little bitch I was when I left university thought I deserved a better job. Not now though. Now I'm a shell of the person I was then. I'm grateful when Dan starts talking first.

"Remember what I said about full disclosure?"

I nod.

"Well I'm going to tell you everything about Astrid and Jed and the investigation and I want you to know that I don't expect anything in return." His warm smile eases my nerves and I am in that moment more grateful to him than he will ever know.

"Thank you," I say softly as I swipe at the tears on my face.

Dan gets up and, from where I have no clue, produces a box of tissues. He hands them to me as he takes a seat beside me now. "You okay?" He asks with not an ounce of pity in his voice.

I give him a nod and a small smile as I dry my face and blow my nose in the most unladylike fashion ever.

"Okay then here goes." He takes a deep breath and dives right in. "So, you know the very basics of this, but I'll start from the beginning. Jed was one of a team of five people I hired to start my business off. He and Tabitha are the only two of those five left."

I nod. "That makes sense," I say thinking of Tabitha when I went up to Dan's office earlier today. God a lot has happened in that short time.

Dan flashes me a quizzical look. "What does?"

"Oh nothing really, I was just surprised at Tabitha's reaction to me being at your office this afternoon. It was as though she already knew everything about us, but I guess that when you are a PA you do know a lot about the person you work for."

He nods his head and smiles. "Yeah, we have a strange relationship. Obviously she does all my bookings for meetings and flights and the like. She's more than just a PA though. I would class her more as a good friend or a kind of... well sister like person. Do you know what I'm trying to say here?"

"I get it. I really do. She probably knows more about you than your own brother does. So, I take it she knows about this Jed and Astrid thing too then?"

"Oh absolutely. Her exact words were, 'I'll put that fucker's balls in a vice'."

I laugh out loud on a stuttered tear laden breath. "I cannot imagine Tabitha saying that. She's so polite and lovely."

Now it's Dan's turn to laugh. "You haven't really gotten to know her yet. Just you wait, you'll never look at her the same again."

"You've met my sister Dan; nothing shocks me anymore."

"Well, when Jed got his promotion last year, he needed his own PA. Tabitha is already overworked with my schedule, so much so in fact that I've offered to find her an assistant. He conducted the interviews with HR and Astrid was the one they all chose. Don't get me wrong she is good at her job, not as good as Tabitha but she can handle what Jed needs her for." He leans forward and reaches for his glass, lifting it to his lips.

"So," he continues, "about six months ago we had a brand-new security software that was in its final weeks of completion and testing. We were doing everything in Glasgow because it's the biggest of our offices worldwide. I had people there on secondment from all our other offices. It was a huge project because it came with an app as well as round the clock monitoring. I had sunk millions of pounds into the planning and development of it. We had a whole new monitoring and call centre facility built in Germany. This thing had been in the works for over two years and it was going to be our claim to fame. It would have put us up there with the biggest of the tech companies."

I can tell where this is going, and I even know what software he's talking about. It takes me a moment to realise I'm sitting looking at him with my jaw almost on the floor. "Oh. My. God. Are you talking about MainSquare?"

Dan's eyes flash like fire at the mention of the name of what can only be described as a game changer in the world of security software. The breath he takes before he speaks flares his nostrils. "The very one," he says through almost gritted teeth.

"Fuck! Dan how the hell can you still be working with those traitors? They must have lost you a fortune."

"Oh yes, to the tune of around five hundred million pounds and billions in future revenue."

I gasp at that exorbitant amount of money and recall my bank account balance of just over three thousand pounds as of this morning.

"I had gotten a frantic call from Tabitha when I was in the south of France with Olivia telling me what she had heard. By the time I got to our Paris office it was too late. The Main Group already had everything and had made significant enough changes to the user interfaces to be able to pass it off as original work. So, the end use was the same as what we had set out to do but how they got there was completely different. They had absolutely everything. Every piece of information from the original outline to the final product to get the project up and running three weeks before we were due to announce ours."

I'm rather shocked at what he's told me so far and I feel terrible for him. Okay so he's not going to be poor or anything, but this is one of those things, like the iPhone for Apple or Windows for Microsoft. A game changer. "Wow." Is all I can muster.

"Yeah. I cottoned on to the fact that Jed was somehow involved after a drunken conversation in my office a few weeks after all the hurrah about this new fabulous software had died down. I was explaining that I had chalked it up to experience. Said I'd be more careful about who I had working on my projects in future. He asked me if I thought it was an inside job, but it wasn't so much what he said as the way he said it and how he reacted when I said yes and that I thought it was someone very close to me. He started sweating and fidgeting. I'm no body language expert but I've known enough liars in my life to know when someone is trying to pull a fast one."

"And how did you figure out that Astrid was involved?" I ask, genuinely interested to know how that nasty piece of shit managed to get herself into all this.

"I hired a company to do a bit of background checking on everyone. And when I say everyone, I mean *everyone.* SecuriSoft employs well over two thousand people across five sites worldwide and I have a few other businesses out with that. I also have my personal staff. You've met a few of them already."

I nod recalling his drivers, pilots, air stewards and Valerie and Nessa.

"Well that's a lot of information. I rented an office space for them so that they could conduct their investigations away from prying eyes. When I got suspicious of Jed I had them delve deeper into his life and that's where the Astrid connection came up. He was spotted with her on a few occasions and I have photographic evidence that will be used against them when they are finally outed. Refill?" He asks leaning over to fill his glass up.

"No thanks, I think I over did it earlier."

He sits back and takes a drink of the whisky. "Here's the kick in the guts on this whole sorry saga," Dan continues. "Astrid's surname isn't really Laurent. It's Jansen. She's related to a guy who used to work at our London office. He left us after he was refused a pay increase and a promotion. If I remember rightly, I was told his exact words as he walked out the door were, '*Tell Dan King he's a fucking tosser and his life would be better if he'd given me what I wanted.*' I now know that his threats weren't empty. He works for The Main Group and I've learned that since the release of MainSquare, he now has a seat on the board of the company. Coincidence? I think not. Astrid is his niece."

"Oh shit." I'm not sure what else to say.

"Indeed. I have a feeling Jed was doomed from the start. Astrid came for her interview with one purpose in mind and Jed is simply collateral damage. But as I said, unless his wife and kids are being held at gunpoint, he is as much to blame. No amount of money is worth that type of betrayal."

There's a sadness in his voice as he talks about Jed. I get the feeling he considered the man a really good friend before all this happened.

"Dan I'm so sorry," I say softly, placing my hand over his. "Now his reaction to signing the NDA makes sense."

"Yeah I am too," he says on a sigh. "It's not something that's going to happen again, believe me. So now you know everything, and I meant what I said about knowing you're good at what you do. You'll go far Nikki and your job is safe with me for as long as you want it. The work you've done so far has been outstanding."

I smile shyly at him. "You've put together an excellent team Dan. They are very good at what they do."

He nods. "Yeah when I read your credentials, I cherry picked the best people from our Glasgow office and gave them all new roles. Each one has a different skillset that complements the others. They jumped at the chance to get their teeth into a new project."

"Well, thank you. It made things so much easier for me. And lord knows I need things to be easier." I shift my gaze to the window. "Dan would you mind very much if we leave my part of this conversation till the morning? I'm exhausted. You've given me a lot of food for thought tonight."

He takes my hand and nods when I look at him. "Take all the time you need. There's four other bedrooms in this place so take your pick. There's a case with clothes and toiletries in the hallway for you. My room is the first door on the right."

I frown at him. "Oh… okay. Well I'll see you in the morning then," I say quietly as I get up off the couch.

Dan lets go of my fingers one by one as I start to walk away from him. "Thanks for listening Nikki," he says with a smile.

I know he's willing me to talk but I'm not sure I'm ready to bare my soul just yet. I smile back at him and make my way out of the living room, lifting my bag off the dining table as I pass by, and towards the bedrooms grabbing the large cherry red suitcase on the way. I don't know why but I choose the room furthest away from Dan's and as I sit on the large bed I'm hit with a huge wall of emotion. I've been a victim of domestic abuse and I'm ashamed of it. I don't know what Dan's opinion will be of me when he learns the ugly truth and it scares me. "Domestic abuse," I say quietly to the room. And I say victim because I'm struggling to keep it together. The last image I have of Mike haunts my every waking hour and more so in my sleep where I can't escape the manifestations of him or his actions. I will tell Dan everything, he's already shared so much about his life with me. I have to give him the chance to know me completely, the good, the bad and the ugly.

CHAPTER TWENTY-FOUR

*T*he white towel lying on the bed gapes open. The two bars of soap inside seem to sparkle in the moonlight. I look at myself in the mirror and I'm smiling.

"Oops, Mike did it again," I say to no one in particular. My voice has a sing song air about it, but my cheeks are wet with tears and my eyes are red.

I watch my reflection in the mirror as a purple stain rises up from my neck and starts to cover my face. I'm screaming but my reflection is laughing, a sickening maniacal laugh.

"Wake up you little idiot," Mike shouts.

I sit up straight in this strange bed and find I'm clawing at my neck. I can't get a breath and I feel lightheaded. Closing my eyes, I think of the only things I can that make me happy right now. My sister and my niece. Georgie's little hands and feet, Charlies smile, both of them together. *Dan.* As my breathing starts to even out and I feel less like I'm suffocating I open my eyes. It's still dark but the moon is giving off enough light to be able to make out the room.

"It's okay," I say to myself although I've never sounded so unconvincing.

I grab my phone off the bedside table and check the time. 03:37. Okay, so I got in a solid four hours. Nice one. The suitcase Dan had waiting for me was filled with all sorts of stuff that had me thankful and uneasy all in one go when I opened it last night. For a start, the clothes he had organised were exactly my style and fit and a nice touch was that they were what I'd normally buy. High street stuff like H&M and Zara. That made me thankful, but it was the same thing that made me uneasy. How did he know? Thankfully, I didn't have the mental energy last night to war with myself over it and now, in this early morning fading moonlight I accept it for what it is, a nice gesture. I know I need to talk to Dan about Mike. I should have spoken to someone about this a long time ago, but he has seen me at some of my most absolute panic-stricken moments lately and if anything is going to happen between us, I need to start being honest with myself and everyone else.

Opening the bedroom door, I stick my head out and listen. The apartment is eerily quiet, but I'm comforted by the muted lighting coming from the bottom of the walls along the floor. It's subtle but practical. Making my way along the hallway I find Dan's bedroom door fully open and see him lying on his back in his huge bed, one arm behind his head and the other draped over his belly. A small globular light on the bedside table gives off the softest yellow glow. I can't help but stare. He is as beautiful in sleep as he is awake. And my God does he look peaceful. For everything this guy has gone through in his personal and work life it surprises me that he sleeps so soundly. I want so badly to go and touch him. To stroke his beautiful face and have him hold me. I startle a little as he stirs, and I move so that I'm out of sight next to the door frame. Peeking round a tiny bit I see that he's up on his elbows, the white flat sheet stretched over his lower body and under his forearms.

"Nikki?" His sleep laden voice questions.

"Hi," I say tentatively, revealing myself in the doorway.

"What time is it?" He asks.

"Almost four. I'm so sorry, I didn't mean to wake you."

"You didn't. Are you okay?"

"Yeah, just a bad dream." And now that I've said that, I know what's coming next.

"Come here," he says as he sits upright.

I shake my head and try to bite my lip against the threatening tears. "I can't," I whisper.

"Yes, you can. Come here Nikki," his voice is soft and inviting but, more than that, there's no judgement behind it.

I go to him and sit on the bed facing him.

He reaches out and takes my hands. "Talk to me Nikki, please. Tell me your story."

I look into his dark eyes and see sincerity and I know it's time. I have to start letting people in.

"Okay. God where to start," I sigh and roll my eyes to the ceiling.

Dan doesn't say anything. He doesn't have to; his eyes say more than he could right now.

"I'm a clever, educated woman Dan. I never thought this would happen to me. Ever." I take a deep breath. "I was in an abusive relationship and it still terrifies me, every hour of every day."

Dan's fingers give mine a tiny squeeze and a hint of anger crosses his beautiful face. "What did he do to you Nikki?"

"It was a casual thing at first. He was my immediate manager and he used to flirt with me a lot. I was young and stupid. I'd not long graduated and it was my first job. I'd had a few boyfriends when I was at Uni but nothing serious. Mike gave me lots of attention and it made me feel good about myself. My sister had moved to Scotland when I was twelve, so I didn't have her, and my parents were constantly busy with work. It sounds clichéd but I think I may have been an easy target for him. You know the little girl craving a father figure's attention." I know somewhere in the back of my mind this is what went on but actually saying in out loud for the first time makes me feel all kinds of sick to my stomach.

"And he knew it didn't he? He took advantage of you." The disgust in Dan's voice is palpable.

"Yeah I suppose he did. Everything was good to start with and I was happy just being... well I guess I was his go to bit of stuff. He told me he'd just got divorced when I started at the company and he said he wasn't looking for anything serious. I was fine with that but then he started treating me like shit at work in front of people. He said it was so that our colleagues didn't find out about us. If we wanted to move up in the company, we'd have to stay quiet about our relationship."

"And that's why you had a hard time with us?" Dan interrupts with more of a statement than a question.

"Dan it was irrational of me to think like that. I know that. He was still nice to me when we were alone at that point, so I took him at his word when he told me that as soon as he got promoted, I'd be too. Never happened. I stayed where I was and got passed over for everything I ever applied for while he just went higher and higher. And that's when things got worse. I was shocked the first time he hit me."

Dan takes an audible breath in and hisses it out through his teeth, but he doesn't say anything, so I continue.

"I had been at his house on a Saturday night. Friday,

Saturday and Sunday were the only days I was allowed to stay and only on the weekends he chose. He said we shouldn't be in each other's pockets since we worked together too. On that particular Sunday morning I woke up and he was sitting by the bed with my phone in his hand. He asked me why I had so many guys numbers in my phone. I had had the same number since I started Uni so all the numbers I ever had were in my phone. I was popular at University, so I had a lot of guys numbers. Most of the people in my phonebook I hadn't spoken to for years, if at all. I told him all that and he said I was a dirty liar and that I must be cheating on him. I told him he was being stupid, and he totally lost it. He stormed into the bathroom and came back with a rolled-up towel and hit me hard three times over the back of my body. I later realised why it hurt so much. He'd put two bars of soap in the towel. The bruises didn't appear for a few days after that but my God when they did, they were disgusting."

Dan swallows hard and rubs at his temples. "FUCK!!" He shouts, and I jump a little. "I want to find the bastard and fucking kill him." His face is blazing with fury.

"I'm sorry, I should never have told you," I say quietly as I run for my bedroom. I know he's not angry at me, but his reaction has rattled me. I close the door behind me and throw myself on the bed curling into the tiniest ball I can all the while saying over and over in my head *'he's not Mike, he's not Mike, he's not Mike'*.

"Nikki," Dan shouts as he bursts in the door and I scream so loudly at the sudden intrusion. "Christ, Nikki I'm so sorry." He's at my side in seconds and I'm gently lifted into his arms as he cradles me against his warm body.

I can't seem to move the pain in my chest as I try to breathe normally.

Dan holds me until it passes and I'm able to function again. "Dan I'm sorry," I whisper against his chest.

"No Nikki, you'll never apologise ever again. None of this was your fault. I won't make you tell me anymore because, if that's how it started, I can only imagine how it ended. I've never understood a man who would use his physical strength against a woman. To me they are cowards and deserve nothing this life has to offer them. I promise I'll never do anything ever again that scares you the way I just did."

"He hit me six times after that," I say. I feel him tense. I know this is going to be hard for him to hear but I trust this man with my life and for some strange reason I feel like telling him will mean that we can start afresh, with no secrets. "You need to know Dan." I release myself from his lap and sit in front of him. I take his hands in mine. "I can't keep this to myself and if I am to be in a relationship with you there are going to be times when you might act as you just have, I would hope not at me, but that sort of thing scares the shit out of me." There are tears in my eyes and as I go to speak again, they fall down my cheeks. Dan lets go of my hand and wipes them away gently with his thumbs.

"It's killing me to see you like this Nikki. I can't imagine the terror he put you through. You must have been so scared."

"I was. But I kept going back to him. I can't even rationalise why. I have no answers. That's why, when my parents said they were moving to the UK, I took the chance and applied for this job. You saved my life Dan. Unknowingly so, but you did. I honestly think I'd be dead by now if I hadn't got out when I did. Either by his hand or my own."

"Nikki," he sighs and pulls me to him kissing me so softly it hurts, and my body physically relaxes into him. He lets me go and moves us both under the covers. I'm pulled into his side and I rest my head on his shoulder, feeling his heat and his heartbeat.

And that's how we stay until the sun comes up and I have told Dan every sorry, sordid detail of my life after I met Mike.

CHAPTER TWENTY-FIVE

*J*always remember my mum telling me and my sister that we used to freak her out sometimes at night when we were young. She said we'd go into her and dad's bedroom and stand beside the bed staring at her till she woke up. She always said it was as if she knew we were there even though she was in a deep sleep.

That's why I've just woken up. I knew someone was watching me.

"Hey," I croak. *God my throat is dry.*

"Hey sweetheart," Dan says softly as he reaches across the bed and strokes my arm.

Sweetheart. I smile. It feels nice to be someone's sweetheart. I don't think I ever have been.

"Everything okay?"

He nods. "Sorry I woke you. I didn't want to leave you. Nikki," he lies down beside me and I turn to face him. "I'm so sorry about last night."

I feel so bad for him. "Dan don't apologise, please. My head is messed up. If I were you, I'd be running for the fucking hills. I'm surprised you haven't actually."

"Nikki, do you realise how strong you actually are? To leave the way you did, knowing how he would have reacted when he realised you'd gone, was courageous.

I smile at his analogy of how I left Mike. "Well I felt like a coward. Sneaking away like that with no explanation."

"He didn't deserve one." He reaches up and moves my hair from my face, tucking it behind my ear. It's a beautifully sweet movement and I feel light and happy. It's been so long since I've felt this way in a man's company that it hurts.

"Thank you for listening Dan, it means a lot."

"I wish my mum had been as strong as you," he whispers. From my position, lying here inches from his face, I feel as though I can see right into his soul. I can see the hurt and pain in those world wise eyes. I can see the young man whose family was torn apart in the most tragic of ways. But more than anything, I see the eyes of a protector. His outburst in itself last night wasn't what had scared me. I see that now. The thing that scared me more than anything was the knowledge that Dan felt so strongly about what happened to me. I know from the fire in his eyes last night that if he got his hands on Mike, he really would kill him.

"Oh Dan, I'm sure your mum thought she was doing the best she could for you and Jason. You said your home life was good considering what your dad had been involved in."

"It was good for us, and it was probably her love for us that got her shot. That's why I understand why you stayed. To try and make the best out of a bad situation. Can I show you something?" He asks, his eyes brightening a little.

I nod and he gets off the bed and disappears from the room for a moment. When he returns, he has his phone in his hand. He sits down on the bed beside me and I sit up with him.

"You see this tattoo?" He points to the soundwave above

the binary date. "This is a soundwave of my mum talking. She was reading a book to Jason and I recorded it on an old cassette recorder we had. Jase and I used to record ourselves singing and play it back at double speed. His wee hearty laugh used to make me smile. Watch this," he says as he opens his phone and holds the camera over his tattoo. I watch the slider move over the soundwave.

"Big nutbrown Hare settled Little Nutbrown Hare into his bed of leaves. He leaned over and kissed him goodnight. Then he lay down close by and whispered with a smile, 'I love you to the moon and back.'"

The recording lasts less than thirty seconds but it is the most beautiful, soothing voice and I know that book well. My own mum read it to me.

"Oh Dan, she had the most beautiful voice. What did she look like?"

He turns his phone to me and shows me what appears to be a photo of a printed photo. The woman in the picture is as beautiful as her voice. "May I?" I ask and hold my hand out.

Dan hands me the phone and I take a good look, enlarging the screen to get a better look. Her dark wavy hair sits just on her shoulders and her dark brown eyes sparkle with laughter. Dan has her eyes and her smile.

"She was so beautiful Dan."

"Yeah she was. She had a beautiful soul. She was an artist and any time you ever saw her she was covered in paint. I always remember the old shirt she used to wear. It had belonged to her dad. He was a big guy, like really big and this shirt used to look like a tent on her. One of the things I loved about our luxury life was how happy it made her to be able to do what she loved. I sometimes find myself wondering what she actually thought about our lives. You know, was she really okay with what he was doing? There was a time when I was pissed at her for staying there and allowing him to do what he did to her but like I've said, we were happy. We never wanted for anything and our parents loved us."

"Dan I can't even imagine what it was like for you and Jason to lose your parents like that. I am really sorry."

He smiles wryly. "It is what it is. It doesn't define me or Jason. We did okay considering."

I laugh a little too abruptly. "Okay? Jesus Dan you have done more than okay for yourself."

He nods. "Yeah I suppose I have. I have a real riches to rags to riches story, don't I?" He takes his phone back off me and places it on the bedside table. "I don't know what it is about you Nikki, but I feel like I could just sit and talk to you for hours. I don't tend to talk too much about my past with people but you, you make it easy. Thank you, sweetheart." He leans over and kisses my forehead.

I feel like I have little love heart bubbles popping over my head right now. He makes me feel so loved and cared for. Just being in his presence excites me.

"I have a surprise for you."

"Dan you do know what you've done already is more than enough, although we've not really spent our time how I'd hoped." I try to hide the embarrassment in my voice but, as usual, I fail miserably.

"Let's think of it as more than it was. Not that it wasn't quite a distressing night. It sure as shit was, but I learned an awful lot about you last night Nikki. And you know what? I want to know more. But first my surprise. I got Tabitha to put in a call yesterday to arrange a lovely lunch for you today."

"Oh really? And where are we going?"

"No not us, just you."

"Oh," I say a little hurt.

"You and your parents."

"Oh wow, Dan. Thank you. I was going to call them today to see if they were free."

"Well you couldn't come to London and not see your parents, could you? Tell me I didn't go too far?"

I get up on my knees and place a kiss on his lips. "No," I say against his warm mouth.

He pulls me to him and kisses me hard. "Can I make love to you Nikki?"

"Why are you asking?" I smile at him.

His eyes blaze and, quick as you like, I'm on my back. I feel as though this could be the start of my real new beginning.

CHAPTER TWENTY-SIX

*L*unch with my parents was a lovely if rather muted affair. What was even lovelier was learning that they are coming up to visit in a few weeks. My dad has a few meetings in Edinburgh, so they are going to spend a bit of time with Charlie. Dad's work schedule is extremely busy, and he rarely gets to take time off. So much so, in fact, that he hasn't actually met his new granddaughter. And that is a bone of contention for mum. All through lunch I could tell she was excited about the trip but also a bit pissed that it had to take a work trip to get him up there.

He was his usual oblivious self. He always has been for as long as I've been old enough to notice. He's very straight faced most of the time. I suppose it comes with the job, but I have seen it get worse as he's gotten older. Especially in social gatherings. I actually want to be there when he meets Georgie because it'll be the most comical thing I'll have seen in a long time and I've been dancing with Damo.

I said goodbye to them around half an hour ago and decided I was going to take a walk. It's a lovely day and Dan is visiting his London office this afternoon, so I have a little time to myself. We are off to a party tonight at The Savoy. I have no idea whose party it is or why we are going. I just know that I have an appointment in an hour at a boutique to pick a dress and a hair and makeup appointment after that. I honestly can't say the last time I felt so content. I'm grateful to Dan for bringing me here this weekend. Since we talked this morning I've been smiling. I know it's going to take more than one night to put Mike behind me, but I mentally feel better equipped to do it now. Finally speaking about it, out loud to someone else, has somehow made me feel that leaving it in the past is the best way forward. I make a deal with myself that I'll speak to someone professional about it. I don't feel that I'm ready to tell my family about what happened to me and I know if I do tell them, their reactions would probably be a million times worse than Dan's and I just can't handle that right now.

I'm around a few buildings from Dan's apartment and notice the entrance to the park that I was looking at last night from the balcony. Wow! I hadn't realised it was Kensington Gardens. I must take a walk through with Dan before we leave tomorrow. As far as I know the weather will be on the warm side this weekend and I intend to enjoy it before we head back to Scotland and ten degrees colder.

I feel absolutely spoiled and beautiful right now as I stand in front of the full-length mirror at the exclusive salon Dan sent me to. The dress I chose at the boutique is simple yet extremely sexy. It's a very dark green satin with the thinnest spaghetti straps. The back is entirely open to almost the base of my back except for the criss-cross of the straps over my shoulder blades. My blonde hair has been styled in a retro 40's movie star style. My make-up has been done to absolute perfection to complement the hairstyle. I'm almost in tears as I look at my reflection. It's been so long since I've felt beautiful. I know Dan will like what he sees, and it makes me smile.

"You okay honey?"

I turn abruptly at the voice behind me. "Oh yes I am thank you," I say to Jennifer, the lovely woman who did my hair and make-up.

"You look beautiful. That colour with your hair is perfect. You've got a kind of Veronica Lake look about you."

My smile widens. I know exactly who Veronica Lake is. My mum and I used to watch a lot of *Film Noir* on a Sunday afternoon. As I got older, those Sundays became less frequent until we no longer spent them together anymore at all. The thought is just about to kill my good mood when the woman talks again.

"So, you said you're off to The Savoy tonight. Have you been before?"

"No, I haven't. My parents have stayed there before but I've never been."

She smiles. "It's lovely, but very posh. I went to an afternoon tea there for my fortieth birthday. It really was very nice but extremely expensive. I'll probably go back when I'm eighty." She chuckles as she walks over to the reception desk in the middle of the Salon. "So, you ready to go then?" She asks as she lifts the phone.

"Sure am," I nod.

"Excellent, I'll get your lift organised."

I watch as she speaks to whoever is on the other end of the phone. I like this little salon, it's so intimate and I wonder how much my hair and make-up actually cost. There is no price list, only a list of services and I notice that the sign says

By Appointment Only. The place is simply decorated and is in no way pretentious or trying to be something it's not.

"Okay," says Jennifer, "your driver will be here in a few minutes. You're going to dazzle the room when you get there."

I blush. "Thank you."

"Oh, thank *you*. Your hair is divine to work on."

I smile touching my hair lightly.

"Now, when you get into the car, just make sure you flatten your dress out under you and hold your seatbelt out a little, so it doesn't crease you," Jennifer says acting out the movements as she speaks. She reminds me of a flight attendant doing the safety announcements. I'm waiting for her to tell me where the exits are.

"Thanks so much Jennifer. For the advice and for making me look beautiful," I say shyly.

"Oh, honey you don't need much work. All I've done is given you a spruce up. Oh, there's your driver." She motions to the huge window at the front of the salon.

I look out the window and see a massive, jet black Mercedes sitting at the kerb. It's blacked out windows gives it a very presidential look and I all at once feel very small.

"Thank you, Jennifer, for everything."

"You're more than welcome. Now go and enjoy your night."

I smile at her as I leave the salon. The driver of the car gets out when he sees me and opens the back door for me. The inside of the car is luxurious. The two back seats are like a huge set of armchairs, the beige and black leather stitched into padded comfort. I get in and sit, fixing my dress the way Jennifer told me to and smiling. It's one of those silly little bits of information that you find out but it's a game changer. I'd normally just throw myself into the car and turn up looking like my iron had broken. The driver takes the car smoothly away from the kerb and we make our way through the streets of London. It still surprises me how long it takes to cross this city.

We are only around three miles away, but it takes us almost twenty-five minutes to get to the Savoy and by the time we pull up outside, I've had far too much time alone to think. I haven't seen Dan all day, since before I met with my parents in fact. I felt beautiful in the salon but now I'm starting to feel incredibly silly. Who the hell am I trying to kid here? I don't belong in this world. I don't get the chance to act on my insecurities as the door of the car opens and I'm greeted with the most wonderful sight. Dan flashes me a huge smile. *God you're beautiful,* I think to myself as I take him in. He's wearing a three-piece blue suit with a green check pattern through it. For some reason I'm sure that's no coincidence.

"My God you're a vision in green Nikki," he says as he helps me out of the car.

I smile at him. "Not so bad yourself. So, whose party is this exactly?" I ask as we start making our way inside.

He gives a little chuckle. "Mine," he says with a smile.

"Oh? And what's it for?"

"A business friend's office has been open one year on Tuesday, so I decided to throw a bit of a birthday party for them while I'm here."

"And you couldn't tell me, why?"

His brows knit together. "I just thought it'd be a nice surprise," he says, his voice sounding a little hurt that I should question him.

"So how will you introduce me then?" My question may have come out a little harsher than I was anticipating it to, but

I had thought things were going to be different. I thought that's why we were here.

"How would you like me to introduce you?"

Oh, hell no! I shake my head and turn to leave but I'm caught by the wrist.

"Don't run Nikki, please."

I turn back to him and sigh. His dark eyes are pleading and in my pissed off state I find it pathetic. "What do you expect me to do Dan?" I say and yank my arm out of his hand. "You promised me things would be different. Fuck!" I shout and everyone in earshot turns to see what the commotion is.

"Nikki, stop shouting, you're causing a scene," he says through gritted teeth.

"I can't do this again Dan." Turning away from him, I walk as fast as I can in my heels but it's like wading through water. I stop next to a huge plant pot holding some sort of greenery. Crouching down beside the pot, I put my head in my hands and cry. This is not how I had envisioned this night going. I looked beautiful when I left the salon. I even actually liked myself a little. Now I'm a mess and I'm crouched down crying outside one of the best hotels in London. And I've just made a roaring fool of myself and hurt a good man in the process.

A cool hand on my bare back makes me jump and I look up at Dan. He holds out his hand and reluctantly I take it. He pulls me up to my feet. "Do you want to leave?" He asks, his voice low and raspy.

I close my eyes, steeling myself. "No," I say quietly as I open them.

Dan places his forehead on mine. "I'm sorry, that was a stupid question to ask you," he whispers.

"No Dan, I'm sorry. What the hell are you doing here with me? I'm all kinds of fucked up in the head."

"You're hurting, there's a difference. I don't want to be that guy Nikki."

"What guy?"

"The one that makes you cry like that. The guy that apologises to you every time he fucks up. That arsehole who makes you feel anything other than love for yourself." He swipes my tears off my cheeks with his thumbs. "This ends now, you're here as my date and that's who I'll introduce you as. That's what I wish I'd gone with."

I can't hide the smile that forms on my lips. "Thank you. And I promise to stop running."

He puts his hand behind my head and pulls me in close, kissing my forehead. "Shall we go inside?"

I nod and he leads us towards the entrance, past the people who stopped to see what was going on when I shouted, the people who now throw accusatory glances my way.

Dan turns to look at me and I see sincerity there, adoration even and feel sorry for the poor guy. I hope he's as strong as he thinks he is.

CHAPTER TWENTY-SEVEN

*W*hat a party this is. The food is amazing, the music is top notch and the venue is stunning. I've been introduced to quite a lot of people and Dan kept his word. I'm his date for the night and now people know.

"I need to use the bathroom Dan; I'll be back shortly."

"Okay, I'll get you at the bar."

I'm taken by surprise when Dan kisses me softly on the lips, in front of everyone in this huge ballroom.

I smile against his mouth. "Mmm. What a show," I whisper.

He leans back a tiny bit. "Let them look. I don't care."

"I would stay here kissing you all night Dan, but I might just pee myself."

He laughs, his chest rumbling against my body. "Off you go, I can't be dealing with pee right now, I get enough of that with Olivia."

I swear his eyes sparkled when he mentioned Olivia. It makes me smile and as I walk in the direction of the toilets, my smile gets wider and a warm fuzzy feeling spreads over my chest. The bathroom is just as beautiful as the rest of the hotel and as I enter, I notice a couple of young women standing at the sink reapplying their lipstick. I smile and politely nod my head at them. I'm a little shocked when one of them, a tall, slim brunette, rolls her eyes at me and looks away with utter disgust on her face. Now, I am not a confrontational person and I would never pick a fight with anyone, except my sister, but what she just did to me was out of order.

"I'm sorry, do you have a problem with me?" I ask from my safe distance.

She turns to her friend and mouths something to her. The friend looks like she wants the ground to open up and swallow her. When the brunette does a slow, patronising head turn and looks me up and down, *I* want the ground to open up and swallow her. She's giving off some really horrible vibes and I realise I've made a huge mistake confronting her.

"What is he to you?" She asks in an extremely posh English accent.

"Excuse me?" I counter, my brow furrowing.

"Daniel. What is he to you?"

Daniel. I've never heard him called that before. Everyone calls him Dan. Who is this woman? "I'm his date," I say a little too feebly.

She laughs, "Daniel doesn't do dates, believe me." She swipes her hands up and down her body. "If he doesn't want this, he certainly doesn't want that," she practically hisses, pointing a skinny finger at me. "You're a conquest love, that's all."

My breath catches and I feel like I'm going to be sick.

"That's enough Bianca," her friend says, but I can tell that standing up to her is not something she does very often when Bianca draws her a most vicious look. I see her visibly shrink back and she genuinely looks worried.

Bianca turns back to me and walks slowly towards me, her model length legs closing the gap between us far too quickly. She leans in close to me and puts her finger on my chest. "It don't mean a thing if you aint got a ring sweetie," she says in a singsong voice.

I know my eyes are wide and I can't breathe, it feels as though she has put her hands round my neck. I'm grateful that she doesn't say anything else and decides to leave me alone. She struts her way out the door leaving me with her friend.

"Are you okay," the friend asks, her voice a little shaky.

I shake my head unable to speak my answer for fear that I'll burst into tears. She puts her hand on my shoulder and I flinch back from her almost slipping on the tiled floor.

"Hey it's okay. I'm really sorry about her. Bianca has been trying to bed Mr King since she first met him two years ago. I'm Casey by the way." She holds her hand out to me. I take it and she gives a soft shake. Her hand is cool against my embarrassingly sweating palms.

"Nikki," I manage to breathe out.

"Nice to meet you Nikki. Where are you from?" She asks and I look closely at her. Her auburn curls and pale skin give her a pre-Raphaelite look and she is very pretty. She doesn't have on a lot of makeup and her pale blue eyes are sincere. I can't help myself but warm to her.

"South Africa."

"Oh nice. So how did you meet him then?"

I'm really not ready to share this information with a stranger.

"How do you know Dan?" I ask her.

"I work at the London office. So does *she*. We were invited here as his guests, along with about thirty others, but Bianca took that to mean he'd finally given in to her flirting.

She goes out of her way to be near him every time he visits with us. In all honesty I was glad when I saw him with you, I thought it would stop her making a fool of herself, but its only made her worse. Now she's going to be unbearable."

"Wow, do you think she needs help? Like professional help?"

Casey laughs, "Oh honey, she's just a little infatuated."

A *little* infatuated? That's an understatement. "Well she really shouldn't do things like that to people it's really not nice. She'll do it to the wrong person someday. I'm sorry Casey I really need to use the toilet, but it was nice to meet you. And thank you." I smile at her and head into the closest cubicle.

Hiking my dress up, taking down my knickers and sitting down on the toilet, I cry silently until I'm finished peeing. I dry my tears and clean up, giving myself enough time to make sure Casey has left, and leave the cubicle. When I reach the sink and look in the mirror I want to die. I look an absolute mess. My makeup is faded, and my eyes are red. I shake my head and sigh. What the hell is it with people? I'm already feeling constantly under attack by hurricane Astrid, I really don't need it from a complete stranger too. Some women are so bitchy. Whatever happened to female solidarity? After trying to fix my face as best I can, I make my way out and back into the throes of the party. I find Dan exactly where I left him and, thankfully, I don't see Bianca or Casey. That makes me happier. I hope they've gone but I want nothing more than to leave here myself. I understand that Dan is used to parties like this and social gatherings in general, but I've never liked it. We used to attend a lot of functions when I was younger because of my dad's job and I spent the whole time feeling uncomfortable, wishing I was home and in my own little world.

Dan's smile when he sees me lights up his eyes and makes me smile too. I need to start living again. He's been so lovely to me and now that he knows what happened to me and hasn't given up on me, I feel I owe it to him, and me, to allow myself to heal and be happy. I make my way towards him, *my* date, with purpose.

CHAPTER TWENTY-EIGHT

*"Y*ou okay sweetheart?"

I turn and look at Dan. Every streetlight we pass illuminates his beautiful face and I feel like the luckiest girl in the world. "Yeah I am. I'm just glad the party's over. I really don't do well in social gatherings like that."

"Interesting. How the hell did you cope all the years your dad was in office? I assume you attended a lot of parties."

"We did and I hated every minute of it. "

"Then I thank you for being there with me tonight. You were the most beautiful woman in there tonight do you know that?"

I felt beautiful. *He* had made me feel beautiful. "Thank you. It's amazing what a good make-up artist and an expensive dress can do."

He reaches over and puts his hand on my cheek. "Those things only work if the canvas is already beautiful." He strokes my bottom lip with his thumb, and I melt into his touch.

"Dan," I whisper.

He answers by pulling me into a soft and sensual kiss. I should be melting into him but all I can think about is what Bianca said to me. I know she's simply jealous. It hurts when you hold a torch for someone, and they don't even acknowledge you exist.

He breaks our contact and leans back slightly. "What's wrong Nikki? You're not okay. You're tense."

"What is this to you Dan?" I gesture between us. "What am I to you?" Bianca's words play over and over in my head. *You're a conquest love.*

"I don't know." His answer wasn't what I was expecting although I'm not entirely sure *I* even know what is going on between us.

"Oh."

"Nikki," he says as he takes my hand in his and kisses my knuckles. "You are a beautiful, intelligent woman. Everything about you turns me on to fuck. I've spent so long trying to protect myself and Olivia from anything that might hurt us that I felt as though I'd lost my way. Then you came along. There was something about you. It was like something was pulling me to you. I still don't really know what it is, don't know if I'll ever find out but it's there."

"There's something about you too Dan. I felt it the first time we met on my first day in the elevator. Your eyes tell a thousand tales." I reach up and caress his face, staring straight into those tell-tale eyes. "Please tell me I'm not just a conquest to you. That I'm not simply someone to fill your time."

"Nikki, you've met my daughter," he says his voice tinged with hurt that I would even suggest that.

"I know Dan and thank you from the bottom of my heart for that. But I know what people will say about me. Our relationship isn't conventional, I mean you are my boss after all."

"Okay. I'm going to lay this down then. Nikki, I'd like you to be my girlfriend, my partner. I can't say where this will go, no one ever can at the start, but I have this need to be with you. Please understand I will never hurt you. I've seen too much of that in my life, I know how it wrecks a person."

If I had any doubts as to what his intentions with me were, they were dashed away by his statement. Unclipping my seatbelt, I slide closer to him on the back seat and am pulled right into his lap. Our kiss is hard and fevered and Dan puts his hands in my hair and holds on tight as though I might float away.

When the driver pulls up outside the apartment building Dan has us out before the guy even has a chance to put on the handbrake. As we head for the door, my heels make it almost impossible to go very fast.

"Hold on," I almost shout, and Dan comes to an abrupt halt.

I bend and slip my sandals off, hooking my fingers through the back straps. The gritty pavement is cool under my bare feet. Dan smiles and grabs my free hand again but, this time as he bolts to the door, I can keep up.

The lift we use is exclusive to the penthouse and as soon as the doors close, he's on me again. Our teeth clash as we kiss, and I'm pressed against the wall by his strong warm body. He snakes his hand down past my waist and round to rest on my bum. I give a little moan when he squeezes my cheek, pulling me in closer to him. His erection presses right into my hip and he groans as he breaks our kiss.

"Nikki," he breathes against my mouth. "Are you wearing any knickers?"

I bite my lower lip, a smile forming on my face. "Uh uh," I shake my head.

"Fuck!"

The doors are barely open before I'm pulled through them and into the apartment. We stop in the kitchen and I watch Dan's chest rise and fall as he rakes his eyes up my body. He stalks forward, pushing me against the island in the middle of the room, his eyes ablaze and my breath catches.

"Turn around," he says, and I do, dropping my sandals onto the tiled floor. Right now, I'd do anything he asked of me.

I hold on to the island as he moves my hair from my shoulders and sets about unzipping my dress the few centimetres it takes to expose the flesh of my backside, ever so slowly, teasing me with every tooth he loosens. When he has it unzipped all the way he runs his finger up my spine and the shiver it evokes tightens my nipples and sends goosebumps all over my body.

"Dan." My voice is low and pleading. This is utter torture but of the most delicious kind.

"You are a vision in green, an angel, my beautiful angel," he whispers as he kisses my shoulder, hooking his fingers in the straps of my dress and letting is fall from my shoulders. I move my hands from the island just in time to let it slide right down my body and I watch as the emerald silk balloons at my feet.

I'm dizzy with need and I hear him suck in a long breath as he takes in my naked body. He takes my hand and turns me to face him. "Angel," he whispers.

"I feel at a disadvantage here Dan." I point at his clothes and smile as I watch him strip in front of me. Each piece of clothing he discards reveals a little bit more of his delectable body. As he unbuttons his suit trousers and lets them fall to his feet, my smile almost hits my ears.

"Dan the man, you went commando too. Nice."

"I'm nothing if not optimistic." He laughs and his dick bobs ever so slightly.

I'm in the middle of a laugh when he steps forward and claims my mouth, his warm hands pulling my naked body against his. He lifts me up onto the kitchen island and I wrap my legs around his waist, pulling him in tight so that his bare cock is sitting against my core.

He shoots me a warning look and I nod. I've never had unprotected sex with anyone, but then again, I haven't given myself to many men. No one has ever made me feel the way Dan does. He worships me and my God is he good at sex.

"You're sure?"

"I've never been surer of anything," I answer and with that he pulls me towards him and pushes his way in.

His guttural groan is hot as hell and I slide myself onto him a little more, feeling him filling me with an exquisite stretch. He pushes himself in to the hilt and stops still, resting his forehead on mine, our noses touching. "We can't do this here Nikki. I'm taking you to my bed." And with that sentiment, he pulls out of me and holds me close, lifting me off the island, taking us through the kitchen to his bedroom.

Dan settles us on the bed and takes his position between my legs. His expression contemplative.

"Are you okay?" I reach up and stroke his cheek.

"Yeah I am. How could anyone hurt you Nikki?" He smoothes my hair away from my face.

I feel a tear run from my eye towards my ear and I swipe it away. "Stop talking, please?" I pull his head towards me and allow myself to be happy in his arms.

"Beautiful," he whispers as he claims my mouth and my body, his hand snaking its way down my torso, his fingers finding my clit. As soon the warm pad of his finger touches my swollen bud my body bucks under him. Every nerve ending is on fire and so help me, but I don't think I've ever orgasmed so quickly in my life.

"Jesus, Nikki," Dan breathes and then his mouth replaces his finger and I almost explode with sensation. He swipes his expert tongue up my soaking wet slit and then goes all out as he pushes it inside, fucking me with his mouth.

"Dan… fuck…" I grab his shoulder before he makes me lose my mind and he rears up over me, his face slick with my pleasure. It's hot as hell and when he kisses me, and I taste myself on him I can't control myself any longer. Grabbing at him and deepening the kiss I lift my hips to meet his cock and he pushes himself right in. Fucking me hard and fast, claiming my body with his. He takes my breast in his hand and rolls my nipple between his fingers hard enough to be on the edge of pain and I move my hips up to meet his thrusts, each one hitting my clit and firing me higher and higher. I can feel myself on the edge of another orgasm and I grab at Dan's tight bum, pulling him in as far as I can, writhing under him and coming like a freight train.

He stills, letting me wring every last morsel from him, then pulls out of me. The cool air hitting my wet core and thighs makes me draw in a breath and as I watch him take his cock in his hand to find his own release. As I lie there, open to him, watching him as he comes in great waves over my belly, I'm struck by just how intimate the scene is. More so because we haven't taken our eyes off each other. I can see the strain in his face as he tries his hardest to hold it together.

Dan puts his head down panting and I'm about to move when he comes to my side and pulls me over on top of him.

"Ew, Dan the… stuff," I squeal.

"Suff?" He enquires, a cheeky grin on his face. He wriggles under me smearing his come all over us.

"You're getting it everywhere."

"I know. Just making sure we need to shower. I want to fuck you in there too Nikki. In fact, by the time we leave here tomorrow I want to have had you in every room in this apartment."

I raise my eyebrows at him. And then I say something that shocks me. Something I'd never have considered ever. "Does the balcony count as a room?" God we're in the middle of bloody London. What has this guy done to me?

"Ooh ya dirty wee minx," he says laughing as he sits us up, throwing his legs over the edge of the bed.

Wrapping my legs round his waist I smile at him and put my hand on his cheek. "Thank you, Dan."

"For what?"

"For bringing me here and making me see that my life isn't over."

"You're special Nikki, in more ways than you realise." He kisses my nose. "Let's go and get clean so we can get dirty again. I want you naked for the rest of the night."

I giggle like a little schoolgirl as he stands, and I slide against him. He gives my bum a squeeze and I pray he gets us in that shower quickly. I never want this beautiful feeling to end.

CHAPTER TWENTY-NINE

*M*y limbs feel heavy and overworked as I stretch out in bed. The early dawn light seeps in through the partially open shades and I turn to look at the beautiful specimen of a man lying beside me. Dan is deep in sleep and I smile. He's treated me like a princess this weekend, never once like a possession and certainly never with anything but respect. It's been wonderful but unusual.

My love life has never been great. I didn't lose my virginity until I was in second year at university and it was the worst. We were both wasted so it was more of a fumble than anything else. Any other relationships I had after that were short lived when they found out what my father did for a living. Then there was Mike. He was selfish. If I orgasmed with him it wasn't because he'd allowed it to happen. And he didn't look at me during it the way Dan has. He hated seeing me having any pleasure and certainly not before him. It usually meant I'd be walking on eggshells for the entire time I was with him.

I move out of the bed, careful not to disturb my sleeping beauty, grab a blanket and wrap it round my naked body before heading to the bathroom in the room I was in on Friday. I check out my reflection in the mirror as I brush my teeth. I've changed. My eyes are brighter, and my skin is glowing. I spit my toothpaste into the sink and wipe my lips.

"You are good, you are kind, you are wanted." I look into my own eyes in the mirror as I say the mantra out loud. I'm done being everyone else's patsy. I'm me and I'm clever, and I *am* a good person. Dan sees that in me and I'm so grateful to him for making me see it too.

Gathering up my toiletries and putting them into the suitcase, I feel a little contemplative. We are heading back to Glasgow tonight and I'm worried that the little bubble we've been in for the last two days is going to pop spectacularly. What if Dan realises he's made a huge mistake with me? What if having a relationship with a member of his staff is too much for him? I don't know that I could cope with that sort of rejection, especially after I told him everything about Mike.

As I'm zipping up the suitcase, I feel Dan's presence behind me, and I can't help the smile that spreads across my face.

"Good morning angel."

I turn my head and look over my shoulder. I'm rendered incapable of speech at the sight in front of me. He's leaning against the door frame with nothing on but his boxers, the material straining over his semi hard cock.

"M...oh." *Engage brain Nikki.* "Good morning."

"What you doing?"

"Packing my stuff up."

"Bit early for that, we don't leave until after six tonight."

I give a little laugh. "Sorry, it's a thing. I like to be prepared; you know in case we end up leaving earlier. I've always been like that; I'd have made a good girl scout."

Dan bites his lip, obviously taking my words and making them dirty in his mind. "Hmm, I like what you're wearing by the way." He gestures to my makeshift blanket dress.

"Oh, this old thing." I make a pretend curtsy and accidentally step on the edge of the blanket, loosening it from under my arm pit and ending up naked as it falls to the floor.

Dan lets out a breath and he walks towards me. "Nope," he says as I move to pick the blanket up.

I stand back up straight and he puts his hand around my waist pulling me into his warm body and now rock-hard dick.

"See what you do to me? So fucking beautiful." He leans in and kisses me and my legs jellify under me. I'm so glad he's holding on to me.

He kisses across my jawline and nips at my earlobe. "Oh," I say on a breath. And he brings his eye back to mine.

"So," Dan says looking past me at the French doors that lead out to the balcony and I instantly know what he's getting at.

I follow his gaze and almost give myself whiplash as I snap my head back and gasp. "Dan no. It's daylight out there. People will see."

He shakes his head. "No, they won't. This building has nothing higher around it and anyway I wasn't going to ask you to go out there starkers." He bends and picks up the blanket, throwing it round my shoulders. "Come with me."

I stick my hand out under the blanket and he links our fingers and leads me out of the room and to the doors at the living room, the ones that look out over the park.

"My God Dan the park? The Royal Family lives in there. Isn't that like a hangable offence?"

He laughs and places a soft kiss on my head. We make our way out onto the balcony and the cool early morning air has me bundling the blanket round me tighter.

I'm guided towards railing and Dan presses his body against my back wrapping his arms around me. I take in a deep breath when he puts his hand through the opening in the blanket at my front.

"Open your legs," he whispers in my ear.

I do as he says, and he slides a finger down over my clit. I feel his body tense when he finds me already wet. "Fuck Nikki," he groans as he edges his finger inside me. When it's joined by another and he pushes them all the way in I can't help but grind my hips, backing up against his hard cock. I'm so lost in chasing my orgasm that I don't even care if I'm being finger fucked on a balcony above one of the most exclusive parts of London. Right now, I wouldn't even care if the Queen was watching.

I can feel that tell-tale heat rise up my chest and I know I'm so close. And so does Dan because he palms my clit, massaging in tiny circles, making me lose my mind. Gripping the tubular metal rail in front of me with everything I have, still clutching the blanket tight, I climax around Dans fingers, my muscles feeling as though they are trying to suck his hand inside me.

I rest my cheek on the soft material of the blanket, revelling in the euphoria running through my body. I wince a little when Dan removes his fingers and rights me, turning me to face him.

"Nikki, you are something else angel."

Spreading out my arms and wrapping us both in the blanket I nestle into his chest, listening to his heart thump in his chest and there we stay, warm and safe in each other's arms. As London comes to life below us, I do too and for the first time in longer than I can remember, I feel genuinely wanted.

"*O*pen," Dan says, holding up a tiny pastry.

I open my mouth like a little baby bird, and he pops it on my tongue. The buttery flakiness is delectable. "Mmm. Where did you get this food?" I gesture to the spread of small cakes and pastries, speciality breads and oils and lots of little Italian tapas bowls. The picnic blanket we are sat cross legged on has been strategically placed enough in the shade of a huge tree to keep us cool. We have champagne and sparkling water with lemons and mint floating in it. It really is the fanciest picnic I've ever had.

"Hmm yeah it really is lovely. I have a friend who owns an artisan bakery. He's very good, been baking since he was old enough to stand. His shop supplies some of the most exclusive restaurants in London, he even catered one of the Queen's garden parties once."

"Ooh you have friends in high places. Wow imagine catering for the Queen. Did he get to meet her?"

"Nope, his wedding was the same day as the garden party. Poor guy was up all night baking then had to go and get married and still be okay for the reception. We found him asleep in the boiler room of the hotel halfway through the party. We were about to call the police at one point. His wife was frantic."

"Oh, that's a shame. My dad met Prince Philip once. When we asked what he was like, all he said was 'interesting'. As we got older and saw reports of some of his slip ups, we understood what dad had meant."

Dan smiles at me as he eats a French Fancy.

"What?"

"Thank you, Nikki?"

"For what?"

"For being here with me, for listening to my woes. For being you."

I narrow my eyes at him and smile. "I should be thanking *you*." I lift the champagne bottle and top up our glasses. "Now would normally be the time I'd have a little panic attack and retreat into myself. You've helped my self-esteem more over this weekend than I've ever been able to in forever."

Dan moves closer to me and strokes my face with his free hand. "You are wonderful Nikki; you should always remember that. Beautiful girl."

I press my cheek into his hand and look deep into his eyes. "You make me feel beautiful, and strong and most of all safe. So, thank you."

He smiles and kisses me softly. Pulling away he gestures at me to open my mouth again and I bite down on the proffered mini Victoria sponge. We wile away the next few hours eating, drinking and chatting away about everything and nothing and by the time we are ready to leave London behind, I've well and truly lost my heart to this man.

CHAPTER THIRTY

$\mathcal{I}$n all the talking Dan and I did yesterday afternoon in the park, the one thing I didn't tell him about was Bianca but now, as I sit at my desk and watch as the shit truly hits the fan, I really wish I had.

The building was quiet when I got to work at seven thirty this morning. I came in a little earlier than usual because Dan got an important phone call just before we boarded the plane last night. The private investigator has finally found a trail that connects Astrid to the intellectual property theft. It has also transpired that Jed is being blackmailed. She has been using him the whole time and when Jed tried to break off the relationship, she told him she had video evidence of their affair. He was so scared his wife would find out that he didn't even ask for evidence, he simply caved and went along with whatever she wanted him to do. When Dan relayed the details of the call to me as we flew home, certain things began to make sense. Jed never asked me for any paperwork by himself, it was always Astrid. She was the one who came to pick up our work at the end of the week and if I ever went to Jed myself, she was usually always there. It wouldn't have been too hard for her to get them anyway since she is his assistant and would have been the one doing all his typing and admin.

"You okay Nikki?" Damo smiles at me as he takes a seat on the other side of my desk.

"Oh Damo, I knew this day was going to come but I was seriously not expecting it this soon."

"What did HR say to you?"

I had been summoned to HR as soon as the place was operational this morning and was shocked when they revealed what had been said about me. They had found out that I'd been away with Dan at the weekend and although he is the owner of the company and can pretty much do whatever, and whoever he wants, it's still frowned upon considering the management position I hold. They said something about it being a conflict of interests. Needless to say, my appraisal has been put on hold.

"Well they know about me and Dan for a start."

"How?" He asks, raising an eyebrow.

"I'll give you two guesses."

"Fucking Astrid. That nasty bitch."

"Hmm."

"Hmm what?"

"Well, it was her who told them, but I have a good idea who told her." I give him the low down on my run in with Bianca.

"Wow that fell right into Astrid's lap there didn't it. I can just imagine her face when she found out. Are you okay?"

"I'm fine honestly," I lie knowing full well what's to come later. Arrangements are being made for Astrid to be removed from the building at close of play today. Dan is in the process of meeting with his lawyers to decide on how to proceed. I have been sworn to secrecy until a press release is put out about the theft. Dan is also considering his options regarding prosecution against the CEO and board of the Main Group since they knew the information they had was stolen.

"So aside from the fact that you've been outed, how was your weekend?"

I think back to our first night. The night I told someone for the first time what had happened to me. I know it's often said that talking about something like that makes you feel better and in a way it has. Dan's reaction was not what I was expecting, however, it made me realise that even though he doesn't really know me that well he still cares.

"It was lovely. We had dinner at the Shard and a picnic in Kensington gardens and the weather was just perfect. I also got to have lunch with my parents which was lovely. Dan certainly knows how to treat a girl." I can't hide my smile when I think about him

"Well he should do," says Damo, winking at me, "he's bloody loaded."

I throw a pen at him. "You make me sound like a gold digger."

"Oh honey, I'm happy for you. I just wish you'd gotten more time together privately before people found out."

"It was inevitable wasn't it?"

As if she'd heard us talking about her, the elevator pings and the doors open revealing the bitch in heels herself. Astrid struts towards us, her long blonde curls swinging behind her. Damo turns back to face me and rolls his eyes and I want to hit him because I want so much to laugh, but she's staring right at me. It's as though she's trying to bore a hole in my face.

"Morning Astrid. What can I do for you?" I try to sound as chirpy as I can without giving myself away too much.

"Hmm. Wasn't actually looking for you. Have you seen

Jed this morning?" I'm pretty sure I hear a hint of panic in her voice.

"I haven't, no. I've been here since before eight this morning. Is he not in his office?"

She stamps her foot like a petulant child, her curls bouncing slightly. "Would I be asking *you* if I hadn't already tried there?"

"Maybe he's phoned in sick. You should go and see HR," Damo says still looking at me, his smile becoming even wider.

Astrid tuts and turns on her heel. "Useless fuckers," she says loud enough for us to hear her.

As soon as the doors of the elevator close, Damo bursts out laughing. I smile at him, but I can't share in his revelry. I know what's in store for her later and finding Jed right now is the least of her worries. Although I am intrigued as to why Jed is nowhere to be found this morning.

"You're terrible Damo. She will know exactly what you were talking about."

"She should be fucking ashamed of herself. I don't know why some people feel it's their right to bring everyone else down. It's like she never left school the way she bullies people. The sooner she's put in her place the better."

Oh Damo if only you knew.

The day has sailed by without incident and its home time. I watch everyone packing up their stuff and wonder how Dan's day has gone. I haven't heard a peep from him all day, but I know he'll be knee deep in all sorts of legal issues so, even though I've been tempted, I haven't bothered him.

"Night Nikki," Ben, who is last to leave, says as he passes me.

"Night Ben, see you tomorrow."

He smiles and winks knowingly at me. I shake my head as I watch the elevator doors close behind him, wondering just what everyone must think of me now. News spreads around these types of offices like wildfire. People talk, of course they do. I used to be part of that gossip before. I just don't like being the subject of it. I decide to head on home since I don't have anything left to do. Dan will be in touch in his own time. I have to let him deal with the Astrid situation without distraction. I turn off the lights and head for the elevator, very much aware of what is going to be happening to Astrid soon. I honestly don't know why but I feel a little sorry for her. She really has no clue that Dan knows what she's done, and I can imagine it will be a bit of a shock when she is ambushed by security and marched off the premises.

I needn't have wondered what that scene would look like as I'm confronted with a wall of noise in the lobby of the building when the elevator doors open. As I'm trying to take in the scene in front of me the doors start to close again, and I fumble with the buttons to try and keep them open. Failing miserably, I stick my hand out and push them open. There are about half a dozen police officers all in different positions just beyond the reception desk, some on their knees, some standing and one talking into the radio on his vest. I don't think I've ever seen so many people in this lobby in the whole time I've been here. The place is absolute chaos and the noise of loud chatter and shouting is deafening.

It takes a moment for my brain to decipher what's going on but as I look at the police officers on their knees, I see a mass of blonde hair and realise Astrid is on the floor and the officers are pinning her down. She's thrashing around like a fish out of water and the female officer holding her wrists shouts to her to calm down. I'm aware of a presence at my side and turn to see Ben.

"My God Ben, what happened?"

"Not a clue. I got off that lift into a war zone. Word is Astrid has lost her mind. According to Steph at the front desk security were escorting her out of the building and she went nuts and started threatening to stab them if they put a hand on her. Have you any idea what's going on there?"

I can't lie to him. I know he knows about my relationship with Dan. I know the whole building will know by now so there's no use in pleading ignorance.

"I do, but I can't say anything right now. You'll find out soon enough though. Let's just say this may be the last time you see Astrid in this building."

Ben smiles slightly, his eyes creasing at the corners. "Can't say I'm too upset about that. I really don't like her. She's so nasty to everyone. I suppose what goes around comes around eh?"

"Mhm. She got to me on my first day."

"Little bitch," he says and we both look back to where the action is happening.

Astrid is still throwing a hissy fit and is now being lifted off the floor by a four-man team of police officers. It feels like something from a TV cop show, not something that should be happening in the lobby of a software company. As soon as they have her out the door, an air of calm returns to the building and I feel myself physically relax.

"I'm going to head home now Nikki; I'll see you tomorrow."

"Okay Ben, here's to a nicer working environment from now on." I hold my hand up and high five him.

I'm about to head out myself when I feel my phone vibrate against my thigh. I pull it out of my pocket. It's Dan.

"Hi," I answer trying to sound calm.

"Hey, are you still in the building?"

"Uh, yeah I'm in the lobby."

"Good can you come up to my office if you're not busy?"

"Sure, I'll be up shortly." I can't really hide my excitement at getting to see him.

In the less than twenty-four hours since I last saw Dan, I've missed him incredibly. I press the call button for the lift and smile to myself. And this time it's a genuinely happy smile. That smile stays plastered on my face for the whole lift ride to Dan's floor. Tabitha has obviously left for the day and Dan's windows are frosted but his door is slightly ajar. I give a soft knock and, opening the door a little wider, I see Dan sitting at his desk. As our eyes lock on each other my smile dissolves and a thick fog of foreboding hangs in the air. Dan has his hands under his chin, his fingers laced together. The look on his face is… well there is no look. His face is completely void of emotion. The straight line of his mouth and his almost dead eyes are very disconcerting.

"Dan, are you okay?" I ask, my voice cracking as I finish the question.

He doesn't speak and I'm starting to feel very uncomfortable at the way he's staring at me. The sound of someone clearing their throat behind me startles me and I snap my head round to see a very thin man with a full head of pure white hair rise from one of the seats at the coffee table. His full height becomes apparent as he stands, dwarfing my slight frame. God he must be over six and a half feet tall. My instant thought as I assess his gangly frame is that he reminds me of that creepy Slenderman character that terrifies little kids. I

233

look questioningly back at Dan who is still sitting as he was when I came in.

"Dan, what's going on?"

"Miss Olsson," creepy man says, and I turn to face him this time. "Mr King has been advised that your acquaintance with each other must be on a wholly professional level from now on and for the foreseeable future."

I feel my brows furrow and turn back to look at Dan. He's changed position and is now staring at the window. He can't even look at me.

"Dan?" The pleading in my voice is more than noticeable but still he keeps his attention on the window. "Dan?" I try again and he doesn't give in.

"Miss Olsson, your help has been very much appreciated during what you can imagine has been a very testing time for the company," Slenderman's voice is soft and higher pitched than I was expecting.

I don't look at him. I keep my eyes on the side of Dan's head and the horrible realisation that I've been used causes a sob to escape from my lips. Now he looks at me and the pity in his eyes is all the confirmation I need.

"How could you?" My body is shaking, and I feel as though I'm going to throw up.

"This isn't personal Miss Olsson, it's what's best for the company."

"Shut up you creepy bastard," I screech at the tall streak of piss, surprising myself that I have managed to stand up for myself to a man, and one of his very intimidating size. "Don't you even dare. You don't know how personal this is."

"Miss Olsson, you should mind how you speak to people in higher office than you if you intend to still have a job in this company."

"Fuck your job and fuck you Dan," I shout, taking off my

lanyard holding my photo ID and throwing it at him. Dan doesn't flinch, even as the strap of the lanyard hits him on the jaw. I take off out the door before anything else can happen.

As I press the button for the lift, I see Dan emerge from his office and start to make his way towards me. "No," I shout holding up my hand.

He stops and I look at him through my tears. "I'm so sorry Nikki," he says his voice rough and tinged with sadness.

I turn back to face the doors and as they open, I take a deep breath. "I'll have my desk cleared out by tomorrow," I say quietly as I get into the lift.

"Nikki," Dan pleads as the doors close.

Leaning back against the wall, the movement of the lift flipping my stomach, I cry loudly as I realise I've lost everything by doing the one thing I promised myself I wouldn't ever do again. I got involved with a guy who couldn't possibly want me, one who would always put me second to his ambitions. I told Dan everything that scared me, everything that happened to me. It was the worst possible thing he could know about me and he couldn't even give me the courtesy of letting me down gently. He had to get that horrible, creepy man to do it instead. Who the hell he was I don't know? Right now, all I want is to get as far away from here, from Dan, as I can.

I exit the building into the damp, drizzle laden air and curse the day I ever decided to move here.

CHAPTER THIRTY-ONE

I have gone through countless scenarios in my head over the last few days as to why Dan did what he did to me. When I think back to how he reacted in London when I told him what Mike had done, I wonder why he was so angry if I really meant nothing to him. He acted as though he truly cared about me. I've ignored his calls and the only person I've really spoken to in the four days since I walked out is Damo. I know I'm going to have to face Dan sooner or later but right now all I can do is wallow in self-pity with a deep-seated feeling of betrayal lying in the pit of my stomach. A loud knock at the door makes me jump but given that it's after two in the afternoon on a Friday I know it'll be Damo.

"Use your key," I shout to him.

I gave Damo a key so that he can come and go in case he can't get hold of me. It was my compromise because he said he was going to camp out on my sofa if I even dared to ignore him.

When the door knocks again, I huff and get up. "For God sake Damo, what's the point in having a key if you're just going to forget it anyway?"

I pull open the door and feel myself physically recoil at the figure standing on the other side. I gasp and try to shut the door but I'm not quick enough as a foot is wedged in the gap stopping the door from closing. I let go of the door and run to the living room. Where the hell I'm trying to run to is beyond me right now, I'm two floors up. Every heavy step that follows behind me fills me with terror. I don't have anywhere to go so I'm forced to turn and face my intruder.

"Mike what are you doing here? You shouldn't be here."

He doesn't say anything. He stands on the opposite side of the living room staring at me.

"How did you find me?"

Mike laughs and a small sneer forms on his lips. "Oh, I have contacts Nik, you know I do. What I want to know is why did you leave me like that?" He takes a step forward and I back up, hitting the wall.

"Mike, please don't hurt me," I say as a tear rolls down my face.

I close my eyes as he stalks towards me as though he is a lion and I, his injured prey. I can feel him close to me, his repugnant aftershave making me want to heave. I jump at the feel of his hand on my face but I daren't move any further. I've been on the receiving end of punches from those hands and I don't wish to feel that again.

"You're so beautiful Nik. I've missed you. Look at me."

I open my eyes and I swear I see a sadness behind his. I'm so confused and so help me, but I feel sorry for him.

"You hurt me Mike. You took everything from me. Why? Why did you hit me?"

"Oh Nik," he says closing his eyes.

"Stop fucking calling me that Mike, my name is Nikki."

He takes his hand from my face and turns away from me, his shoulders slumping slightly. "You've gotten strong since you've been away Nikki. You have to believe that I've changed." He turns back to face me. "I'm getting help. I want to make a fresh start with you. Will you come back with me? Are you able to?"

I think about how fucked up my life has become here and how Dan has treated me. What he has done has made me feel a million times worse than anytime Mike laid a hand on me. Bruises heal, but broken hearts are scarred forever. Right now, I'd like nothing more than to get away from here. In the back of my mind, I know I shouldn't be giving Mike the time of day but what choice do I have now?

"Where are you staying?" I ask him, and I can't hide the defeat in my voice.

"The Holiday Inn at the airport. Look, I know this is a little presumptuous, but I bought you a ticket back to South Africa. I had hoped that when you saw me, you'd realise that you still love me, and I've already told you I'm getting help. I'll be a better man, I promise."

I honestly must be out of my mind, but I nod at him and he comes back to me, kissing me fervently. I put my hands up to his chest and push him back.

"I'll come back with you Mike, but I need time to get over what's happened, and you need time to prove that you've changed."

"Thank you," he says almost sincerely, and I hate myself for it, but I somehow believe him.

"Okay, when is the flight?"

"Tomorrow morning, eight fifty. Come to the hotel with me, please Nikki. I want to make things right. I need you."

"Let me gather up some clothes and stuff. I'll need to make arrangements for the flat and things too."

"Do it from home."

I shake my head. "I thought this was going to be my

home," I say solemnly. "Give me time to pack Mike. Show yourself out, I'll meet you downstairs in the courtyard."

As I go to walk away, he grabs my wrist. I look down at his hand on my arm and a fleeting memory flashes in front of me. I bat it down. I have to get away from here and I have to believe he's changed.

"Thank you, Nik, sorry Nikki. I'll try to remember." He smiles at me.

I shake my arm and he releases my wrist. "I won't be long," I say as I make my way to my bedroom and begin packing my stuff into a bag with tears in my eyes. It's like I'm replaying the day I left his apartment all over again, only this time I truly am heartbroken. I can't believe I'm even contemplating going back there with him but in a messed-up way I seem to have convinced myself that it's a good idea.

*C*an we stop at an ATM? I have no cash on me."

"Sure," Mike says as we get into his hire car.

"Thanks. There's one not far from here."

We set off and I feel at odds with myself. Deep down I think fear is making me do this. I'm still scared of him. I turn and look at his profile. That cocky smile is back on his face. Gone is the sincere, '*I'm sorry*' look. The atmosphere between us has changed too and I realise in this moment that I've made a huge mistake. He hasn't changed one bit. As Mike pulls up next to the ATM, I grab my bank card from my bag and get out. There's a woman at the machine in front of me and I stand behind her. My palms are sweating and I'm shaking. This doesn't feel right. I look back at the car and Mike smiles at me. But it's not a nice smile, it's a smile that screams of control and I've seen it on his face many times. I have to get away from him, but my bag is still in the car with my phone and all my clothes. I need to get it before this woman finishes. I turn back to the car to pretend I need a different card with the full intention of getting my bag and running. My self-assuredness disappears in an instant as I open the door and see him sitting there with my phone in his hand and his face contorted in a way that's reminiscent of the look he had every time he was about to hit me.

"Get in," he demands.

"I n…need to get a different card," I say trying my hardest to plead innocence.

"Get in the fucking car Nik."

I take a deep stuttering breath and do as he says. I need to get my phone back and I'm scared of what he'll do if I don't comply.

"Is… is everything okay?" I say plastering as much of a smile on my face as I can.

The clunk of the door closing is like the sounding of a death knell and a feeling of pure terror hangs over me. Mike keeps my phone in his hand, clutching it against the steering wheel, as he speeds off before I can even put my seatbelt on.

"Who the fuck is Dan?"

I feel every bit of colour drain from my face and a horrible cold feeling courses through my body. I can't answer him.

"Fucking answer me," he shouts.

"My boss." My voice sounds so weak and I know I've shrunk down in my seat. I chance a look at him and see that his jaw is clenched tight, his face reddening.

"Your fucking boss. Your FUCKING BOSS!" He screams at me.

His driving is becoming increasingly erratic and given that it's only mid-afternoon on a Friday, the streets are filled with people. I'm worried there could be a fatal accident if he doesn't calm down. I manage, with extremely shaky hands, to get my seatbelt clicked in place

"It meant nothing…"

"Shut up and don't treat me like I'm an imbecile. I read the messages, that wasn't nothing." He throws the phone at me and it hits my chest before falling to the floor and sliding under the seat.

"I thought you said you'd changed Mike." I don't know why my warped brain is deciding it would be a good idea to antagonise him further but it's out there now and I have a feeling I'm about to regret it.

"Fuck you, you little bitch," he shouts as he all but stands on the breaks propelling me forward, the seatbelt digging into my neck. I'm pushed forward again as there's a sudden impact from behind us. "FUCK!" He shouts. "FUCK! FUCK! FUCK!"

His voice is deafening, and I put my hands over my ears. "I'm going to fucking kill you," he says through gritted teeth as he grabs my neck and pushes me against the door. I can't breathe and I genuinely feel as though I might die. I honestly don't think it's an idle threat. He really would kill me.

"FUCK!" He shouts again and loosens his grip on me. The gasp of air I take in burns my lungs.

As he gets out of the car to assess the damage, I hold my throat where his hands were. I should run I know I should, but I can't seem to make my legs move to get out of the car. My whole body is shaking. I let out a huge sigh of relief when I look in the wing mirror and see a police car arrive. I watch as the male and female officers get out of the car and start to speak to Mike and the man who ran into us. Mike is smiling at them with the fakest innocent look on his face and it fires up a strength in me that I didn't think I had. I grab my bag and my phone, get out of the car and walk towards the police officers, determined that I'm going to get Mike for everything he's ever done to me.

"Ah here's my wife now. I was just telling these officers we are on our way to the airport sweetie. We'll just let the hire company's insurance deal with this. Get back in the car, there's nothing much we can do right now anyway." His voice is saccharine sweet, and I feel like I want to vomit.

The male officer nods at him and smiles. His fucking wife? Over my dead body. I'm never going to get away from him and I know how manipulative he is so there's no point in me telling these officers anything in front of him. The look Mike gives me is a warning shot and I know if I don't do something now, I'll never be free of him. In the split second it takes Mike to look between me and the two cops, I lift my fist and punch the male one right on the jaw. I'm not a violent person, far from it and I would never have dreamt of hitting anyone let alone a police officer, but I need to get them to arrest me, to get away from him, and this is the only way I can guarantee it.

There is complete and utter chaos in the aftermath as I am handcuffed and read my rights then placed in the back of the police car. I watch as the officers talk to Mike, who looks like he's seen a ghost, and as they take statements from everyone who witnessed the punch. When they are done, they get back in the car and as we move off, I look Mike right in the eyes. The look on his face is priceless and it makes me happy. For the first time in a long time, I genuinely feel free of him and I smile and physically relax. He looks like he's going to blow a fuse. I watch the male officer rub his cheek as he talks into his radio. I feel awful for him. The poor guy was only doing his job, but I wonder if he'll ever know that he may have saved my life. I'll tell these officers everything that Mike has done to me and now that I know his hotel and flight plans, I hope my disclosure to them will result in his arrest. I don't want any other woman to suffer what I have at his hands. If he gets back to South Africa that will never happen. I slouch down in the seat and worry about what's to come, if I will be believed and, God, the worst part of all, what my father will say.

*T*he lighting in this police station is stark and painful on the eyes but I'm happy to be standing in front of this desk with a sergeant reading over my case. He's just had a rundown of what happened and has decided there's enough evidence to charge me, although it was a foregone conclusion. You don't tend to punch a police officer and get a slap on the wrist for it. I've had my rights read to me again and now the sergeant is reading off a checklist.

"Do you have any medical conditions that require medication to be administered?" He asks as the officer beside him marks off my answers.

"No."

"Do you have any injuries?"

"No."

"Do you have any food allergies or allergies to medication?"

"No."

"What is your nationality?"

"I have dual nationality, South African and British."

The sergeant raises his head and a slight frown appears on his brow.

"My father works for the Foreign Office," I offer.

"Ah I see. Okay then I think we are good here. Is there anyone you'd like us to call for you?"

"No."

"You are entitled to have a solicitor informed of your arrest. Do you wish us to inform one for you?"

"No."

"Okay then. Officer Gilland here will take you through and have you processed."

I'm taken to a room further into the station and the female officer accompanying me does a search on me, checking my pockets and anywhere she thinks I may be concealing anything illegal. She asks me to take off my jewellery, belt and shoes. I feel tears bubble up in my eyes and I let out a small sob as I kick off my trainers.

"This is an overwhelming situation for a first offender. Are you okay?" the officer asks.

"No, I'm not. I didn't want to hurt anyone, I just needed to get away from him."

"From who?"

"The man I was with was my ex-boyfriend not my husband. You'll notice he hasn't shown up here. If I was his wife he'd be here. He's not here because he's an abuser and by now he knows why I did what I did."

The officers face changes from indifference to extreme concern. "Nikki, have you been subjected to domestic abuse?"

I nod my head as a tear runs down my cheek. "Yes, and right before the officers turned up to the accident we had, he tried to strangle me and told me he was going to kill me. I know he didn't mean it as a figure of speech. I really believe he wants to kill me."

"Okay, I'm going to move you to a cell right now, for your own safety, while I run this information by the custody sergeant. We take domestic abuse very seriously so believe me when I say we will do all we can to help you."

I can say I have never felt relief like this in my whole life. I don't know what I was thinking letting Mike talk me into going back to South Africa with him. He managed to find me at my most vulnerable and used it as he always has. As I sit down on the bed in the cool cell, I'm struck by the realisation that I may just be able to start living a normal life. If I end up getting prosecuted for hitting that officer, it's a small price to pay for my freedom.

$\mathcal{I}$ feel like I've been lying on my back staring at the same piece of peeling paint on the ceiling for hours when I hear the lock of the cell door turn. I sit up as the female officer from earlier enters the cell with a plastic cup and a pre-packed sandwich.

"Hi Nikki, would you like something to eat and drink? I have tea and a chicken sandwich here if you want them."

"I'll take the tea, but I'm not hungry. Thanks," I reply taking the cup from her.

"Okay, I'll take this away and I'll be back to take you through to the interview room so that we can talk to you about your allegations."

"Do you believe me?" I ask as she heads back to the door, my voice shaking. "Will anyone believe me?"

The officer stops and turns to me, her eyes full of compassion. "Believe *me*, people will believe you. Domestic abuse is never okay and that goes for women who attack men too. Please don't worry, we'll do everything we can to help you. Are you sure there's no one we can call for you? You'd probably feel better if there was someone here with you."

I sigh and close my eyes. There are only three people I know of who can help me here. Two of them will go absolutely ballistic when they find out what happened. The other already knows and has already gone ballistic over it. I'm not ready for my dad or my sister to know about this.

"Damien Shaw," I tell her. "But I don't know his number, it's in my phone."

"Who is he to you?" She asks.

"My friend," I reply. God what a sad, sorry situation this is.

"And you're sure that's who you want us to call? What about your family?"

"No. Please I don't want my parents involved. They live in London anyway so it wouldn't be feasible for them to be here. There's no point worrying them. My sister has just had a baby and she's in Edinburgh." I shake my head. "No, Damien is who I'd like you to try and call if you can." I know he's going to panic but I really need a friend right now. Someone who won't judge me.

She nods. "I understand," she says as she closes the door behind her.

I stare at the back of the door as the realisation of what has happened finally hits me. It also occurs to me that Mike may have been here for a while. The roses, the balloon, the constant feeling that someone was watching me. I shake my head. *How did I let this happen?*

CHAPTER THIRTY-THREE

*M*y whole body is a whirl of emotions right now as I sit in the waiting area of the police station. I've finished recounting my traumatic relationship with Mike to two police officers from the Domestic Abuse Unit. I've been here for hours and fatigue is taking over. The officers told me that although they can't take any action on the offences that took place in South Africa, they sure as hell can for what he did to me today. Their take on the situation I found myself in this afternoon was that it was coercion, which is now considered an offence in this country. Also, because he put his hands on me, he is now wanted for assault. As much as I thought I was free from him because I had left him, he still had a hold on me because he had worn me down for over a year. It appears I couldn't say no to him even if I'd wanted to and he knew it.

The police officers were very nice to me and what's more they believed me. That was the one thing I was so worried about and it was nice to know that people didn't treat me as though I was stupid or made it feel like it was my own fault. Mike did that a lot. Every time he would hit me, he'd apologise by first of all saying something like *if you hadn't* or *if you'd just.* It was always me, always my fault that he'd done those terrible things to me. Now, having spoken at length to these specialist officers, I realise that is classic behaviour of an abuser. They will never admit that anything is their fault. They always blame their victim to justify what they've done.

Now as I sit in this police station with my belongings in a plastic bag, waiting on Damo to turn up, I'm starting to think it wasn't such a good idea to get him involved. I don't know what he can really do to help me. He doesn't even drive so we'll need to get a bus or a taxi back home.

"Nikki," Dan's voice envelopes me like silk and I turn to see him standing at the door.

As soon as I lock eyes with his, I break down in uncontrollable floods of tears. "Dan wh… what are you doing here?" Tearing my eyes away from him I look down at my pathetic little bag. "I'm so sorry," I whisper as my body shakes on a sob.

"Oh Nikki," he says as he comes to me and pulls me up into his arms, "you have nothing to apologise for. Damien called me."

As I stand against him with my head on his chest, I feel safe again. I love Damo to bits; he did the right thing. I can't believe Dan actually came to get me. I can feel his heart beating in his chest as it rises and falls against my head.

"Miss Olsson," the male desk sergeant says from behind us.

I reluctantly pull away from Dan and acknowledge the man. "Yes," I reply swiping tears from my cheek.

"You are free to leave but I'd like to inform you of a few things first. Take a wee seat and we can talk."

Both Dan and I sit next to each other and he takes my hand, a gesture that is neither forced nor expected. A rush of sensation runs up my arm and my breath catches. He squeezes my hand and rubs my knuckles.

"Okay," the officer starts, "we have to send a report to the Procurator Fiscal, our prosecuting authority here in Scotland. It's only a formality because you were charged with assaulting a police officer. PC Sharp is okay by the way, and he completely understands why you hit him. He's already given a statement to that effect. As it stands right now, we plan to take this case against you no further than that."

I take a huge shaky breath in and nod my head at him. "Thank you," I say, my voice croaky.

"You'll receive written confirmation from the PF's office stating that there will be no further action taken. Now on the matter of Mr Hunter. We have officers on their way to arrest him at his hotel and I have to inform you that you will be called as a witness, obviously you being the victim in this, that is a given."

"I understand," I reply. "I honestly am just glad that he won't be able to do this to me again, or to anyone else."

"We will be sending a report to the authorities in South Africa and if he is convicted here, he will be deported so he won't be able to return here."

That makes me feel so happy and I look at Dan who is regarding me with a frown on his face.

"Okay so you get yourself home and we will keep you informed of any developments."

We say our goodbyes and I thank the sergeant again before we make our way out to the car park. Its dark outside now and the older style sodium streetlamps bathe the cars in a dull orange glow. Dan has obviously driven himself here as he directs me to his car. He opens the passenger door for me, and I get in, sighing as I sit back in the plush leather seat. Dan gets into the driver's seat and doesn't immediately start up the car. I can feel him looking at me, but I can't face him.

"Nikki?"

I close my eyes and will myself not to cry.

"Nikki," he says again.

I turn to face him, the orange glow of the car park lighting casting angular shadows over his face. "Why did you come here Dan? I was under the impression you wanted nothing more to do with me."

"Damo called me; he was absolutely hysterical. After I'd managed to get the story out of him, I thought it best that he didn't come. I didn't think it'd do you any good to have to deal with his meltdown as well as your own problems."

"I'm glad it was you that came. You're the only one who really knows what happened to me. My sister would have hit the roof and I couldn't tell my dad. In fact, I don't know that I'll ever be able to tell my parents. I feel so stupid."

"You're not stupid Nikki. He manipulated you, got inside your head and he twisted until you broke. No, you're far from stupid. You were in a vulnerable place and I was to blame for that. I was expecting you to turn me away me after what I did?"

I should have sent him packing given how humiliated I was, but the truth is, I miss him. I sound utterly pathetic, I know that, but a week ago I thought I was finally getting on with my life and by Sunday I was happier than I have been in so long.

"Dan why did you do that to me?"

He shakes his head and stares out the window. "I have a lot to explain to you Nikki, a hell of a lot and I don't know what you're going to think when I've finished."

When he looks back at me, he has tears in his eyes, and I can't help myself but reach out and touch his cheek. He closes his eyes and nuzzles into my hand as a tear runs over my thumb.

"Oh, Dan what happened?"

"Can I take you home with me?"

Looking down at my hands I sigh. "Do you really think that's a good idea?"

"I understand why you don't want anything to do with me…"

I cut him off. "You had someone else tell me we were finished. That my services were no longer required. Do you have any idea how used I felt? When I saw Astrid being escorted from the building on Monday, I was so happy that we could finally put all that rubbish behind us. But to be spoken to like that… well it was like someone had punched me right in the gut. And you know what made it a million times worse was that you couldn't even do it yourself."

"I'm so sorry Nikki. I promise you I never meant to hurt you but there's…" He sighs. "This is what I need to explain to you. Will you hear me out? If, after I've explained everything, you still feel the same, I'll let you go, and I'll make sure you're looked after financially until you get another job."

"Dan, I don't want to work at SecuriSoft anymore regardless of what happens here tonight," I say solemnly and wince at the hurt look on his face.

"What are you going to do?"

"I honestly don't know. I hadn't thought that far ahead. I just know that I can't be around you anymore. If we were still together, I couldn't handle the whispers and if not, well I couldn't handle seeing you every day and not be able to touch you, hug you, kiss you. It's just too hard. My head is seriously messed up right now. It has been for a long time and I know it was a mistake to even become involved with you. It wasn't fair on either of us."

"I don't want to lose you Nikki."

"I don't know what to do. You made me fall in love with you Dan and then you squashed me as though I was a fly bugging you. You crushed what was left of me."

"Nikki, I can't begin to imagine what this has been like for you but, believe me I understand how hurt you are. Please let me explain. I promise, you'll see things differently."

I turn and look out the window, focusing on the reflection of an overhead light on the car next to us. My heart and mind are at war with each other. I can't take anymore hurt, I'm so emotionally drained and I don't know if I have room in my head for anyone else's problems. But what if I don't give him a chance to explain? Would I end up regretting it for ever?

"Ok," I whisper, relenting and hoping I haven't just made my life a whole lot more complicated.

"Nikki."

I turn to face him and feel my bottom lip tremble as a wave of emotion hits me like a ton of bricks.

"Let's get out of here. Come home with me and we can talk for as long as need be so that I can explain everything to you."

I nod at him. It's all I can do right now. He takes my hand and rubs my knuckles and his eyes say a silent thank you.

"There's somewhere we need to go first. I have someone you need to meet so that I can start to explain."

"Okay," I manage to say and I'm all at once intrigued and apprehensive about where this night may lead my life. I hope against hope that this will finally be the day I start to live again.

CHAPTER THIRTY-FOUR

*D*an and I have more or less sat in silence on our drive to what looks like an old country estate house. The red sandstone brick and, from what I can see in the dark, beautiful gardens reminds me of National trust houses my parents took us to whenever we visited family in the UK on the rare occasions my dad wasn't working. Dan brings the car to a stop outside the front entrance and turns off the ignition. I turn to him and watch as he takes a few steadying breaths before he turns to face me.

"What is this place Dan?"

"It's a care home."

"Who lives here?"

"My mother," he says as his voice cracks.

I feel the colour drain from my face as I try to process what he's just said. "I thought you said your mum was…" I'm about to say dead but then I remember that he's never actually said the word dead when talking about his mum.

"She survived the shooting Nikki."

"But the report I found on the internet said she was dead," I say, and I can't hide the confusion in my voice.

He nods. "I know it did and there's a reason for that. This is what I need to explain to you but first I want you to meet her. I don't know if she'll understand who you are. I've talked about you though, so she might. Her brain was severely damaged by the shooting. Her cognitive functions don't work as they should, and she can't speak."

This is a lot to take in. It must be heart-breaking for him to see his once vibrant and active mother as ruined as she must be now. I feel so terribly sad for him.

"Come, let's go in."

We get out of the car and make our way into the building and stop at a set of closed glass doors. Dan presses a button on a panel at the side and within less than a minute a young woman in a carers outfit comes to greet us.

"Oh, hi Dan," she says as she opens the door. The waft of warm air that escapes is scented with some sort of disinfectant.

"Hi Amy. This is my friend Nikki. I'm bringing her to meet mum. How has she been today?" *His friend.* His words strike a pain in my chest.

Amy nods. "She's doing okay today Dan. We weren't expecting you this late. I thought you'd scheduled for this afternoon."

"I did but something came up," says Dan as he looks at me.

He put off seeing his mum to come and rescue me. I all at once feel special and utterly wretched. I can't believe he did that.

"Not to worry. You'll have to make do with half an hour now though, it's almost bed prep time."

"That's fine. I'll make it up to her on Sunday's visit."

"Okay then, she's in her room so you just make your way in. It's nice to meet you Nikki."

"And you Amy," I say as we move past her and head down a long hallway, past a communal sitting room, dining room and a couple of offices.

Dan stops as we reach a bedroom door. "Thank you for doing this Nikki, for letting me explain. As I said, Mum can't speak, and she has limited movement. If you feel uncomfortable in here at any point please just say and we'll leave."

"I'll be okay," I reassure him, and I can see that it helps to put him at ease.

In the short time I've known him, I've never seen him look so vulnerable. It's a sobering sight and I know this can't be easy for him. He opens the door and we step into a beautifully furnished room. It is decorated in grey and white and has all sorts of little blingy accessories dotted all over. In fact, it reminds me slightly of Dan's bedroom at his big house and I wonder for a second if that's so that he can feel a sense of attachment to her. The juxtaposition of all the beautiful décor and the mechanical hospital style bed is striking. On one hand you could mistake this room for that of a boutique hotel but when you look a little closer you realise what the purpose of it actually is.

"Hi mum," says Dan and the frail face of the woman sitting in the chair by the window twitches slightly when her eyes fall on him. It's the tiniest of movements but it is a smile. "This is Nikki. She's the one I was telling you about last week." She smiles again, obviously remembering something he said.

"Hi," I smile and give a tiny wave to her.

"This is a short wee visit today mum, but I promise I'll come back on Sunday and we'll have a picnic in the garden. The weather's getting much nicer now."

I watch as he sits on the seat facing her and takes her pale, fragile hand in his. It's tiny compared to his and it makes her frailty seem all the more pronounced. Her once beautifully thick dark hair hangs limply over her shoulders, greyed with age. The right side of her face is sunken and scarred and her mouth is distorted on that side too. Her gunshot wound. By the look of it, she's lucky to be alive. "So, Jase," Dan starts, and I watch Anna's eye twitch. "Sorry, Jason."

I laugh. "Ah Anna you want your boy called by his given name, don't you?" Her lip rises on the left side in answer.

"She doesn't like me being called Dan either." He says smiling. "She's never called me Dan, have you mum?" Her lip lifts again.

"Quite right."

"So anyway," Dan continues, "Jason wanted me to tell you he was bringing his own friend to meet you next week. He keeps telling me this guy is '*just a friend*' but I can see a wee romance starting there with them. He's a nice guy. It's good to see my wee brother happy."

I watch as Dan talks to his mother and every now and then he lifts her hand, placing a soft kiss on her bony knuckles. He tells her about his work, Olivia, what Jason has been up to and generally filling her in on all the small, normal aspects of his life.

I don't talk much for the rest of the half hour we spend with Anna, mostly due to the fact that I'm close to tears at the sad sight I'm witnessing. Having seen a picture of Dan's mum, and knowing how she looked before this tragedy happened, I feel a profound sense of loss for both of them. Dan lost his mother, his nurturer and Anna lost herself and her children. Her scars must run deeper than the physical ones that are extremely apparent. There is no mistaking that this woman has suffered a trauma to her head, but I wonder how anyone can possibly know what she may be feeling inside. She can communicate, but not to the extent that she can tell anyone how she feels. I wonder if she'd be happy to be sat here all day every day, knowing there's never going to be anything else. Does she remember the person she used to be? And worse still; does she remember every day what happened to her?

We say goodbye to Anna when our time is up and before we leave, I watch as Dan places a soft kiss on his mother's cheek. "I love you mama," he whispers to her. As he turns away from her, a tear rolls down her cheek and, in this moment, I feel like I am going to die of heartache for her. As soon as we are outside her door, I let go of all the emotion I've felt whilst I've been in Anna's company.

"Hey, Nikki, what's wrong?" Dan steps towards me and pulls me in close to his chest.

I take a huge shuddering breath and savour the warmth and protection of his body. "Oh, Dan I'm so sorry." It's all I can manage before I am sobbing hard.

"Let's get out of here. It was wrong of me to bring you here after what you've been through today. Come on we really need to talk."

He takes my hand and leads us back out of the building to the car. Our drive to the country house is silent. Neither of us even glances at the other. It's a strange atmosphere and I feel an uneasy sense of foreboding about what's to come tonight.

CHAPTER THIRTY-FIVE

*D*an's home is eerily quiet in the dark. More so than it was the first time I was here. I sit at the huge breakfast bar in the kitchen and watch as Dan makes coffees for us both. Given that this place is huge, and he has to have any number of staff that would probably do this for him, he moves around the place with such ease that it's clear he doesn't take advantage of that. I take a sip of the steaming coffee and he's made it exactly as I like it. Shit! Hugging the warm mug into my chest, I watch as Dan sits down on the stool next to me. I daren't say anything and I'm extremely grateful when he breaks the silence.

"Nikki, I want to apologise for everything right off the bat here. I behaved incredibly unprofessionally towards you and I'm sorry. You are a very talented woman and, even though you haven't been with SecuriSoft long, I can see you have the potential to go far in this industry, whatever you plan to do."

"Dan, I'd be a pitiful fool to blame you. Do you think I didn't want any of this to happen? You're an attractive man, no sorry, you're fucking insanely hot. You were under my skin the minute you stepped into that lift."

It's true. The moment I saw him I knew there was some-thing about him. I still do and being so close to him right now and not being able to touch him is hellish. I've stroked the taught muscles that now strain against his rolled shirt sleeves. I've writhed under that sculpted body and been kissed in places I'd never known existed by those talented lips. I've seen the beautiful soul behind those eyes and as much as his actions hurt me, I know there's more to it than what I was led to believe.

"Why did you hurt me like that Dan?"

He sighs and shakes his head. "Oh Nikki," he says raking his hand down his face. "I have an explanation and it's going to sound crazy. This is the reason I wanted you to meet my mum. She's where it starts."

"About that. What the hell went on there?"

"She survived the shooting and a lot of money was thrown at keeping her safe."

"Who put the money up?"

"My grandparents were multi-millionaires, and she was their only child. When they passed away, which was within around a month of each other, she was the sole beneficiary of their entire estate. But it was put in a trust and she was never allowed to access the money directly. My grandparents were never happy with her choice of husband. They knew he was bad news and didn't want him getting his hands on their money. She was given a payment of a thousand pounds a week and that was all she ever got. She would have had access to the whole lot within a year if she'd divorced my dad or if he had died and she was still able to make decisions for herself. Neither of those things happened so the money stays where it is. I sometimes think that was my father's plan all along. If he couldn't get his dirty hands on that money, no one could. There was, and still is, a set of trustees who deal with the money and they take care of my mother to this day. The man who spoke to you in my office is one of those trustees."

I can feel my brows furrow hard. "Dan, I think I know where this is going."

"Tell me your theory and I'll tell you if you're right," he says with a smile.

"You were given money to start your business from your mother's trust fund, but there was a catch. The trustees either had to have a controlling stake in your business or they had to form part of your board."

He smiles and nods his head. "Well done Miss Olsson, I knew you were smart. Yeah, they are my entire board. In actual fact I control very little of my own company."

"Wow, I really wasn't expecting to be right you know. But why was I kicked to the kerb like that? What had I done wrong?"

"You got too close to me. Simple as that. These people have become extremely over-zealous when it comes to controlling the company. They've lost sight of what my mother would actually have wanted. She doesn't have the mental capacity to do any of that herself, so I'm stuck with them until I'm able to walk away from the business or until she passes away."

"Why would you walk away? Can't you just buy the trust out? Or contest it. SecuriSoft is an amazing company, you have so many amazing people working for you. God, isn't it worth fighting for?"

"Not when it's ruined the only chance I ever had to be truly happy."

I let out a sharp breath at his words. He was happy with me. Truly happy. And the crazy thing is, so was I. I had, for want of a better word, an epiphany sitting in that police cell tonight. I finally realised that I'm worth a lot more than I have allowed myself to be in such a long time. Hearing everything the police had to say made me see how much Mike had worn me down. How much his actions had damaged me to the point where I wasn't able to distinguish what was love and what wasn't. Mike never truly loved me. He loved the control he had over me and it must have almost killed him when I took that away. The thought makes me smile.

"You think you could be truly happy with me Dan?"

"I do. I'd move mountains to make you happy, keep you safe. I'd never make you feel like you were worth anything less than you deserve to be. You are a beautiful human being Nikki. What that fucker did to you was despicable beyond belief. He deserves to rot in hell. Any man who thinks it's his right to take away a woman's rights doesn't deserve to walk this planet. It's only money. I have lots more where that came from and I can easily start again."

His words hit me full force. "Dan I…"

He puts his finger on my lips. "Nikki, I can't remember the last time I wanted more with anyone, not since Irena. I realise now that I never really had anything with her. I know how hurtful it is to feel used and I know you felt exactly the same way on Monday. I hope you can forgive me for that. I never want to make you feel like that again."

I put down my mug and get off the bar stool. Moving in between his legs I run my fingers down his cheek and skim his stubbly jawline.

"I love you Dan," I whisper.

His lips part on a sigh and he leans into my touch, his eyes never leaving mine.

"I love you too Nikki," he says, and his pupils dilate as he sucks in a long, slow breath. I watch as his nostrils flare slightly and before I know what's happening, he grabs my hips and stands taking me with him. His lips crash into mine and we kiss like a couple of horny teenagers as he carries me through the house and up the stairs. My need for him to fill the overwhelming void I've felt since we last saw each other is almost killing me. He sets me down when we reach his bedroom and it appears neither of us can wait to be naked as we each strip ourselves, clothes flying around the room in rather a comedic fashion. We stand looking at each other for a few seconds before Dan charges at me, flinging us both onto the bed.

"I've missed you," he says on a ragged breath as he kisses me hard.

Our warm bodies writhe against each other and I can take the anticipation no longer. "Please Dan, I need you." My words come out stuttered and I fear that my impending tears will put an abrupt end to this connection that my body so desperately needs.

He lets me go long enough to put on a condom and then he's back, looming over me. His presence all at once intimidating and fiercely protective. He readies himself at my entrance and looks at me for an agonising second. I can't take the anticipation any longer. Raising my feet behind him, I pull him slightly towards me, urging him on and it seems it's all the encouragement he needs as he rams himself right into me, pushing me up the bed slightly.

"Oh," I gasp as goose bumps form on my skin and my body jerks up to meet his thrusts.

"Nikki," he whispers as he thrusts harder and harder, the bed shaking under us and it doesn't take much until he comes on a great wave and I watch as beads of sweat form on his forehead. I reach up and stroke his biceps.

"Are you okay?" I ask knowing from the look on his face that he's anything but ok.

"I'm sorry," he says, his voice cracking as he pulls out of me. "That was incredibly selfish of me." He turns and sits with his back to me.

"Hey," I say as lightly as I can and lean on his back, putting my arms round his waist. He is warm and slick with sweat. "It just means you owe me now," I smile against his back, kissing his shoulder blade and tasting the salty tang of his sweat.

"Come here," he says pulling me round from behind him so that I'm sitting in his lap. He moves my hair away from my face and runs the back of his hand down my cheek. "How could anyone ever hurt you? You are a beautiful person inside and out. You should be worshipped."

A tear slips from my eye and he swipes it away with his thumb.

"Thank you for saving me," I say on a tiny sob and he pulls me in close, the heat of our bodies melding us together.

CHAPTER THIRTY-SIX

*M*y feelings of safety and thinking that Mike couldn't hurt me again were short lived when I received a call from the police just after six this morning. As I sit in one of Dan's huge formal reception rooms holding a piece of paper in my shaking hands, I wonder just what kind of cruel joke the universe is playing on me. I'm trying not to look at it, but I can't stop. The words *'This is your fault Nikki'* taunt me in their jagged scrawl. Mike wasn't done with me when I was arrested and he decided, in the worst and most final way possible, to make sure I'd never forget him.

"Nikki are you okay?" The female police officer asks, her voice soft and soothing.

"How could he do this? It's just so… oh God I think I'm going to be sick." My stomach is flipping and my mouth watery. I swallow hard and try to compose myself. From nowhere Valerie appears at my side with a glass of water. I try to take it from her, but my hands are too shaky, so Dan takes it. Valerie puts her hand on my shoulder and gives a little squeeze before she leaves. The police officers have just finished recounting how their operation to arrest Mike ended with them having to deal with a suicide. The piece of paper I am holding is a copy of Mike's suicide note and, just as he always did, his last act was to make sure I knew I was to blame for it.

My Darling Nik,

I love you and I can't live without you. You've hurt me in the most unimaginable way possible and I can't forgive you for that. It was one thing to run away without telling me but to have an affair with your boss was as bad as stabbing me in the heart.

You say you love the rain,
But you open your umbrella.
You say you love the sun,
But you find a shadow spot.
You say you love the wind,
But you close your windows.
This is why I am afraid,
You say that you love me too.

This is your fault Nik. My death will leave blood on your hands and I hope you never forget, for the rest of your life, what you did to me.

All my love

Mike

That bastard must have found out where I'd gone pretty soon after I left, because that's the same thing that was written on the roses I thought Dan sent me. I'm now certain the balloon was his doing too. I'm starting to wonder whether I was imagining being followed or whether he had been here the whole time

"Nikki," the female officer says, breaking into my thoughts. "You have to understand that this is all part of an abuser's tactics. Mike knew his game was up and that he'd very soon be arrested. I have to admit suicide is a very extreme way of dealing with that and it's not something we see very often, but it is the ultimate way to try and hurt you and make you feel guilty. I'll say it again, you are not to blame for this."

"I can't believe this," I say shaking my head. For some morbid reason I can't take my eyes off the note.

The male officer clears his throat. "Do you know someone called," he pauses to look at his notebook, "Astrid Jansen?"

Dan and I shoot a look at each other.

"Yes, she was an employee. She's actually under investigation for intellectual property theft," says Dan. "Why do you ask about her?"

"We found numerous text messages in Mike's phone between the two of them. The first one dated second of April."

This is getting worse by the second. "What were they talking about? I had only been here around three weeks at that point. I hadn't even met Astrid yet."

"From what we can glean from the conversations they were having, Mike had found out where you were working. His first text to Astrid told her that he had got her number from a friend who was related to her. He never mentioned a name but having pieced the evidence together it seems that he enlisted her in taunting you."

"That's why she took an instant dislike to me, but worse than that, now I know she's the reason he found out where I live."

"I think she'd have been the same even if Mike hadn't got her involved," says Dan. "She's a truly bad person but it's obviously that fact that hid her real motives with you. No one would ever suspect anything because she was horrid to everyone." He drags his hand down his face. "I'm so sorry Nikki. If I'd known…"

"Dan please don't apologise. This is not your fault."

"Unfortunately, we can't take any action against her because ultimately she didn't break any laws," the female officer says as she leans forward and hands me an envelope. "This is a list of names of some really good counsellors and I'd definitely try and see someone if I were you. You have a lot to process and talking to a professional will help."

"Thank you," I whisper as my head starts to swim in all different directions.

"What happens now?" Asks Dan.

"Well that's the one other thing I need to talk to Nikki about." The female officer looks at me. "We've contacted his next of kin. His wife."

"But he said he was divorced. She wouldn't be his next of kin."

"Unfortunately, he wasn't divorced, and his wife was under the impression that he was simply working away when he wasn't at home. It appears you had unwittingly become his mistress. I have to tell you that we found out he also had a child and his wife is also around six months pregnant with a second."

My stomach coils and now I actually am going to be sick. I stand up and run for the door we came in earlier, but this house is so huge I have no idea where I'm going. When I push open a door off the kitchen that may be a bathroom, I find myself in a huge laundry room. Thankfully there's a sink and I lean over it, throwing up the minuscule contents of my stomach.

"Nikki?" I can hear Dan's voice in the kitchen. "Nikki, where are you?"

He hears where I am when I run the cold tap and spoon

some water into my mouth with my hand. He opens the door and steps inside.

"Hey angel, are you okay?"

"He had kids Dan," I say as I start to cry, uncontrollable tears and sobs take over my body.

Dan comes to me and wraps me up in his big warm body. "Nikki this isn't your fault."

"But it is Dan. How could I not have known?" I lean back from him, noticing the wet patches my tears and the water from my face have left on his T-shirt. "How the hell was I with him for a full year and not know he had children? What sort of person does that? His wife assumed they were still married, still a happy family. I could have coped with them just being separated, but she had no idea. And his poor kids."

"Come back through and listen to what the officers have to say. I think you'll be able to forgive yourself after you do."

When we enter the reception room, both officers give me a sympathetic look and I feel so wretched.

"Are you okay Nikki?" Asks the woman.

"Yes, I'm sorry. That was just a shock to hear, I wasn't prepared for that."

"We completely understand. Are you okay to continue?"

I nod and she lifts a notebook I hadn't noticed before. She flips a couple of pages and starts talking again.

"So, during our enquiries to find Michael's next of kin, we contacted the police in Johannesburg. They told us some interesting things about him and his wife, and I think they may be relevant to your relationship to him."

I know I look puzzled, but I'm also intrigued to find out what they know about him.

"The police told us that for around a year before he started a relationship with you, Michael's wife had filed and redacted six reports of domestic abuse. From what you've told us, it appears from the time he started his relationship with you, those reports stopped. There wasn't another one until March this year."

"That's when I came to Scotland." As I say the words, I instantly feel awful. "He started abusing her again when I left."

"It appears so. This time when she reported him it was escalated because she is pregnant, and their younger child seems to have been hurt too."

I look at Dan and find his eyes ablaze with anger. He takes my hand and rubs my knuckles. "It's okay," he whispers.

"There are family liaison officers with her now and she is being taken care of. Michael was under investigation and shouldn't have been out of the country, so I assume there will be an investigation conducted in due course but as far as you are concerned, we won't really take this case any further here. I highly doubt they will call on you as a witness or anything. It will more than likely be a fact-finding investigation. Had anything happened to you because he had been allowed to leave the country, we would be in a very different position right now. As I said before, please get some professional help. You can't know how all this is going to affect you in the following weeks." She nods at Dan. "You have an important role to play as a friend. Be there as much as she needs you."

"Absolutely," he says and gives my hand a light squeeze.

"We will keep you updated as much as we feel is necessary but, in all honesty, I don't think you'll hear from us again. I really think you need to put this all behind you and get on with living your life."

$\mathcal{T}$he door I'm trying to push open is jammed so I put my shoulder into it and force it. Something shatters behind it but it's so dark I can't see. I fumble for a light switch, but when I find it and switch it on it's like a spotlight on a stage. Mike's body lies under its beam, smashed into a thousand pieces apart from his mouth, upturned in a sneer and a horrible maniacal laugh echoes around the room. "*This is all your fault Nikki,*" the mouth says as the body starts to come back together around it, clinking and crunching as it does. I try to turn and run but my feet are sinking into sand. As I slip further and further down, Mike's body takes its form again and as he reaches out to touch me, I scream and slam into something hard. Opening my eyes wide and fighting in a tangle of fabric, I try as hard as I can to breathe but it just won't come. I can feel my head becoming woozy and I feel as though I'm about to pass out.

"Nikki." Dan's voice is welcome in the haze of the nightmare I've just woken from. It's only when he sits down beside me that I realise I'm on the floor. "It's okay I've got you, just breathe. Take it slow, look at me."

I do as he says and watch as he takes deep steadying breaths and I copy him, eventually calming down enough to make sense of what's just happened.

"Are you okay?" Asks Dan, his face pale and his voice shaky.

"No," I cry and put my head in my hands. "I'm not okay. I'm glad he's dead Dan. I'm a horrible fucking person. I am actually glad someone has died." I'm crying so hard and loud that anyone listening from the outside would think I was being murdered.

Dan pulls me into his lap, blankets and all and holds me against him until I've spent every tear that can possibly come out of me. My tears have dried but my body jerks involuntarily on a sob every so often.

"I'm sorry," I whisper.

"Don't you ever apologise Nikki. You have nothing to be sorry for. I'll tell you what I think. I think you inadvertently saved that woman and her children's lives."

I lean back so that I can look at his face. "What do you mean?"

"When he was with you, she was safe. I know you weren't, but she was. It would be all well and good saying that she should have taken her reports further and allowed the police to investigate him, but you know better than anyone how hard that is. Your sacrifice kept that woman alive and in my eyes that makes you a hero."

I get up from his lap and pull the blankets round me as I walk to the window. The setting sun casts a warming orange glow over the sprawling gardens below. I sigh and my breath stutters as a sob escapes.

"Dan I'm no one's hero. I should never have been with that sorry excuse for a man. I thought being with him would get me a better job. That's not heroic, that's downright disgusting and verging on prostitution."

I feel Dan's heat behind me, and he turns me to face him. The strip of sunlight coming through the window reflecting off his beautiful dark eyes gives him an ethereal look and I feel something that I haven't allowed myself to feel in a long time. Hope.

"It's only natural that you would feel like that about yourself Nikki. I don't think for one minute that you went into that relationship with the sole aim of getting a better job and I also know that at some point, whether misguided or not, you did fall in love with him. Don't ever put yourself down like that sweetheart. You are worth a million times more than that scumbag ever gave you credit for and if you'll let me, I'll show you exactly how you should be treated. Like the beautiful, intelligent and kind woman you are."

I was wrong when I thought I'd cried the last of my tears as I feel my cheeks wet and my eyes go blurry. "Oh Dan," I say throwing my arms around his neck and as he kisses me soft and tenderly, I know my life can only get better from now on.

EPILOGUE

The July sunshine beating down on my face is glorious as I lie on a tartan blanket with my head in Dan's lap. We've been properly dating for just over two months now and I'm happier than I've been in so many years. If I'm completely honest with myself, and my counsellor has made me realise this, I haven't been truly happy since my sister left home when I was twelve. I was at an age where I really needed her because, although my parents love me to the ends of the earth, they never really had time for me. My dad's job kept him extremely busy and my mum was too busy being the dutiful wife of the diplomat. Looking back on my life in South Africa I wish I had followed my sister and come to Scotland earlier but then I wouldn't be where I am today, with this wonderful man and his beautiful daughter.

A day out to see the Kelpies in Falkirk is just what the doctor ordered today. The sunshine and happy carefree mood it brings out is glorious. Dan has decided it would be a good idea to get out and about with Olivia this summer because she's starting her new school in August. A private school not very far away from the country estate. I was right about her not being with other children and after discussing it with Dan one night he agreed that it would do her good to be with her peers and get the social skills she so clearly craved.

"Daddy look at me," squeals Olivia.

I sit up as Dan and I look in the direction of the swings. Olivia is flying through the air, her brown curls bouncing as she is pushed back and forth by her nanny Nessa. Her giggle is infectious and we both smile at her.

"Woo hoo, you go my little sweetheart," he shouts to her and her response is to demand that Nessa push her higher. Of course, she obliges. Who couldn't resist that beautiful girl?

"You know something Nikki?" Says Dan.

"What?" I turn to look at him and take off my sunglasses.

"I dreamed of this. Of feeling this sense of happiness. I couldn't be more grateful that you came into mine and Olivia's lives. You gave me a new perspective on things and that little girl has benefitted greatly from it."

It's true that Dan has changed a lot about his life in the last few months. Since Mike's suicide in May we've both gone on a life cleansing mission. Dan gave up his final share of SecuriSoft. Only the Glasgow office mind you, because his solicitor found a loophole in the trust fund deeds that meant he got to keep control of every other arm of the business. The only part they got to control was the part they gave him money to start. Every single other office was set up using money that had no links to the original business. Dan opened those with money he made through investments when he was nineteen, before SecuriSoft was even an idea. He didn't become Scotland's youngest billionaire by relying on the profits of one company. As soon as he was free of the business, he changed the name of the rest of the business and the nature of the company so that it didn't have anything whatsoever to do with SecuriSoft.

He doesn't make security software anymore; he's now working on developing computer games and has his brother sharing the business with him. It's something they've always wanted to do and as I understand it Scotland is already at the forefront of the video games industry so it's already a strong market to be in. Most importantly though is that he doesn't have a board of directors to answer to anymore. Dan and Jason are the owners of this new business and the only directors. It's given them both piece of mind that no one can take it from them. SecuriSoft won't last long without Dan at the helm, his name is too well known and as soon as it starts to go down the tubes his plan is to buy it back at a reduced rate and carry on where he left off. It's risky, but if it works his business will be colossal. If it doesn't work, it's no great loss. Both Dan and Jason are also taking steps to contest the trust and try and get the money their mother was always entitled to. Their solicitor has said it can be done. The sooner he is free of them the better.

As for me, well, I have a new job. I'm now my own boss. I decided, after a lot of soul searching to do something I've wanted to do for years. I am in the process of finalising my own tech based online magazine. It's geared more towards women in the industry because I have always felt it to be a very male dominated business. There are some really intelligent, forward thinking women in I.T but they always seem to be overlooked or disregarded for their male counterparts. It was when Dan decided that he was going into video gaming that I really took notice of that fact. Out of the hundreds of video game developers in the UK only a handful are led by women, and it is the same regardless of which branch of the I.T industry you take a look at. I got myself into a rut in the security software game and every decision I made seemed to make me hate it a little more every day. The day I decided I wanted out of it all together was the day I truly felt free. And the best thing about it is that I still get to work with my new best friend. As soon as Damo learned that Dan and I had gone from SecuriSoft, and that the ensuing legal battle between Dan and the firm would probably result in its demise anyway, he left his job to come and work with me. He's a wonderful friend and a fantastically efficient PA so it was the least I could do for him.

I have seen a huge change in Dan over the past few months too. He no longer carries the day to day worry that his company could be taken away from him, he's called the shots on that front and I know it's the best thing that could have happened to him and Olivia. He has invested heavily in my new business venture, although I had the reimbursement of his investment written into the contract. No matter what happens with our relationship, I will never be financially tied to anyone. Mike's death didn't only free me from the constant fear and anxiety that he could still hurt me, it gave me back my independence. Yes, from time to time I get flashbacks to some of the violent incidents that were inflicted upon me, and I still have the odd nightmare here and there, but I'm slowly getting myself back with the help of a great therapist. She is a survivor of domestic abuse and chose to go into therapy to help others suffering the same. When you know you're not alone and that you were in no way to blame for what happened to you, it's easier to heal.

"So, do you want to come back with us for dinner tonight? Valerie is making Olivia's favourite, mince and tatties. She always makes enough to feed an army so you're more than welcome." Dan's voice interrupts my thoughts.

"I'd love that. My mum used to make us mince and tatties when we were younger, but I haven't had it in years."

"Excellent, Olivia will be so happy, you're her new

favourite person," he laughs as he watches the little girl laughing and playing with Nessa.

"What can I say, I'm adorable."

"That you are sweetheart, that you are," he says as he kisses the top of my head.

I close my eyes and bask in the warm glow of affection and glorious sunshine, safe in the knowledge that I am finally truly loved and cared for.

The End

INFORMATION

If you have been affected by any of the issues in this book there are excellent organisations worldwide designed to help. These can be readily found with a quick search on the internet.

Here are a couple for the UK and US to keep in mind:

UK: Women's Aid - www.womensaid.org.uk

USA: National Domestic Abuse Hotline - www.thehot-line.org

It's okay not to be okay, and sometimes it helps to talk.

Cx

ACKNOWLEDGMENTS

First and foremost, I offer a huge thank you to my family and friends who've been my rock throughout this journey. Your continued support and love keeps me motivated

My immense thanks to Liz, my wonderful friend and maker of magic. I'll forever be amazed at how you take my words and help turn them into something beautiful.

Thanks to my beta readers, in particular Samantha and Rukaiya. You guys are fabulous. Your no-holds-barred approach to the book made it even better in it's final edits and I thank you for keeping me on the right track.

To all the bloggers, fellow authors and readers who took the time to share the cover reveal and release for this book. I was blown away by the support and I'll always be forever grateful.

To my new ARC team. Thank you for taking the time to read my book and I can't wait to work with you all again on future projects.

The cover for The Intimidation game was produced by Natasha Snow and OMG she blew my socks off with the final design. Isn't it stunning? Thank you Natasha you are an absolute pleasure to work with.

And last but by no means least, my thanks has to go to you, my readers. Without you there would be no other books and I'm so happy to see so many people loving my stories.

I hope you loved reading Nikki's story as much I loved writing it.

Thank you all from the bottom of my heart.

Claire x

ALSO BY C.L STEWART

The Soul Series:

Shattered Soul

Saviour of The Soul

Heart and Soul

Standalone Novella:

My Summer at The Pink Flamingo

PRAISE FOR SHATTERED SOUL

This story took me on an emotional roller coaster, and I enjoyed it so much, instantly buying the whole series. I adored the Glasgow setting and felt every twist and turn of the story. Go buy it. You won't regret it.

Jolie Vines
Author of the Marry the Scot Series

Wow this book was utterly amazing! The characters in this story are strong, courageous, brave and completely made for each other... Can they both repair their fractured lives... I sure hope so... Loved this and cannot wait to read more.

QueenOfBooks88
Goodreads Reviewer

I thoroughly enjoyed this book and managed to get through it in record time because I simply couldn't put it down. Lots of drama, twists and turns had me hooked and I can't wait to find out what happens next.

Anonymous
Amazon Reviewer

Read on for an excerpt of Shattered Soul (Book 1 in The Soul Series)

SHATTERED SOUL

PROLOGUE

$\mathcal{B}$EING WOKEN UP IN the middle of an already restless night is bad enough but now I'm looking at these two people, two police officers, on my doorstep. What the hell are the police doing here at this time of night? Christ, it's after one in the morning. I'm willing myself to wake up. It must be a bad dream. Yes, just a dream, their faces are going blurry…I must be waking up.

"Mrs Connor, I'm PC Stanton and this is my colleague PC Davies."

I can't see anymore. Where am I? I can hear voices, but I can't see. The voices sound like they are coming from the end of a tunnel. Oh God, I'm so scared. Where are you Aiden?

"Mrs Connor, Mrs Connor are you ok? Jesus… Mike radio control and get some medical help."

Who is Mike? There is only blackness now. I think I will sleep. Yes, sleep. Just sleep. See you in the morning Aiden.

"*H*ello ma'am, can you hear me? It's okay you're in safe hands."

Light flutters through my eyelids. This is one seriously weird dream.

"Can you open your eyes?" The voice sounds sweet and calming, female, not from around here. My eyes sting as they open and my head thumps.

"There we are. Can you tell me your name love?"

I see a mass of red curly hair as I take in my surroundings and realise I am in my own hallway. A flashing blue light emanates from behind the angel in green.

"Hey love, focus here." I hear clicking fingers and I follow the sound until I am looking into a beautiful set of jade green eyes.

"That's better, now what's your name?"

I can feel my mouth opening but the words don't come out. Gina Connor. Gina Connor. GINA CONNOR. My throat is so dry, I need water.

"...ink," I try to ask for some, but it comes out wrong.

"Daz can you get the lady a drink of water?"

I hear footsteps.

"Right love we're getting you a glass of water. Do you know your name? Just signal with your head."

I nod. Northern Irish, that's her accent. Her voice is lovely, and she is very pretty.

"Right, here we are, take a drink of this." She holds the glass up to my mouth. My hands are shaking as I try to hold the glass and the water sloshes everywhere.

"It's alright I've got it. Try and take a few sips."

The cool water slides down my throat easily. As I close my eyes to savour it the glass is gone, and the snapping fingers return.

"Better?"

I nod.

"Right darlin' let's try again. What's your name?"

"Gina." Although a little croaky my vocal chords actually work and produce a viable sound.

"That's great Gina. What's your full name?"

"Gina Connor." I am aware of movement all around me, but I can't take my eyes off this woman.

"Right Gina. My name is Ava and I'm going to help you. Do you know where you are?"

"At home."

"That's great Gina. I'm just going to check you over. You fainted and have a wee bump on your head. I need to make sure you don't have a concussion or anything serious. Is that okay?"

"Yes. Why did I faint, what happened?" I'm so confused, why are there all these emergency workers in my home? Where is Aiden?

"Where is my husband?" I ask Ava. The sympathetic sorrowful look on her face says it all. I know in my heart that something is wrong.

"Gina I just need to do a few little checks on you then these police officers need to speak to you okay?"

I am numb. My head nods but I don't feel it. I feel as though I am floating, watching everything from above, disconnected from my body, from my life. I am poked and prodded. Ava speaks to me and I answer automatically. As she finishes, I feel a sense of foreboding. I am led into the living room to sit somewhere more comfortable.

"Alright Gina honey that's me finished checking you out. You don't appear to have a concussion and all your vitals are fine. If you feel light headed or dizzy over the next 24 hours you need to get checked out, okay? Contact the A&E department at the hospital. Just because we don't see anything now doesn't mean that something won't crop up later."

I nod in response and she puts a hand on my shoulder and gives a little squeeze.

"The police need to speak to you, so I'll leave them to it."

As she moves away, I grab her arm. She turns and smiles. "I don't want to be alone," I whisper as I feel tears run down my face.

Ava puts her arm around my shoulder and pulls me in to her side. "I understand love. I'll stay until someone comes to be with you."

"Thank you Ava."

This woman doesn't know me from Adam but is willing to sit here as I break into a million pieces. Looking down at my hands I notice that I am clutching my left hand in my right and squeezing my wedding ring tight, giving it a little twist every few seconds. I feel Ava tense and looking up I notice the two police officers from earlier approach me. I am shaking and finding it hard to breathe.

"It's okay Gina I'm here, you have to stay calm. Breathe in deeply and let it out slowly." Ava's soothing voice calms me enough to listen when the officer starts talking.

"Mrs Connor, my name is Shaun Stanton. I'm a family liaison officer. This is my colleague Mike Davies. Is your husband Aiden Connor?"

I nod.

"Mrs Connor I'm really sorry but I have to inform you that Aiden was involved in a serious accident this evening. Emergency services were called and arrived within a few minutes but there was nothing they could do, and he was pronounced dead at the scene."

I can't hear what else he is saying. There is a high-pitched animal-like wailing ringing in my ears. It takes me a few seconds to realise that sound is coming from me. Oh God, this cannot be happening. What am I going to do?

"Gina," Ava says quietly. "We've had a call in and I need to go. You're in good hands here and your mum is on her way okay? I'm so sorry for your loss honey. Stay strong and remember to get medical help if you feel you need it."

Ava's eyes are teary. All I can muster is a quiet thank you. Moments later she is gone and I am left alone with the two police officers. There is an eerie silence between us all as I try to absorb what has happened. My whole world has imploded, my heart shattered. I feel numb. My whole reason for being is gone.

CHAPTER ONE

*S*ix Months Later

I have never thought of myself as pretty, at least not compared to the beautiful celebs and models that are splashed all over the media. I am average, normal and look ok with a bit of make-up on. My long brown hair and blue eyes are a bonus and I have curves in the right places. I know I will never be a svelte size 8 it's just not in my genes. I am healthy and that's all that matters to me. My husband thought I was beautiful; I think he was biased. He always made me feel loved and wanted. If I felt terrible, he would always do or say something to make me laugh. Anything from funky facial expressions to putting dirty words into songs and singing them out loud to me.

The last six months have been hard, and grief has taken its toll on me. I feel older than my 31 years; damn it I look older. Catching a glimpse of myself in the mirror on my dressing table I feel tears start to well up from my heart, a heart that is still pained every time I look at my empty bed. I close my eyes against the stinging of the salt water. I can see Aiden walking in and wrapping me up in a big bear hug, telling me I am beautiful. I squeeze my eyes tight sending trickles down my cheeks. In the distance the revving of a car engine brings me out of my reverie and I open my eyes. I look at the mirror and there is only me with my arms wrapped round myself painfully wishing that he was here. I miss him so much.

It is just after midday and I have to get ready for my weekly grilling by Dr. Nathan Dempsey (Nate), my therapist, who is not much older than me. I think that is why I have stuck with him for so long. He is easy to talk to and doesn't rush me or dismiss me. I never wanted to go in the first place. I didn't think I needed it, but I had gone to keep Dr. Parsons off my back and stop him from prescribing anti-depressants. I am not depressed, I have too many other things to occupy my mind to be depressed, or so I like to keep telling myself. The good doctor had come to see me a week after Aiden's funeral, I highly suspect at the insistence of my mother-in-law, and sat looking at me with pity over his thin wire glasses. He is possibly in his late 50's and always looks like he got dressed in the dark. He told me that the reality of my 'situation' had not yet hit me and that I should try to speak to someone. Apparently, I have a mild case of Post-Traumatic Stress Disorder. I thought that happened to people who had been in an accident or had witnessed something terrible or had experienced some sort of physical trauma, so when it was directed at me, I was shocked. It took another few weeks of persuasion and threats of the dreaded 'Happy Pills' before I finally agreed. It was only an hour a week on a Tuesday afternoon. I really didn't have any excuse not to go and Dr. Parsons knew it. He knew I didn't have any children or commitments.

Aiden had said he wanted to wait for our careers to take off before we started a family. I have a degree in business and economics, but photography was my passion and I had aspired to be a hot shot photojournalist, travelling the world photographing the rich and famous, stunning places and interesting people. My dream was to live and work in New York. Turns out there are too many people already doing that and I was a bottom feeder compared to most of them. I found my vocation doing portraits from my little studio in the high street. I photographed weddings, parties and other social events. In the end I had to give up the studio and have fallen into a rut since, I have no motivation to photograph happy people. My poor camera is neglected. Aiden qualified in structural engineering and was destined for great things. He got a part time surveyors job at the local council offices while he waited for his big break. Part-time turned into full-time and as he moved up the ranks he found it harder to honour his aspirations. We had discussed having kids but there was always something going on and it never seemed like the right time. A part of me now thinks it was just as well we didn't, I don't know how I would have coped on my own with a kid; I can barely keep myself going. Who knew we were not going to be together forever? We thought we had all the time in the world. I was comfortably complacent and oblivious to the fragility of life and it was ripped from me in a few short minutes by the side of a country road.

So, here I am off to talk to Nate for an hour to see if he can help. I usually take the bus in to town on a Tuesday afternoon because parking is highly coveted and costs an arm and a leg if you are lucky enough to get a space. Nate's office is in a tall sandstone building with large sash windows and a beautiful set of pillars on either side of the main door. It is in the west end of Glasgow, a very affluent part of the city, near the University and sits inconspicuously on a tree lined avenue overlooking Kelvingrove Park. I sometimes take a stroll through the park before I go home just to clear my head.

There are 3 floors in the building. The two offices on the ground floor belong to a private dentist. I always grin as I pass and see the little set of teeth on legs smiling at me from the sign on the front door, 'Sparkles Dental Practice'. I have never seen the dentist, but I imagine her to be tall, blonde and perfectly groomed wearing a pink uniform with diamantes spelling out her name. My imagination is ridiculous; *it's not a beauty salon for God's sake*. Just above the teeth on legs is a new sign I haven't noticed before. It would appear that they now do Botox. This makes me laugh. From the look of me today I should probably keep this in mind, I may get to meet 'Dr. Sparkles' after all. An architect and an accounts consultant occupy the second floor. They don't have funky names. The architect is S. Parker and the accountant is D. Todd, not a lot to imagine there. The only images I can conjure up are two short, bald, old guys who look exactly the same wearing the same bland suit sitting behind identical desks. This floor is far too boring for my liking.

I arrive at my destination, on the third floor, and am greeted by Nate's receptionist and my once a week impartial friend Fiona. She has blonde curls to her shoulders and a flawless complexion like a little china doll. She is always cheerful and has a smile for everyone. Then again, I would always have a smile on my face too if I worked with Nate, he is an extremely handsome man and Fiona's husband.

"Oh, hi Gina," Fiona chirps, her beaming smile makes me smile as well. Apparently it's infectious.

"Hi Fiona, looking lovely as ever," I reply, she always looks perfectly preened.

"Oh you're too kind Gina. You look happy today, it's nice to see your smile."

"I just saw the sign on the dentist's door on my way in and it made me laugh."

"Oh the Botox! Nate had a laugh at that on the way in this morning too and the cheeky sod told me that I should bear it in mind. I may be husbandless by the end of the day...Oh I'm so sorry Gina, the words were out before I knew what I was saying," Fiona cries as she clamps her hand over her mouth.

I flash her my biggest smile to reassure her as inside my heart sinks. I hate people walking on eggshells around me. "Fiona don't apologise, I'm fine. I'm early today, is Nate with someone just now?"

"Thank you Gina, I'll try and link my brain to my mouth in future. He's with a new client right now so the session may overrun a bit"

Her eyes are so full of apology, I could never have been mad at her even if I wanted to, she's just so lovely.

"No problem, I'm going to go and grab a bite to eat at the deli on the corner. Would you like me to get you anything?" Thinking back to my first session with Nate I know I could be waiting a while.

"No thanks, I've already had lunch and if I drink any more coffee I'm likely to pee myself right here in this chair." We both have a chuckle at that as I head for the door.

"See you shortly."

As I reach the front door of the building, I can feel the cold, end of November air greeting me with its harsh bite. I pull my coat around me and tighten my scarf then proceed out onto the steps. I have my head down fishing in my pockets for my gloves when I feel an almighty thud hit me square on. My head shoots up just in time to see a brown-haired figure in an expensive looking grey three-piece suit tumble down the stairs. Jesus...he is gorgeous. This should not be my first thought after knocking him down the stairs but...WOW! He has eyes like Paul Newman with a bit of young Marlon Brando thrown in for good measure. His skin is slightly tanned, and he is clean-shaven. His hair is so perfectly styled it looks like it wouldn't move even in a tornado.

"Oh my God I am so sorry, are you ok?" I rush to his side and put my hand on his arm, oh my, what a nice arm that is. I feel a little buzz and the hairs on my arms stand to attention, as do other parts of my anatomy. I immediately let go, shocked at my reaction.

"I didn't even hear you I'm so sorry." My voice is uncharacteristically high, and I am talking too fast, but I can't seem to control myself. What the hell is wrong with me? *'Get a Goddamn grip Gina he's just a man…gorgeous but just a man.'*

As he gathers himself and his briefcase up, he looks at me with the most beautiful deep blue eyes I have ever seen. He holds my gaze, I can't tear my eyes away, I am mesmerised.

"Please be more careful in future missy, you could have caused some serious damage there." He looks at me like I am a naughty child being told off for running in the school corridor with an open pair of scissors. I don't know what to say. How bloody dare you, you cheeky bastard. Missy, MISSY! He doesn't even know me. As I stand there seething at this complete stranger's total dismissal of me, he turns on his heel and walks into the building without a backward glance. All I can manage is a shake of my head as I stand there in utter disbelief. I can feel tears well beneath my lids. *'Stop it right now Gina, he is not worth it,'* I tell myself without much conviction. I apologised for goodness sake. What did he want me to do? Fall to my knees and beg his forgiveness like he was some sort of God. He was rather hot and, as much as I hate to admit it, those eyes were amazing but like most hot guys he was full of himself. I hope his butt cheeks hurt…moron. He is probably having the accountant on the second floor fiddle his books. Although the exchange only took five minutes I feel as though I have been outside for an hour. I'm freezing and not even hungry anymore...I'm too mad. I decide to go back inside and have a coffee in the waiting room, scowling and sticking my fingers up at the accountant's door on my way past.

CHAPTER TWO

*M*y session with Nate goes well. As usual we discuss how I am feeling, how I am filling my days, whether or not I am seeing friends and family, am I keeping active and the like. I respond automatically. I am fine, I am going to the gym, swimming, reading etc., seeing my friends and my mum a few times a week. Of course, none of this is true, I just don't have the energy and I only speak to people on the phone now and again. In actual fact my only real human face-to-face interaction is with Nate and Fiona every Tuesday. I had so many visitors in the days following the accident and after the funeral that I just wanted peace and quiet. I thought that would only last a few weeks, but it seems to have become routine now, I actually like my own company. I suspect that Nate knows I am lying; he wouldn't be very good at his job if he didn't. I am sure he is humouring me at the moment. In all honesty I enjoy our little hour together, it's good to talk to someone who doesn't pity me all the time.

It is now 3.30pm and the sky has a mauve hue to it. I don't like the winter nights and the closer it gets to Christmas the more I hate them. Aiden and I used to cosy up with each other on these cold dark nights after we had spent the day Christmas shopping in town. This year Christmas can take a hike, I am not interested. I am lost in my thoughts as I walk towards the bus stop. Looking up I notice a tall man with his back to me. He is wearing a black overcoat and is fighting with his briefcase lock next to an absolutely stunning jet-black Aston Martin. The registration plate is simple: SP1. Very expensive. I didn't notice it earlier, I would have remembered since it is my dream car and that plate is hard to miss. As I get closer the click click click of my heels makes him turn and look in my direction. My heart constricts, oh Jesus Christ, it is that moron from earlier. I don't want another confrontation, so I look down at the ground and walk faster. I really want to punch the bastard, but I don't want to get myself arrested.

"Excuse me." The voice calls to me. I carry on walking. Fuck you asshole, I am not in the mood.

"EXCUSE ME!" Much louder this time. Still I ignore him.

"Excuse me MISSY!" He is laughing now. That's it, I stop abruptly and spin on my heel ready to take aim and knock the idiot to his arse again.

"Do not EVER call me Missy again you condescending bastard," I shout at him. I must look like a mental case bawling at a complete stranger in the street. I try my best to control myself, but I can already feel the tears welling up in my eyes and I know it won't be long before it all comes flooding out. I am shaking, not from the cold, from pent up emotion.

When I look at him again, he is still smiling and that tips me over the edge. My mind detaches itself from my body and before I know what I am doing I lift my hand and crack him on the jaw with a slap that makes some birds in the tree across the street from us take flight. My legs choose that moment to give up on me and I collapse in a heap on the cold hard ground, sobbing uncontrollably with my head in my hands. I feel him kneel down beside me and put his arm around me. He is warm and smells so good that I want to snuggle in to him; then I remember he is a cheeky bastard and is the reason I am now slumped on the pavement. But, then again, would a complete moron comfort a crazy lady who had just slapped him in the middle of the street? I look up at him and into those deep blue eyes and feel like I could get lost in them.

"Are you ok?" His voice is sincere and not as harsh as it had sounded in our earlier exchange.

"I'm fine." I really don't have anything else to say to him and I am slightly embarrassed. I really don't think he deserved to be slapped like that. Now I feel like such a bitch. He helps me up and brushes off my coat for me. He gently moves my hair, which has got stuck in my tears, from my face. As his hand brushes my skin, I feel a little buzz again. I close my eyes and savour it.

When I open them he is looking at me, smile gone, with his face full of concern. Good God he is gorgeous, I can't take my eyes off his beautiful features. Holding out his hand for me I gratefully accept, happy to get off the cold damp ground.

"I have to apologise for the way I spoke to you earlier, I'm so sorry. I thought the 'missy thing' had annoyed you that's the only reason I used it. I knew you were going to ignore me, but I really didn't expect to get a slap for it; I thought you would see the funny side. I was in a rush earlier after an exceptionally heated meeting with a client, so I was not in the best frame of mind when we bumped into each other." His voice is lovely and calming and not patronising at all. I can feel my face flush crimson.

"Yes, I'm sorry for that, is your cheek okay?"

"I'll live I'm sure."

He holds out his hand in a handshake gesture, "My name is Steven by the way."

I take his hand; his big warm hand and give it a little shake.

"Georgina... eh Gina." Damn, I can't believe I gave my Sunday name first. Only my mum uses my full name. I am starting to feel giddy at his touch. Am I a bloody hormonal teenager or a grown woman?

"Well nice to meet you Gina. I assume you are heading home; would you like a lift?" I look at Steven's face and his smile is back, softer this time and without an ounce of pity.

"No, it's fine, really, I can catch the bus it goes right past my house." I really don't think I should accept a lift from a complete stranger. He could be a raving lunatic using his charm and flash car to lure unsuspecting females to his lair.

"Are you sure? It's cold and dark and I don't think my conscience will let me leave you to get home on your own" And there it is, the patronising voice again as if I am a fragile little girl and can't get myself home. I am not amused.

"You can drop me at the bus stop and wait till my bus arrives if that makes you feel better." That's my compromise. He is a stranger so the bus stop where there are other people about will do nicely. My mind is going into overdrive playing scenarios of me being found chained up in his basement after being tortured to death. I have honestly got to stop watching gory horrors on my own this is getting ridiculous.

"Good, at least I'll know you're safe. This street is a bit creepy when you can't see into the park, you just never know what strange people are lurking in there." His smile reaches his eyes. The street is now dimly lit with the orange glow of street lamps but even in this subdued light I can see he is very knicker rippingly gorgeous.

"Shall we?" He grins hooking out his arm in an 'I'm a Little Teapot' fashion. I take his arm and we walk to his car.

Steven presses a button on the remote and the interior lights up. From where I am standing, I can see the seats are black with bright red stitching. The gear paddle on the steering column is covered in red leather. The luxuriousness of it all has me conjuring up scenes of espionage, car chases and a man who knows how to handle the ladies. The red against black is enchanting, very James Bond-esque. I shake my head and banish those thoughts. '*Enough*,' I scold myself; '*you've just been to therapy because your husband just died'*. Steven opens the door for me; very charming, probably one of his ploys. I smile at my over active imagination.

"What's so funny?"

"Oh nothing, I was just admiring your car it's very nice."

"It's an Ast...

"Aston Martin, I know it's actually my dream car." Damn, as if his head isn't big enough already. He is smiling like a child who has been locked in a sweet shop overnight. Boys and their toys. Aiden was the same whenever he talked about his bike. That damn death trap that got him killed. With a slight shake of my head I return to the here and now. I get into the car as ladylike as I can in heels and a dress; the seats are so low that I think I may have flashed my knickers slightly. Judging by the look on Steven's face that is most likely. I blush; thank God it's dark.

Removing his overcoat and suit jacket Steven throws them onto the back seat along with his briefcase. He looks even better in his shirt, tie and waistcoat. I feel a familiar sensation between my legs and abruptly squeeze them shut to try and stop it as the car roars to life. I can feel it rumble beneath me and, oh my God, that is just making things worse. I try to find something to distract me and settle on watching Steven press icons on the little touch screen which has magically appeared from the dash board. His iPhone is showing as connected and a multitude of playlists come up on the screen. He selects one named 'driving music'. The speakers' spring to life and the car is filled with a beautiful and calming sound. I recognise the soft piano music from various TV ads and programmes. Any man who likes this type of music surely can't be an axe murderer. '*Although Hannibal Lector enjoyed his fair share of classical music*'. I swear I am going to give myself a stroke.

"This music is nice," I whisper; I don't dare to look at him for fear I may implode.

"Yeah, great for relaxing you after a hard day."

I feel him looking at me and am compelled to turn and face him. He has a boyish grin on his face which is making him look even hotter. I smile involuntarily. Holding my gaze for a moment Steven says: "You have a beautiful smile Gina."

Oh bugger, where the hell did that come from? I quickly turn my head away and look out the window again. My face is flushed, not because I didn't like what he said but because I did. Steven reaches over and puts his fingers on my chin forcing my face back towards him.

"What's wrong?" His voice is full of concern, tinged with worry that he may have said something wrong. His touch pulses through my skin. I have to get out of here.

"My bus will be on its way. Can you please take me to the bus stop?" It comes out all harsh and wrong; I need to keep a clear head. Steven looks wounded at my sudden change in demeanour.

"Not a problem," he says dryly. We get to the bus stop in record time and in silence. The purr of the car's engine and the soft strains of the piano are all we can hear.

"Thanks for the lift Steven and I'm sorry again for the slap."

I give him one last look and before he can say anything I am out of the car and standing in the queue. The other people waiting in line are all gawping at the stunning vehicle I have just alighted. I can see the headlights of the bus approaching and start praying that it will get here before he has the chance to get out and talk to me again. I am a little shocked and disheartened that he doesn't even look at me, speeding off in a blur. Not even a goodbye wave. Deep down I was hoping he would beg me to get back into the car. What I was hoping would happen after that I don't know but right now I am reeling at how stupid I have just been. For goodness sake I don't even know his last name or anything about him except that he drives the most beautiful machine and likes piano music. Oh, and he is seriously hot. He could be one of the strangers waiting for the bus; I probably know more about them. As the bus pulls to a stop I think about that for a moment. The old lady getting on first is a regular. She only travels two stops, but I have spoken to her on a few occasions and I know that her name is Martha. Her husband died twelve years ago, and she has no children or other immediate family. Just her friend down the road and her wee dog. Good God I could be looking at my future looking at her.

I take my usual seat right at the back. It has started to spit with rain and the windows of the bus are steamy. I can see the outline of a heart with initials in it. It makes me think of being in love as a teenager; little did we know how cruel life and love really is. I am destined to be alone like Martha. I feel like such an idiot. Steven seemed really nice and I blew it because I'm fucked up. I don't even know if I will ever see him again. Something changes in me at that very moment. It is like a little light has been turned on inside me as I realise that things need to change. Right now, in fact. I get off the bus at the stop next to the train station. The rain has gotten heavier and is now turning to sleet. Oh, winter is definitely here. Inside the station I am faced with that familiar diesel fuel and sulphur smell mixed with coffee and cookies. The overhead display boards show that the train I am looking for is on time and will leave in 12 minutes. Just enough time to get a coffee and head to the platform. As I get closer to the Starbucks kiosk the smell of the freshly ground coffee makes me feel warm inside. I wish coffee could cure everything.

"Welcome to Starbucks, how can I help you today?" Says the overly happy barista whose badge is telling me she is named Lucia.

"Skinny Mocha please." I smile back. "Just a small one thanks."

"What's your name for the order?" She asks holding the iconic white cup in one hand and a Sharpie in the other.

"Gina."

My hands are cold, even inside my gloves, so when she hands me the coffee I am grateful. The steam coming from the little drinking hole is comforting. I can actually feel myself smile. I look at my name on the cup and see that Lucia has put a little heart next to it with a smiley face inside it; my smile becomes even wider.

"Have a nice day," Lucia beams.

"You too, thanks."

I wonder, for a moment, what someone like Lucia would have done in my situation. She looks about 20, a student more than likely, I bet she would never have run for the hills at the drop of a hat; but then would any student? I used to be one, I know what they are like.

As I make my way to the platform, I pull out my phone and call the one person I know who will make me feel better. The phone is answered on the third ring.

"Hello?" The voice on the other end makes me feel like I am being wrapped up in a fleece blanket.

"Hello mum, how are you?"

"Oh Georgina! How lovely to hear from you. I'm wonderful. Dad is off to pick up some take away because I can't be bothered cooking tonight and he has some project or something to work on. Oh darling I've missed you. How long has it been since I last saw you? Three weeks or longer, my goodness we need to catch up before I forget what you look like. Where are you it sounds busy?"

That's my mum, once she starts talking it takes a while for you to get a word in.

"I'm in the train station mum, just about to get on the train to Bearsden. I was just calling to make sure you were home."

"Oh, that's wonderful, I'll try and catch Dad and get him to bring more food. Is Chinese ok?"

I try to tell her I am not hungry, but it is in vain, she just keeps going. She mentions something about a new car and my cousin being pregnant before I can eventually get off the phone and get on the train.

I choose a seat near the doors facing the direction I'm travelling in. I have always felt weird travelling backwards. It is after rush hour now, so the train is not that busy. I pull my earphones out of my pocket and plug them into my iPhone. Shuffling the playlist, I go for a lucky dip. The song that comes on makes me think about earlier today. A song called Runaway: *'Take your time; don't go running away from this.'*

Yes, that's what I did, I ran away from something that scared me. It shouldn't have, but it's been so long since I felt like that around anyone else that I didn't know how to handle the situation. Now Steven probably thinks I am a lunatic. You win some, you lose some but losing this one has had an effect on me. I can't stop thinking about him.

END OF EXERPT

DOWNLOAD YOUR COPY NOW
SHATTERED SOUL

http://hyperurl.co/c3becu

ABOUT THE AUTHOR

For as long as she can remember, Claire has been a hopeless romantic. She can always be found dreaming up HEA's for her characters.

Claire lives with her husband and three children in Lanarkshire, Scotland (bet you're thinking of rolling hills, castles and men in kilts, Outlander style). Her love of her home city of Glasgow is more than apparent in her books so far.

If you loved The Intimidation Game and want to keep in touch Claire, would love to hear from you. She can regularly be found on Instagram and Facebook and if you like to get your hand on exclusive material you can join her Facebook reader group, Claire's Glasgow Kiss and sign up to her newsletter.

facebook.com/clstewartauthor

twitter.com/CLS_Author

instagram.com/clstewart_author

Printed in Great Britain
by Amazon